SAM WOOD

Civil War

BY

HENRY E. PEAVLER

To argue with a person who has renounced the use of
reason is like administering medicine to the dead.
— Thomas Paine, 1737-1809

Copyright 2022

Paperback ISBN: 978-1-953686-16-9
eBook ISBN: 978-1-953686-17-6

Library of Congress Control Number: TBD

Living Springs Publishers

WWW.LivingSpringsPublishers.com

Cover design by Jacqueline V. Peavler

DEDICATION

Nina Simone 1933-2003

Alabama's gotten me so upset
Governor Wallace made me lose my rest
And everybody knows about Mississippi,
Goddamn

Lord have mercy on this land of mine
We all gonna get it in due time
I don't belong here
I don't belong there
I've even stopped believing in prayer

"You don't have to live next to me
Just give me my equality.

Prologue

In 1854 the Kansas-Nebraska Act repealed the 1820 Missouri Compromise which banned slavery west of the Mississippi (Except Missouri) and north of Latitude 36 30 N. The act provided for 'Popular Sovereignty' meaning, in theory, voters (white males who owned property) would ballot to decide if the future state would be slave or free. The powers that be in Washington had already determined Kansas would be a slave state, like it's neighbor Missouri. Nebraska would join the northern free states thereby maintaining the legislative balance of power in existence at the time. Problems arose because the politicians failed to inform the pioneers pouring into the Territory of this sham—the voters took the wording of the act literally—the devil was in the interpretation of what constituted a voter. Missouri citizens crossed into Kansas Territory to vote in the Territory elections. True Kansas voters objected, and the conflict began.

Other issues were involved, including expansion of the railroads west of the Mississippi promising lucrative paydays for the politicians and businessmen. But slavery was the issue that hung like a storm cloud over the land.

People came to Kansas Territory--at first a trickle, then a steady stream--intent on claiming 160 acres of land through the Preemption Act of 1841 (also called Squatter's Rights). The cost--$1.25 per acre.

It was a complex time. The simple explanation that the Abolitionists came to eradicate slavery and the Border Ruffians came to ensure slavery is one-dimensional but for our purposes it will suffice. Sam Wood was an abolitionist. He didn't come for the land—he came to eliminate slavery--not just in Kansas but throughout the nation.

The roaming mobs of Border Ruffians and Missouri 'militia' wreaked havoc among the Kansas pioneers. President Pierce insisted that Kansas be a slave state and he didn't care how it was accomplished. Sam Wood was accused of being a traitor then indicted for Treason by the Kansas Territorial Grand Jury, a pro-slavery group appointed by the President. Kansas Territory was, by any definition a lawless frontier with justice defined by the club, fist and gun.

Drought parched the prairie in the years 1854 and 1855. During the winter months of 1856-1857, storms crashed down the western slope of the Rocky Mountains, roared across the Kansas prairie encasing everything in a frigid shell of ice and snow. A family in wagon or on horseback stranded on the frozen wasteland of an endless plain with no food, water or shelter; no sense of direction in the blankness of the blowing snow, faced a slow spiral to an ice-covered death.

The persistent threat of sudden attack undercover of the intermittent blizzards meant a constant watch by the settlers on farms and in the villages. Tempers were short, food was scarce. This was all a coordinated effort by Missouri Senator

Atchison and his cohorts, most dangerously, former sheriff Samuel Jones who achieved an exalted status among the pro-slavery thugs by dint of his slash and burn, take no prisoners approach to policing the territory. There was no pro-slavery crime too shameful to attract his attention and no free-state protest to minor to merit a charge of Treason.

The bitter cold left settlers exposed in their meager shelters; even the finest Lawrence home was poorly insulated against the weather. Flour, wheat, beans and all other staples were in short supply; deliveries from the warehouses in Westport and Kansas City could not get through, delayed by blizzards and preyed upon by the highwaymen who were just as desperately cold and hungry as the settlers. The antelope, deer, and pheasant were hunkered down, yet the men were forced to hunt and fish, often losing their way and their lives in the blinding whiteness of a 'blue norther'. Life on the Kansas prairie was played out in the death throes of the old and feeble, the young and weak. Doctors were unable to reach patients because of the weather and unable to provide much relief when they could. Yet life continued. Families grew and faced all the challenges of creating a life on the frontier.

Part One

KANSAS TERRITORY
1856-1857

They were the best of mankind and the worst... Abolitionists and Border Ruffians. Fighting on the hills and plains of Kansas Territory in a battle of good versus evil to determine if Kansas would be a slave or free state. Each side trusted that God, the Supreme Being, the Prince of Peace... sanctioned their point of view and they quoted bible verses to prove it. And each side sincerely believed they were the good and their opponent was evil. It was a week until Christmas in December 1856, a cold blustery day; just two weeks until the new year. "Dear Lord Jesus, please let the new year bring Peace on Earth to Kansas."

At Fort Riley the parade ground was awash in ceremony due a visiting dignitary on the western edge of civilization, in this case newly appointed Governor John Geary. The fort sat on a prominence at the convergence of the Smokey Hill and Republican Rivers about 12 miles west of the small village of Manhattan. On the parapets and bastions regimental flags fluttered in the brisk breeze. The Army band stood poised for the parting ceremony.

Governor Geary arrived that morning for a meeting with Commanding Officer, Nathanial Lyon.

Geary reviewed the troops in the company of the General, his second in command, Lieutenant Matt Rodgers, and Major Henry Sibley the officer in charge of Geary's military escort. Geary, at 6 feet 7 inches towered over the soldiers. Large with a wide girth impressive in its mass, he commands notice because of his size and his outgoing personality. After shaking hands with General Lyon, he saluted the troops, raised one foot to the coach footrail then hesitated when the icy prairie wind set the American Flag flapping. The halyards banged against the flagstaff, a lonely sound on the full but silent parade ground. He glanced up at the banner, blue canton of 31 stars with the red and white bars brilliant in the clear sky.

"I helped bring California into the Union back in '51', Major. God only knows if I can do the same for Kansas."

Major Sibley glanced at the waving flag as the Governor pulled himself into the coach with a farewell smile and nod to General Lyon. Cymbals crashed, horns blared, and the band struck a rousing Military March startling the horses, propelling the coach forward.

From the steps of Army headquarters, General Lyon raised a gloved hand, "I wouldn't have that man's job for all the money in Washington, Matt." They watched the Governor's entourage pass through the double gates accompanied by twelve dragoons from Ft. Leavenworth, the Governor's specially designed coach and two baggage wagons.

Lieutenant Rodgers admired General Lyon as a boy might regard an eccentric uncle, awed by his presence but uneasy about the impression the General made on people, especially important people like Governor John Geary. Rodgers thought to himself, 'The General needs a bath, his boots are still dusty from maneuvers last summer, and his insignias are duller than a mud puddle. God knows I've given him enough hints.'

"Nice fellow, didn't you think?" The General turned to go back inside expecting Rodgers to follow. Lyon stood no more than five feet six inches; the six-foot Rodgers loomed over him.

"Yes Sir, but that fellow Woodson seemed a bit down at the mouth. He probably would have been impressed with your battle ribbons and medals had you worn your formal uniform."

"Ahhh, don't mind Woodson, Matt, he's with that Atchison bunch. They don't much like anyone who wants Kansas to be a Free State. That and he's mad because he wasn't appointed Governor."

"I thought he was Governor at one time," Rodgers held the door open allowing Lyon to proceed.

"Acting governor and the ignorant fool almost started a war. He had the Border Ruffians attack Lawrence before Governor Geary arrived. If John Brown and Jim Lane wouldn't have rallied the Kansas Militia, Lawrence would have been burned down again." Lyon put his hat on the rack near the door and sat down, pointing at a chair for Rodgers.

4

"We've never discussed it Matt, but where do you stand on this slavery matter?"

Rodgers scowled, "You want the long story or short?"

"I'm not going to judge you one way or the other, I'm just curious."

Rodgers stared at the floor before speaking, a heavy southern accent forecast the answer, "I'm from Arkansas, Sir. Slavery is a way of life down there. The only Niggers I ever knew were field hands; none of em' would survive if they was on their own," he hesitated to gather his thoughts. "Niggers just ain't very smart. That's about all there is to it."

Lyon nodded for Rodgers to continue, "You believe that slavery should be allowed in Kansas?"

"Well Sir, all said and done, I just don't know what to think. You can't just free em'; they won't survive on their own, plus nobody I know will live next to one. I damn sure won't. The people in Arkansas...they'll fight. I guarantee they will."

"I'm afraid that's what it's going to come to, Matt. I wasn't an abolitionist when I came here but Sam Wood has opened my eyes. Him and John Brown. People like them are going to force a war. What side you going to fight on?"

Rodgers glanced out the window at the dismissed soldiers returning to their duties, "Like I said, Sir. I'm from Arkansas."

***

Major Sibley ordered the twelve Dragoons to form columns of two, six in front, six in back escorting the governor from Ft. Riley. General Lyon's troops stood at attention on both sides of the large Federal coach emblazoned 'KANSAS TERRITORY'. Sibley climbed inside; his horse tied to the rear boot.

Geary waved at the men as the coach swayed away jerking him back in the seat. The sky was clear, almost springlike, but the cold wind stole into the coach forcing the men to stay bundled. The Ft. Riley honor guard presented arms as the coach pulled abreast. The band played exuberantly making up in noise for lack of skill. Geary saluted as did Major Sibley.

The Governor was accompanied by his friend and physician, Dr. Jack Gihon, the Governor's personal secretary, J. H. Jones known to everyone as 'Shorty' and Territorial Secretary, Daniel Woodson who pulled his coat tight, slumped down with the collars hauled around his ears.

"Well, what do you think, gentlemen?" Geary asked.

"I hope we don't have to call on him to dispel a rebel uprising. His intent was very clear. He's with the Abolitionists," Woodson growled, "plus, he looks like a tramp. How anyone would promote that man to General is beyond me."

Major Sibley, a career officer possessed of a full head of brown hair, a stern handlebar moustache and a fierce gaze when provoked turned abruptly to Woodson, "I served under Nathaniel Lyon in the Mexican War. There is not a finer officer in the United States Army. Every man under his command will attest to that fact." He continued to stare at

Woodson who glowered out the window without responding.

The Governor observed Woodson thoughtfully. First impression upon meeting the man was unfavorable. Woodson, at 30, seemed to be eternally scowling. A wispy black moustache appeared an attempt to look older. Geary assumed the staunch pro-slavery supporter must have something on President Pierce to be appointed as Secretary of Kansas Territory with no political experience. Woodson was a printer by trade.

Geary turned to Gihon, "What do you think Jack?"

"Seemed a very reasonable man; and I don't believe the Abolitionists are the bad guys in this mess, Dan."

Woodson continued watching out the window, silently composing a letter to President Pierce, 'Franklin, I am forced to write this painful letter. You sent me here to make certain that Kansas is admitted as a slave state. I assumed you appointed Geary for the same reason. He is not who you suppose. He is firmly in the Abolitionist camp. If you don't act soon, he will expel all of our militia groups and we will be in grave danger of falling to the Abolitionists. To secure your historical legacy you must take immediate action. Quit appointing Governors who profess to be good American's, yet they side with the rebel Abolitionists and vilify the true Americans who are following the letter of the law; God fearing men who believe in the southern institutions that made our country great; men who want to do what is right for the entire nation and not just a few northern anti-slavery do-gooders--all guilty of Treason. DO SOMETHING BEFORE IT IS TOO LATE!'

Woodson glanced back at his traveling companions. They were all glaring at him. He turned back to the window, 'Well, I won't hide my feelings. I've got the President of the United States on my side.'

As if reading Woodson's thoughts Geary addressed Sibley, "Major, my primary purpose is to ensure that only qualified voters from Kansas vote in the elections. I don't care what the outcome is, but I will not abide Missouri citizens coming to Kansas to cast an illegal vote."

"Christ Almighty, most of those men aren't even Missouri citizens, the Border Ruffians are from the deep south," Gihon turned a little to his left better able to see Geary.

"Yeah, south of Hell," Shorty's voice was a nasal whistle like blowing through a newly carved willow flute. Barely five feet four inches tall and 125 pounds he glared at Dan Woodson daring him to say something. Woodson ignored them all.

The coach rocked on, wagon springs creaking, muffled shouts from the driver encouraging the horses, "Catch up Little Blackie, hie Sampson." Geary watched the scouts' race ahead then back with reports. He wasn't terribly concerned; the highwaymen recognized his Territorial Coach. Most of the 'militia' gangs pillaging the territory had been disbanded back to their homes in Missouri. Renegade groups of Border Ruffians still roamed the territory looking for plunder, stealing horses, livestock, anything they could get their hands on. The past six months had been total chaos with several deaths, many injuries and constant strife.

Geary pulled the shade down and latched it, blocking some of the cold air, "Thank God most of the thugs are gone," he said quietly. To Jack Gihon he added, "We've still got many problems ahead of us."

Gihon nodded in agreement looking pointedly at Woodson who continued to ignore them, pretending to read government documents.

"Major, we are much indebted to you for the comfortable tents. They've made this trip almost enjoyable," Gihon said.

Even Woodson could agree with that remark and did so enthusiastically, "I hope you've patented your design, Major."

"That I have and very near finalizing negotiations with Washington on licensing the Sibley Tent for Army use."

"That should be profitable," Shorty Jones leaned toward the Major hoping to gain more information. Sibley merely nodded affirmation, disappointing the diminutive Secretary. Geary smiled, 'mighty feisty for such a slight fellow. I'm glad he's on my side. I think the Major considers him insignificant,' "What are your thoughts so far, Shorty?"

"My thoughts are that you've done an impressive job of ridding this Territory of the Border Ruffian scum. Those men shouldn't be hired to dig a latrine let alone be soldiers. We'll be a lot better off when the likes of Atchison and Stringfellow are eliminated from this Territory."

Major Sibley turned his gaze on Shorty. Geary noticed an appreciative gleam in his eye. Woodson scoffed, "Those are decent law-abiding citizens you're maligning, Shorty," the nickname snorted in contempt, "just because you don't agree with them politically doesn't mean they have to leave. They have as much right to be here as you do, Shorty."

"No one is denying that, Dan," the Governor shifted around to face Woodson, "but Atchison is a Missouri Senator. The men they bring to vote in Kansas live in Missouri. That's what I'm talking about," he raised his voice, "and you can't deny you are as much to blame as anyone... ordering Atchison to attack Lawrence."

"I was acting Governor then...and I had good reason. Sam Wood, Jim Lane, Charlie Robinson—they're all rebels, criminals. They should be in jail," Woodson was getting agitated.

"For what?" Shorty sniffed.

"Treason for one thing. They were all indicted."

"By your stooges in the courts," Shorty argued.

Woodson waved Shorty away, addressed Geary, "We've been together for three weeks on this inspection. There's something I want to know, Governor." He leaned forward aggressively, "do you honest-to-God believe that Niggers are equal to us White people?"

"Where did that come from?" Gihon turned to Woodson.

"It's a legitimate question. You seem to me to be siding with the Abolitionists. Don't they believe the Black race is equal to the Whites? Sam Wood believes they are--so does John Brown." Woodson glared at Geary, "What about you, Governor?"

"No... Negroes are an inferior race but that doesn't mean they should be in chains treated worse than animals."

"See, that proves that you don't want Kansas to be a slave state?" Woodson gloated.

"That isn't a logical conclusion, Dan. I just said that I don't care the outcome of the vote in Kansas. I just want to follow the guidelines in the Organic Act of Congress that created Kansas and Nebraska, dammit," he pounded his fist on the bench, "It's clear as hell...Popular Sovereignty...how can you misinterpret that. The citizens of Kansas vote for slave or free state...not invaders from the south. All I'm trying to do is ensure a fair election with true Kansas voters."

Mayor Sibley fidgeted, obviously wanting to make a point, "No sane man believes that Niggers are equal to white people. This entire matter has been blown out of proportion. Niggers are just not worth all this fuss. I'd like to see the Nation stay united, but the South will secede, and I'll be right there with them. We have the right to run our lives as we see fit."

Gihon sat back, "Major, you mean to tell me you'll abandon your military career to fight with the south?"

"I will if it comes to that. How can you sit there and tell me a bunch of ignorant Niggers are worth going to war? They don't have feelings; not like we do. For white people to turn their back on their own kind is beyond my understanding."

"I have to disagree with you. I've seen Negroes treated worse than the family horses in Kentucky. Living in nothing more than tarpaper shacks with dirt floors. It's criminal, inhumane the way they are treated."

"And the dirty little secret nobody talks about," Shorty said quietly.

They waited for him to continue. He looked up to see the confusion in their faces, "The sexual abuse of the women," he explained as if it were obvious.

Sibley laughed, "Well, Mr. Shorty, I wouldn't call it abuse. I've partaken of that little pleasure myself. Ain't nothing better than a Nigger wench on a cold night. My old man used to call em' belly warmers...'You want a belly warmer for the night, boy', he'd say. Oh, the memories."

Geary turned away looking at Dr. Gihon, the rocking of the coach couldn't mask the Governor's revulsion. Gihon finally said, "That is a disgusting sentiment, Major. The Negroes are not animals. They have feelings. What you did is rape."

"Ah, bullshit," Woodson fumed, "if they're so abused why don't they do something about it? I'll tell you why...because they are perfectly content right where they are. It's the Northern whites who are stirring things up. Traitors like Sam Wood and John Brown."

Shorty, angry now, waved his finger in Woodson's face, "And that fellow Sherrard is nothing but a drunken bully. Why do you want him to be sheriff?" Woodson turned away, as Shorty stood, barely able to maintain his balance, "I'll tell you why... because he'll do exactly what you slaveholders want and keep harassing the Free State men."

"That doesn't have anything to do with this discussion, Shorty," Woodson dismissed him with a wave of his hand.

"It may not, but we're going to have to deal with that issue and soon," Geary insisted.

"He was appointed by the Territorial Council and approved by Judge LeCompte."

Gihon held his hand out as if to stop Woodson, "The Territorial Council is not a legitimate body. They are not elected officials and have nothing to do with Douglas County."

"You'll play hell convincing President Pierce of that," Woodson shouted back.

Geary raised the window shade again. The cold air seemed to freeze the conversation out of all of them. Tensions eased as they rocked on to the East. Shorty left Woodson's side and sat between Gihon and Geary.

The Governor took a deep breath and reflected on his success in clearing the countryside of the organized 'armies' of Senator Atchison, Bogus Sheriff Jones and General Stringfellow, the leaders of the Border Ruffians. Still, bands of thieves terrorized travelers. 'Civil war', Geary wrote in letters back to

Washington. His first trip from Leavenworth City to Lecompton was like traveling through a battlefield, farmhouses smoldering, only the chimney's standing, crops plundered, no sign of life; the occasional dead cow or horse to complete the gruesome scene. "It damned sure didn't look like the America I know," he said aloud startling his traveling companions.

He glared at all of them, "Think about it. Freight companies forced to hire armed escorts to protect shipments. Settlers have to band together before venturing anywhere. That's no way for civilized people to live."

"And all the Territorial Judges are in the pocket of the Pro-Slavery bunch," Shorty shook his head looking at the Major.

Daniel Woodson shook the paper he was reading to make a point, "The Judges are upholding the laws of the United States. Slavery is legal."

"Not in Kansas Territory it isn't," Gihon countered.

"I have to agree with the Governor," Major Sibley said, "it hasn't been determined if Kansas is to be free or slave. I make no bones about my opinion, but fair is fair."

The coach lurched to a stop. A trooper opened the door, "Major, a tree has fallen across the ramp to the low water crossing. Governor, you want to stretch your legs?"

"Thank you, Corporal. Where are we?" Sibley asked.

"Almost to the village of Manhattan, Sir. Just over the next rise you'll be able to see the valley."

"I've heard it's a beautiful place," Gihon said.

"It is, Sir," the trooper agreed, "be a great place to have a farm," he glanced at his commanding officer hoping he hadn't overstepped his authority, "people who think Kansas is flat need to come to Manhattan."

They climbed down squinting into the bright winter sun reflecting off a thin blanket of snow. Patches of prairie grasses lay quiet in brilliant splendor, purplish fox tail barley in the shallow ditches, the blue stem in its Fall copper coating and reddish-brown buffalo grass lying dormant awaiting the return of spring. The coach rested in the lee of a hill near Kings Creek about a mile south of the Kansas River. Geary turned his face to the sun, shielded his eyes, guessing the time to be near one. Even though the prairie wind was brisk, a pleasant sensation of warmth washed over him. He could hear the soldiers sawing and chopping at the fallen tree.

Constant strife between the abolitionist and pro-slavery factions was taking a toll, mentally and physically, 'I've got one friend here', he lamented, looking at Dr. Gihon. 'Franklin Pierce misled me when he said to make certain the people of Kansas decide the fate of Kansas. The entire Presidential Cabinet wants Kansas to be a slave state regardless of the wishes of the majority of citizens and the wording of the Kansas-Nebraska Act. How can they misinterpret popular sovereignty? Seems simple enough,' Geary lamented, 'but no one could foresee the Border Ruffians who don't give a damn what the law says. They decided to make Kansas a slave state with guns and knives and I guess Pierce supports them.'

"Lord, give me strength," he said to the heavens, eyes closed.

"Praying, Governor?"

"Asking for the strength to carry on, John. I hope the President lets me finish the job I've started here. We're just beginning to make some progress."

"Don't get too discouraged, you have good friends in Lawrence and Topeka. Charlie Robinson, Sam Wood, those are men that will back you."

"My God, can you believe the monsters President Pierce has loosed on this land? These Boarder Ruffians, I've never witnessed anything so vile, so disgusting..." Geary shook his head in frustration.

Gihon nodded, "You've done everything humanly possible, Governor. Don't criticize yourself and don't listen to him," Gihon gestured toward Daniel Woodson climbing back into the coach, "he and Senator Atchison are using the Border Ruffians to rid the territory of free-state voters."

"You know, Jack, I'm six feet seven inches tall, 280 pounds, I'm not afraid of anyone, but William Sherrard, the fellow Jones and Atchison want to be sheriff. He's a whole different kind of bad news."

Gihon nodded agreement, "Say, where's Shorty?"

Glancing around the coach, they couldn't help but laugh. Shorty was on the downhill side of the grade, the double-bladed ax seemed bigger than the man swinging it. He worked in tandem with a solder on the uphill side. They alternated strokes. Two other soldiers were at the opposite end of the tree, chopping and at the same time trying to steal a glance at their opponents. It became a race. Troopers were cheering them on, picking a favorite; even a few wagers made.

"Look at the little fellow swing that ax. Shorty can hold his own, can't he?"

"He's amazing, and a hell of a mind too. I couldn't get along without him."

"Let's go help."

They draped their coats on the door, grabbed a large limb, and began hauling it to the side. Cheers erupted as Shorty and his partner chopped through their end of the tree. Soldiers crowded around enjoying the diversion. Shorty raised his ax in victory.

Daniel Woodson watched from the coach, eyes narrowed, lips puckered. Reaching under the seat he produced paper and pen to begin the letter exposing the disloyalty of Governor Geary.

***

Almost seven months earlier, May 1856, bogus Sheriff Sam Jones torched Sam and Margaret Wood's home at 7th and Massachusetts Street during the Sack of Lawrence. It was, according to Jones, "One of the happiest moments of my life." He hated Sam Wood. After Sam rescued Jacob Branson in November of

1855, Jones pursued him with warrants accusing him of interfering with a lawful arrest, assaulting an officer of the law, insurrection and most damning, High Treason. Sam eluded Jones by going East to work with John Fremont in his campaign for the Presidency. Meanwhile, the Wood family built a new brick home in West Lawrence on Michigan Street between fourth and fifth.

Sam stood for a moment on the front porch after seeing to the livestock. Stars shined brilliant in the crisp cold air. He leaned against a corner column looking at the dark canvas dotted bright with pinpoints of light. The cold air drove him inside where the fire burned low, yet the house was cozy warm from the heated stones. Several children were bundled up asleep on the hearth. David and Punch, Caleb and Missy plus assorted neighborhood friends. Stephan Wood and his wife were upstairs asleep along with Sarah. Margaret sat in the rocking chair before the warm fire the baby at her breast. Sam slipped behind Margaret leaning over to gaze at the newest addition to the Wood family. Margaret leaned her head against his cheek.

"Tired, Meg?"

"Exhausted and we've got a busy day tomorrow."

The baby lay sleeping, mouth open, parents gazing fondly, "We'd best sleep down here. I think Stephan and Caroline are in our bed."

Sam nodded, taking the baby, gently patting away any discomfort. They crawled into bed. Sam kissed the baby, then his wife, and fell asleep instantly. Margaret rested on her side the baby lying between them, her arm lying on Sam's chest. She lingered lost in thought of all that needed doing the next morning. Sam snored causing the baby's lips to move searching for mother's breast. Margaret smiled and brushed a lock of hair from his forehead, warmed by a memory of the first time she saw him at her parents' home in Ohio some 9 years earlier. She was coming down the stairs in her under garments. Oh, the look on his face. She laughed, reached out to touch Sam's face, lay back contented and the next thing she knew it was morning.

***

Margaret let dangle her crochet hook to gesture toward the men and women gathered around the table, "Have you ever seen such a to-do over a baby?"

Sarah Wood and Mrs. Sally Thompson nodded briefly but quickly returned to their tasks; Sarah with her tatting shuttle applied vigorously to the lace. Sally attended to the decorative hemstitching on the long cotton gown for the baby. She used a pink thread in a diamond pattern, her hands flying from years of practice.

The Wood home was crowded with the first guests of the new year after being winter bound by deep snow and brutally cold temperatures. The visitors, indicated by Margaret's casual gesture, stood in a circle around the table gazing into a small box recently crafted by John Thompson, husband of Sally. His was one of the faces frozen in the scene described above. A dark man, handsome with smooth chestnut skin and lively eyes basking in the glow of his God child, an infant of indeterminate sex who lay in an angelic repose of slumber, swaddled in a long white cotton nightshirt folded back at the hem to provide additional warmth. An unbiased observer would not be wrong in applying a certain religious connotation akin to an event almost two thousand years earlier. Though this child was female, her father, Sam Wood, would not have argued with the notion that she was blessed.

A Nathanial Currier lithograph, Hunter in the Woods, hung provocatively on the wall enticing the guests with visions of the coming spring. Through the window icicles dangled from the eves, water dripped diamonds sparkling in the sun and children played gaily in the snow. Their childish laughter stirs even the hardest heart with hopes and dreams of a new beginning. Isn't that what spring suggests? Especially for these Kansas settlers who just experienced a dreadful year of turmoil and terror. Many friends and neighbors were murdered or driven from their homes, yet these folks, against all odds, seem to expect better times ahead. To these frontier optimists, dreaming just comes naturally, like the first breath of the baby. They couldn't survive without dreams of better days entrenched on the frozen edge of civilization. Each gazed with wonderment at Francis in her peaceful sleep.

Charlie Robinson turned to his wife, Sara, "Well my dear, it appears I owe you a bolt of silk."

"You should never bet against Margaret's premonitions," John T cautioned in a good-natured way, his hand on Charlie's shoulder.

"What would you have won had she been a boy?" Jim Lane pulled a fat cigar out of his vest pocket.

"Jim!" Mary cried startling the baby.

"Oh sorry," he put the cigar away with a guilty glance at Florence.

Margaret set her handiwork aside and gathered up the fussing child, "Francis is hungry," she moved toward the stairs followed by the entire group of ladies except for Sarah who carefully placed the three knitting projects in the proper bag, then stored them in the utility closet on the back porch. A blast of cool air filled the room as she quickly closed the door.

"What would you have won, Charlie?" Caleb Pratt asked as the men found chairs or stood near the hearth.

"A very nice felling axe from McCoy's in Westport."

"I'll wager you end up with it anyway," Judge Wakefield said, trying to find a comfortable position on the hearth for his heavy body. He would need help getting up.

"I'll bet he does too," Lane said a mischievous gleam in his eye, "but who is going to swing it? Charlie has never found a tree he couldn't get someone else to chop down." That brought a round of laugher from everyone except Charlie, glaring at General Lane while pulling his chair closer to the fire, "Gentlemen, the time has come to make some hard decisions. Our backs are against the wall. Governor Geary has done all he can to calm the situation; the rest is up to us."

Clarke Pomeroy agreed and added, "We've got to organize the Topeka Convention Delegates and proceed with our plans to form a Free State Government."

"And ignore the Pro-Slavery Legislation at the same time. Nothing has changed, truth be told," Sam Walker took his knife and a piece of kindling, shaving the bits into the fire.

This elephant-in-the-room had been on their minds all winter. The Senate and House of Representatives in Washington failed to enact the Topeka Constitution submitted by the Kansas Free State Legislature the previous summer when Charlie was elected Governor. President Pierce installed a pro-slavery panel of Judges as a territorial Supreme Court and a group of pro-slavery appointees as the Territorial Council. Many of them were men from the Slave State of Missouri. The pro-slavery legislation was enacting laws that the Free State citizens ignored causing them to be labeled 'rebels' by the law enforcement officers.

"To begin with, what are we going to do about this fellow, Sherrard? Atchison and Jones are pushing him to be the new sheriff. I assume because he'll terrorize the Abolitionists just like Jones did." Jim Lane glanced up the stairs as he lit his cigar, blowing the smoke up the chimney. He gestured to Wakefield with the cigar case.

Wake took a cigar, held it for a light, "We cannot allow him to become the sheriff, he's nothing but a drunken bully," he said between puffs.

Sam Walker jumped up to relieve Sarah the burden of a bundle of firewood as she struggled to open the door, "I thought Governor Geary refused to seat him," Walker said setting the wood in the bin and throwing a log on the fire.

"He did," Charlie agreed, "but he was overruled by the Territorial Council; all of them pro-slavery men."

"The Governor stopped by here last week," Sam leaned against the back of Charlie's chair, "have you spoken to him since our last meeting, Charlie."

"No, I haven't."

Judge Wakefield blew smoke up the chimney, rolled the cigar lovingly, "There is an indignation meeting in Lecompton next week to protest Sherrard's appointment...weather permitting."

"We all have to be there," Pratt stated emphatically.

"We need to get as many Free State men to go as possible. If this weather holds, the roads will be dry enough to get a good representation." Sam pulled a chair closer to make a quiet point, "Governor Geary told me that Sherrard has threatened to kill him if he opposes his appointment as sheriff."

"Why doesn't Geary have him thrown in jail?" Walker asked.

Charlie raised his hands in frustration, "By who? We wrote a letter to General Smith at Fort Leavenworth. He said he can't do anything about

Sherrard making threats. He can only act if Sherrard commits a crime."

"It'll be a little late by then, won't it?" John T offered, met by silent agreement; a silence broken by the sound of raucous laughter from above. They all looked to the stairs.

***

"How did you know Francis would be a girl," Cora Wakefield asked, peering at the sleeping baby just finished nursing at mother's breast.

"Don't tell Sam, he thinks I willed it," Margaret giggled, "he thinks I'm a seer." They all broke into furtive laughter. "The truth is I carried her different from the boys."

"I wish you were clairvoyant," Mary Lane lamented. She stood at the window watching the children playing outside, "I wonder what's going to happen to us here in Kansas."

"We'll survive just as we have the last three years," Margaret sighed.

Marlee Tappan came up the stairs, "Sorry I'm late, Oh, my goodness," she reached for the baby. Margaret gladly passed her over. "What a darling, I'm going to tell Tap that I want one."

"Get Margaret to put a spell on you. She can pick and choose," Mary winked. "Otherwise, you'll be taking your chances like the rest of us."

"I think she needs changed. Where are the napkins? I'll do it," Marlee nuzzled the baby.

"I wish there was more that John and I could do," Sally took the baby's things to the bed.

"What do you mean, Sally?" Sara Robinson asked.

"It just seems that everyone is working so hard to free the slaves. I'm a former slave and I can't do anything to help, at least here in Kansas. If I was in the east, I could make speeches like Frederick Douglass or Harriet Tubman."

"Sally, you and all the Negroes in Lawrence are important to what we are doing," Marlee handed the baby to June Walker.

"I tell her that constantly," Margaret added, "I still think your speech at the July 4th celebration converted many people to our cause."

"And almost got me killed," Sally said, rubbing the bullet scar hidden by her dark hair.

"All I know is you and John T help remind me of what we're fighting for. I'm mighty glad you're here with us," Sara took her by the arm.

"We have a long way to go, ladies. When we become a State...Jim wants to be our first Senator," Mary Lane said.

"So does Charlie," Sara Robinson countered.

"But Charlie will be Governor," Marlee held Flo to her shoulder, patting her back.

"Well, there will be two senators."

"So does Clarke Pomeroy, George Dietzler, Andy Reeder, and Mr. Parrott," Cora added, "I suggest we wait until we become a state before we worry about it. That's a political issue left to the voters."

"Jim deserves it more than anyone. He led the Kansas Militia against the Ruffians."

Margaret took the baby, "Sam deserves it as much as anyone else."

"SAM," they chorused, all laughing, "Margaret don't be silly. If someone disagrees with him, he'll whack them on the head with his cane."

Margaret didn't feel silly, "Sam almost got John Fremont elected President. He rescued Jacob Branson. He's worked harder than anyone to make Kansas a Free State."

"Yes, and left Jim here alone to fight the Missouri trash that attacked us," Mary Lane folded her arms and tapped her foot.

"That is unfair," Margaret scowled.

"And Charlie was in jail, Mary," Sara Robinson had tears in her eyes, "you know he would have fought if he could."

Margaret put her hands on her hips with a ferocious glare, "Jim left the Territory just like Sam did. In fact, Jim told Sam to stay in the east. He could help the cause more there than here. He brought more Free State settlers to Kansas than anyone."

"Ladies, please, we can't fight among ourselves. Compose yourselves," Sally urged. Silence filled the room as they turned away looking out the window or fussing over the baby until Margaret turned to Mary Lane with her arms extended. They embraced, "I'm sorry I got carried away. let's go join the men," she moved toward the stairs arm in arm with Mary.

The wives trooped back down to a scene of embarrassed guilt as Judge Wakefield and Jim Lane quickly tossed their half-smoked cigars into the fire. Too late, both Cora and Mary eyed their husbands with looks that foretold a serious discussion when they got home. Jim had been warned not to smoke in the house, Margaret forbade the practice and Sam did not smoke. The Judge was under doctors' orders and Cora intended that he would follow those orders religiously.

"Where's Sarah?" Margaret asked. Sam had no idea.

"She's on the front porch, staring down the road. Looking for Hal Barnett," Sally pointed out the window.

"Oh, for heaven sakes, she doesn't even have her shawl. She'll freeze to death. I told her that the Barnett's would be late if they come at all."

"Sarah, come wait inside," Sally said, opening the door. "It's too cold out here without your coat."

"Hal said that he would come even if the rest of the family didn't. You don't suppose he ran into some Border Ruffians on the way do you, Sally?"

"Well, if he did, I feel sorry for the Ruffians. Hal can take care of himself. Autumn told me that they would be here if her brothers guard the farm while they are gone. Harold won't leave the place unattended, and you can't blame him."

"Sally, here they come," Sarah waved happily as the wagon pulled by a fine four horse team came into sight. Hal leapt from the wagon wrapping Sarah in a firm embrace as she giggled and pretended to resist.

The children ran from their snow games to greet Carol.

Harold and his wife Autumn were influential in the abolitionist movement and among the farmers in the area. They owned about 800 acres south and west of Lawrence between Hickory Point and Bloomington. Autumn was of Shawnee heritage. Her two brothers, and their sons agreed to come stay at the farm while the Barnett's visited neighbors.

The children laughed, made snowmen, threw snowballs, enjoyed all the winter games children love. Barring another winter storm, the warming weather would soon turn the snow to water, overflowing the rivers and creeks, washing the detritus of the horrible winter away. If only it would wash away the foul men who vowed to make Kansas a slave state.

***

Sam, Margaret and Sarah sat at the table engrossed in varied tasks; light from the single lamp reflected the paleness of their weary faces.

"Who are you writing to?" Margaret didn't look up from the pork cut she was salting.

"A letter to the Republican Planning Committee for the Presidential election in '60'."

"That's a lot of letters," Sarah smiled as she ground black pepper with the new mortar and pestle recently gifted from Autumn Barnett.

"It would be if I were going to write them all but I'm going to the office tomorrow and have Bill typeset it and print them off."

"Is John Freemont going to run again?"

"Yes, but he doesn't have much support; I think Salmon has the best chance. I'll nominate him again, but Abe told me he is seriously considering it, and Ed Bates is getting a lot of support."

"I like him," Sarah added, "ever since he won the Freedom Suit for Lucy Delaney."

"He's a good man," Sam agreed.

Margaret wiped the salt from her hands with a wet rag, "Why would Lincoln want to run against Salmon, isn't everyone for him?"

"No, not everyone. I think Bill Seward..."

"From New York?"

"Yes, he has some support. A few Chicago businessmen want to build a convention hall to house the nominating convention. That's what I'm helping to resolve. I'll have to go back to Ohio and meet with the committee this summer. After we settle the Topeka Constitution issues."

"Sam, I worry you're taking on too much. We really need to resolve the state and local matters first."

"But Meg, I've got you and Sarah to do all the work. I'm just a poor humble public servant."

She hit him with the wet towel, "I'm just glad Jones isn't sheriff anymore. At least you don't have to hide from him."

Sarah poured the newly ground pepper into the container and replaced it on the shelf, "I hope things calm down a little around here. Too many people being killed over politics."

Sam stared at his sister, "Sarah, don't wish for something that is beyond our power to control. Make no mistake about it, there will be a war."

***

"Margaret...Sarah, ya'll go on about your business and leave this here to me. I been washing out clouts fore either of you was born. The boys can haul water from the well or melt some snow. Just get a good fire going on the stove before you leave," Beulah wasn't looking at either lady, busy as she was, sorting clothes, getting the washtub down from the wall and supervising the boys hauling water.

Margaret was exhausted. "You're a Godsend, Beulah," she hugged her, took off her apron before leaving to walk to her mother's house.

Beulah had been busy all winter trying to keep the Wood's, Thompson's and Lyons from starving or freezing to death. She deserved a lot of the credit for easing the hardships of the harsh winter months. A fact she foretold almost a year earlier when announcing she and Silas were coming to Kansas Territory to get things straightened out, because the 'white folk wasn't doing such a bang-up job on their own.' That general indictment included John and Sally Thompson although they were most certainly not 'white folk'. Beulah lumped them into the mix because they spent most of their time 'hobnobbing' with the bigshots in Lawrence, "You all gettin' way above your raisin'," she scolded. Truth was she couldn't have been prouder of John T and Sally and everyone knew it. Though she couldn't read herself, Beulah insisted that Sally read to her from the book she was writing about the slaves passing through on the Underground Railroad.

Beulah placed the round metal washtub on a tree stump John T cut to just the right height so she wouldn't be breaking her back bending over. She was a large woman with high shiny cheek bones, short tightly curled black hair, normally under a scarf, and dark sparkling eyes that can only be described as playful. She managed the children with a firm but loving hand, chastised Sam and John for laxity in disciplining their children, Caleb and Missy Thompson and Lloyd, nicknamed Punch, and David Wood. She need only give an order once to be obeyed. Sam and John T would coax, bribe or just pass the task off to the ladies when it came to getting the children to do something. Yet the children loved and respected her, and baby Flo would be no different. Silas and Beulah were born free. Yet they worked with runaway slaves all their lives. They were not strangers to the cruelty of the slaveholders. Knowing that Sam was leading the movement to make Kansas a Free State she said, "I'd work for Margaret and Sam Wood for free if it helps my brothers and sisters lose their chains."

David and Caleb hauled a bucket of water from the shared neighborhood well, trying desperately not to splash it all out before handing it to Beulah. She poured it in the large pot on the wood stove. It was going to take a lot of water to wash all the clothes that had piled up during the cold winter. Through the worst of the storms, only underwear, nightclothes, and the cloth 'napkins' were rinsed in cold water then hung to dry on the hearth. There was a constant earthy smell in the Wood home especially after baby Flo arrived. Her wet napkins often hung unrinsed on the hearth to dry for reuse later that night.

"It's warm enough to hang em' on the clothesline," she announced. Both boys loved the smell of clean laundry drying in the sun. Beulah's hands were rough and calloused from years of using lye soap, washing in hot water, rinsing in cold. She never complained, it was just a fact of life, "until someone invents a machine to wash the clothes for you," she laughed.

Sam had nearly forgotten what it meant to have a baby in the house. David was almost nine and Punch seven. They were very proud big brothers, a little overawed, maybe, "Aunt Beulah," David said lifting the pail of heavy water as high as they could reach, "Flo sure does use up a lot of napkins. I wish she wasn't so messy."

She gave him a look, "Listen to you child. You was just the same. I cleaned your messy bottom from the day you was born, Caleb too. You just don't remember it."

Caleb scowled, "Well, I sure don't plan on having no babies. Too much trouble."

"You best not be making that kind of decision till you got a little more room between them big ears," she grabbed his ears like handles.

David and Caleb trudged off to draw more water, holding the bucket between them. Caleb was dark skinned, like his father whereas sister Missy was much lighter even than her mother, Sally, a mulatto, what some called a 'high yaller'. Missy was so light colored; the southerners called her a 'White Nigger." Sally was a product of the rape of her mother by the white overseer of the plantation where she was raised and was not shy about proclaiming that fact. Well educated and opinionated, it was not her fault, nor her mother's fault, these details of her birth.

Sam moseyed out of the house after finishing some legal papers, "Where is everyone, Beulah? Why isn't someone helping you?"

"First off, I don't need no help washing clothes, second off, everyone's got something else to do, what with the sun shining and all. Sarah's taking care of Flo, Silas and Mr. Lyon are off doctoring some sick cow, Margaret just went over to her mama's house to help skin an antelope Paschal Fish brought by."

"That was sure nice of him."

"I think that's your payment, doing those legal papers for selling his land."

Sam chuckled, "He's going to have plenty of money to pay me when this land deal goes through. I need to walk over and see Charlie. Tell John T I'll be back in an hour or two and we can go get that firewood."

He walked off toward Charlie's house higher up on Mt. Oreod, oblivious to Beulah watching him, "Yeah, you bout as much help cutting firewood as Flo."

Sam strolled along enjoying the good weather, many things on his mind. A gradual slope from the City Park turned into a steeper climb. He stopped to gaze over Lawrence. The new Eldredge Hotel almost complete, replacing the Free State Hotel burned down in the Sack of Lawrence. Several new businesses in town, a new clothing store, a dentist office; Brook's Mercantile had been expanded. Sam could hear hammering and the workers shouting to each other. The Baldwin ferry crossed the Kansas River at the end of Massachusetts Street carrying a brougham pulled by two white horses. A beautiful sight. 'I wonder whose it is?'

The last 100 yards to Charlies' house he reviewed an agenda in his mind including the Free State Delegate Convention scheduled in two weeks in Big Springs. That was the first item of business. They also had a meeting the following week in Lecompton to discuss the appointment of the new Douglas County sheriff, William Sherrard, by all accounts a poor choice for the job.

"I don't know this fellow, Sherrard, do you, Charlie?" Sam took a vacant chair on the south facing front porch. Sara brought coffee and a pitcher of water. "Do you know this fellow Sherrard?" he repeated to her.

"No, not by that name. I guess you'll meet him Friday night. From what I've heard he's a very violent man. Drinks a lot, always looking for a fight at the saloon in Westport across from McCoy's or at that horrid Red Dog Saloon in Leavenworth."

Her husband looked surprised, "Where did you hear all that?"

"Mrs. Brown told Maisey Epcot and she told Sarah Wood and she told Mrs. Brooks and she told all of us at choir practice Tuesday night."

The men looked at each other, "Maybe we should pay a bit more attention to what the ladies are doing," Charlie laughed as he sipped the coffee. They sat quietly looking over their town. Charlie's house occupied a prominent vista on Mt. Oreod, rebuilt on the same lot after Sheriff Jones and the Border Ruffians burned his first home. This one was an improvement, brick on the first floor and wood frame above.

"Sam, I want to discuss something with you," he looked at the floor trying to find the right words. "I'm going to resign my position as governor."

"What?"

Charlie took a deep breath, "I'm going to go to Washington to plead our cause. I think I'll have more influence as a private citizen than I would as the Governor of half the citizens."

"Charlie, I've argued with Pierce until I'm blue in the face. I'm not sure why you think you'll have better luck than I did ."

Robinson shifted uncomfortably, leaned forward to make his point, "Sam, you worked wonders campaigning for the Republican Party. I truly believe Fremont received half again as many votes as he would have without you. But you rub the President the wrong way. Pierce just hates you, let's be honest."

"Well, I'm not sure that hate is the right word," Sam chuckled, "I think, though, a lot of his impressions come from Senator Atchison and that man does hate me and the feelings are mutual. He should be in jail for the things he's done. To have a town named after him is an insult to any intelligent human being."

They sat quietly for a moment, "I guess it wouldn't hurt for you to give it a try, Charlie. You might have some influence going through our friends in the House and Senate, but President Pierce insists that Kansas be a slave state and Buchanan will be the same when he takes office in March. It's that simple. That's why the Border Ruffians are allowed to terrorize us, that's why Senator Atchison was able to raise an army and burn Lawrence down. But if you think you can be successful, more power to you."

"I'm going to leave tomorrow, weather permitting," Charlie scratched at his beard, "I hope to God I'm doing the right thing."

"What about the County meeting Friday and the Free State convention at Big Springs?"

"I've given, Lt. Governor Roberts a letter resigning my position as governor. He will be the acting governor and the convention should go on as planned. You'll be there, Caleb Pratt, Sam Walker, George Dietzler, Clarke Pomeroy," he took a sip of coffee to gain time before he finished, "I'm distrustful of Jim Lane. He seems to be posturing more to be a Senator when we achieve statehood than focusing on the issues now."

"I've seen a little of that myself," Sam agreed, "remember, he came here as a Democrat and only changed to the Free State side when he saw we were going to be successful. Regardless, we'll have to work with him. Are you sure you want to go through with this trip to Washington?"

"I feel strongly about this Sam. If I don't try, I know I'll regret it forever."

"If you've made up your mind, then that's that," Sam stood, extended his hand, "I'll let the others know what you're up to; you'll have our hopes and prayers riding with you. Godspeed, Charlie."

***

Hal Barnett, Junior, an oversized, well-proportioned young man of 25, known to his friends and family as Bull, was not to be crossed if one valued his health. Bull, strong of mind as well as body was ferociously devoted to family and friends and, like his father, a terror to those who offend him. Together with Harold Senior, his mother, Autumn, and four brothers and sisters he farmed and grazed land near Bloomington, a village five miles west and south of Lawrence.

The settlers in Kansas were, for the most part, ordinary citizens who immigrated from the United States to settle on the American frontier on land claimed according to the pre-emption law of 1841 whereby a squatter on federal land could 'claim' up to 160 acres and pay the equivalent of $1.25 per acre for the right. The settlers around Lawrence and Topeka were no different except that in addition to the land, they came to prevent the advancement of slavery into Kansas Territory.

Harold senior stood 6'4" and weighed 250-pounds, a gentle giant who turned vicious if his Indian wife and children were insulted in any way. His son, Bull, was known as Hal by his girlfriend, Sarah Wood, a young lady of 22, full of feminine energy and determination. They developed a romance the previous summer amidst speculation by the entire community as to their plans. Although friends and family assumed marriage was imminent, no one seemed to know for sure. Bull decided, without consultation with his fiancé, to build a home on the Barnett family land for himself and his future bride.

One bright sun filled day in late January of 1857, Bull met with his friend, the blacksmith and carpenter, Eric McCrea to discuss this planned new home. Eric was well known in the territory having created a furor the previous March when he killed a Leavenworth City pro-slavery citizen by the name of Malcolm Clarke. Some claimed it was cold-blooded murder, some claimed it was self-defense. The pro-slavery faction declared, without benefit of a trial, that it was murder and sentenced young McCrea to be hung. The Free State settlers knew it to be self-defense. Regardless, Eric vacated the area and only came back during the Siege of Lawrence when the citizens focus was on protecting themselves from the Border Ruffian invasion. His situation was forgotten or ignored.

The trip to Leavenworth City was to pick up a load of building materials for the new home; mainly iron for the hinges and lintels, beams for the ceiling and planks for the flooring. Both Harold's dad and Eric's father-in-law (and business partner), Riley Tanner, felt it was too wet and cold to attempt the trip.

"You should wait a week and see if the weather clears a bit more, maybe dry the roads some," Riley volunteered as he stoked the fire in their forge. Business was good for the Tanner-McCrea smithing and carpentry business, "You can't start the foundation yet anyway."

"I talked to Mr. Baldwin, he said the road is clear all the way to Leavenworth and the ice isn't a problem in the river. We won't have any trouble...any way, it's going to take two or three trips," Eric finished the list of items he expected to find at the docks and grabbed the Bill of Laden for the delivery from St. Louis.

It was early, just light and they were anxious to get on the road. They took the blacksmith shop's large Conestoga wagon converted to a freight truck drawn by six mules. The return load would be heavy. They drove to Paschal Fish's ferry near the confluence of the Wakarusa and Kansas River. It was larger than Baldwin's ferry and would hold the entire rig.

"Hey, Cricket," Bull hollered at his brother, cupping his hands. They were passing Chief Fish's house when his brother and cousins set off on a hunt into the prairie. Cricket, Billy and Eudora Fish waved back.

"Isn't it still a little early to chance this weather?" Eric said.

"They'll be fine. Cricket's an excellent hunter. He won't go that far." They watched the hunters ride off whooping and yelling. Hal and Eric had a good laugh at their exuberance, waved at Chief Fish at his door and drove toward the ferry. Once across, they could relax and enjoy the trip. Though cold, it was clear with no wind. They were well provisioned and warmly dressed.

"When's the big day?" Eric asked.

Hal looked confused, "What big day?"

Eric laughed, "Your wedding, dummy. Haven't you set a date yet?"

"I haven't even asked her yet," Hal grinned, "but I don't think she'll turn me down, do you?"

"Bull, you just never know. If I were you, I'd make it official; women are funny about things like that."

They rode a while in silence, "Did you hear Katie is expecting again?"

"No, I didn't, congratulations. You hope for a boy this time?"

"We don't care, just want Tammy to have a brother or sister to play with."

The mules plodded along, Eric barely holding the lines, "You going to the hearing next week?"

"Sure, aren't you," Hal took off his heavy coat and placed it behind the seat, "We can't let this guy Sherrard become sheriff."

"You know him?"

"No, but everyone says he's worse than a Border Ruffian. I don't know what that makes him, but it's bad."

Eric nodded, "I can't believe some of the stories. He whipped three or four guys in a saloon in Westport just because one of them asked him to quit bumping his elbow. Ralph Brown was there and saw the whole thing."

"He threatened to kill Governor Geary if he doesn't approve the appointment."

"The problem isn't the Governor, it's the pro-slavery legislation. They want him because he'll be just as bad as Bogus Jones was. I heard they're going to arrest any of us that try to meet for the Free State Legislature."

Hal thought about it for a moment, "If they do, Sam'll whack someone with his club and that'll be the end of it."

Eric laughed, "I'm sure glad he's on our side. If this guy Sherrard is as bad as they say, Sam'll take care of him one way or the other."

The road was still frozen making travel easier than traversing mud. Snow drifted across depressions in the road and would have been an impossible impediment to their voyage if someone had not cleared the drifts.

"I suppose work details from Fort Leavenworth," Hal said.

Some of the drifts were as high as the wagon with just room for the team to pass through.

"Good thing they were here before us, I don't know that I would have wanted to dig through all of that snow and I'm not sure we can turn around."

The Leavenworth City docks grew considerably since the summer of 1854 when the settlers began arriving in large numbers. The wharfs at Westport Landing and Kansas City had also grown yet it was easier for the Topeka and Lawrence citizens to fetch their deliveries from Leavenworth, even though they had to cross the Kaw River, more and more known as the Kansas River, to get home. The number and quality of ferries had increased significantly making travel easier on both sides of the river.

"Looks like we'll have to wait," Eric said pointing to a line of wagons, maybe four or five, waiting to enter the loading area. Hal jumped down and walked to the freight office at the entrance to the dockyards. The ground was chewed up from wagon wheels, horse hooves coming and going, black men and boys scooping manure, hauling dirt to smooth out ruts and hauling wagon loads of snow to dump into the river. Wagons were pulled into the yard by teamsters, loaded by dockhands then delivered to the owners at the freight office.

"The queue is about two hours, Mr. Barnett," Lewis Dashwood announced as Bull entered the freight office.

"What? What is about two hours?"

"The wait, sir, in England we call it the queue. Here in America, you say line."

"I didn't know you was from England, Lewis. I just thought you talk funny.'

Lewis took no offense at the slight, "Whatever we call it, plan on two hours until we can get your wagon into the yard. Probably have you loaded and ready to go home about two this afternoon."

When Bull reported the situation Eric replied, "That will put us home after dark. I guess we could stay at our house on Stranger Creek, but it will be pretty cold. I don't know if there is any wood or feed for the mules."

Eric and his father-in-law owned 320 acres on land between Lawrence and Leavenworth that they leased to Ralph Epcot. Eric had not visited the land since before the storm.

"Let's walk over to Grandma's Kitchen and see what she's got on the stove," Hal started that way.

"Wait," Eric pulled his arm, "I have to be careful not to get recognized."

"I don't think anyone will recognize you with that bushy red beard," Hal started off with Eric in tow.

The restaurant was busy, a lunch crowd of settlers and businessmen from town. The rougher crowd, the Border Ruffians and laborers frequented one of the saloons or bars.

They finished their meal of beef stew with potatoes and carrots, a rare delicacy during the winter months.

"I guess they still get deliveries here even when we don't in Lawrence."

Eric nodded as he drank the last of his coffee, "As long as the river's clear, they get freight from as far south as Memphis. Now that the army cleared the road, we'll start getting more supplies in town."

"Let's mosey on back to the freight office. Maybe they'll let us help load."

"I doubt that. Those boys on the docks are jealous of their jobs."

They stepped into the bright sunshine and turned toward the port about a half mile southeast of the village.

"Hey, isn't that Ralph Epcot and his family," Eric pointed to his neighbors passing in front of the Red Dog Saloon. The saloon door burst open; two drunks stumbled out running into Ralphie Epcot knocking him down.

"Watch out you little turd," the biggest screamed then kicked the boy in the side. Maisey rushed to her brother's aid. The drunk grabbed her hips and pressed his groin against her backside, "how's about a little poke darlin'," he mumbled.

Ralph punched the man in the face. The giant Border Ruffian was barely fazed by the blow. He pulled a pistol and fired. Eric and Bull jumped into action as Ralph spun around and fell to the plank board sidewalk, his wife and children screaming. Eric reached the man first jerked the pistol from his hand while Bull flipped the heavy man and knelt on his back. His companion sat down in a drunken stupor.

"Get the sheriff," Bull shouted to the gathering crowd.

"And a doctor," Eric yelled kneeling beside Ralph.

***

Ralph Epcot farmed next to the Tanner and McRae land near Stranger Creek between Lawrence and Leavenworth City. The previous year, Epcot leased the Tanner/McCrea tract when Eric and his father-in-law moved their blacksmithing business into Lawrence. They were good friends as well as business partners. Eric became enraged at the sight of Ralph shot down in cold blood in the middle of Leavenworth City; yet he needed to exercise caution lest someone should recognize him for the Malcolm Clarke death a year earlier.

Mrs. Epcot cradled Ralph's head while Eric applied pressure to the wound in his left shoulder only relinquishing the duty when the doctor arrived from his office just up the street. At the same time the sheriff came running up. Hal pulled the drunken fool to his feet while waiting for the lawman to apply handcuffs to the criminal.

"What the hell is going on here?" deputy Marshall Donaldson demanded when he realized who Hal had detained.

"This man shot Mr. Epcot and attacked his children."

"Is that true Bill?" Donaldson obviously knew the shooter.

"Self-defense!" the man was sobering up fast. "That bastard punched me in the face," he pointed at Ralph lying on the ground in obvious pain.

"I saw the whole thing," Hal protested. "You need to put this man in jail. He tried to kill Mr. Epcot."

"I'll take him with me, but it's his word against yours and this is Bill Sherrard the new sheriff in Douglas County."

Hal and Eric stared in disbelief as Donaldson walked off with the drunkard.

"That's Big Bill," Eric stammered, "he was Sheriff Jones deputy, remember?"

"I know you from somewhere," Big Bill's friend staggard to his feet. "It'll come to me cause I seen you before," he turned and pointed at Eric then stumbled after his friends.

"We need to leave," Eric said.

Doctor Starr stood up from tending the wound, "Well, you're a lucky man, Ralph. That fool missed all your vitals, and the bullet went through clean. Let's get you into my office and I'll wash it out and sew it up. It's going to tighten up and be sore, but you'll be fine in short order." He grabbed Hal by the arm. "I'll give you some free advice...let this matter drop. That's William T. Sherrard and the State Legislature has appointed him sheriff in Douglas County, he'll have authority over Lawrence. He's one mean son-of-a-bitch, excuse my language Mrs. Epcot, but I'm serious. Just let it go."

Eric was obviously nervous, "Let's get Ralph into Doctor Starr's office, Bull. We need to get out of here."

"We've got to take Ralph and his family home after Doc sews him up."

"We will but let's get back to the wagon. I'll explain then. Ralphie, where's your rig?"

Ralphie crouched by his father sobbing, "It's over behind the hotel."

Eric put his hand on Ralphie, "Are you ok?"

"My side hurts. That man kicked me for no reason."

Hal looked toward the Marshal walking away with Big Bill, "This is just wrong. That guy should be in jail. You want me to go with you Ralphie?"

Ralphie nodded, 'yes', looking at his father.

"Go get it, son. I'll be all right."

They got him to his feet then supported him into the Doctor's office. When settled, Eric hurried to the door, looked cautiously around then started for the dock. Hal looked at Mrs. Epcot, "I don't know why he's in such a hurry but wait for us if you get done before we get back. I want to take you home to make sure there isn't any more trouble. Maisey, are you ok?"

"I can't wait to tell Diane what happened."

"My sister will want to hear the whole story," Hal assured her as he hurried after Eric. "What's up Eric. Why the big hurry?"

"That drunk who said he recognized me. His name is Johnson, he's the guy stationed at the door the day I shot Malcolm Clarke. He's the one who lied and said Bill Phillips had given me the gun. He really did recognize me."

"He probably won't remember when he sobers up but let's find the wagon...get out of here," Hal agreed. A cold blast of wind startled them as the northern sky suddenly filled with angry clouds and snow stinging their faces. They took off at a run for the freight office.

***

"Lord have mercy, where did that come from?" Beulah pointed out the window. The wind rattled the panes; snow began to fall, blowing sideways by the time Margaret could observe the storm sneaking in like a thief from the northwest. The shutters began banging back and forth.

"Oh my," Margaret placed her hand on the rattling window, "David, run outside and fasten the shutters. Be sure to lock them down tight." Then to Sarah and Beulah she added, "Better bring in more wood. No telling how long this will last; it looks like a bad one."

"Where's Sam?" Sarah asked.

"With Silas at the barn. They better get themselves back here pronto or stay there until it blows over," Beulah opened the door to a blast of frigid air and blowing snow. The ladies hurried to the wood pile, about fifty feet from the back porch, gathered wood into burlap bags and turned back to the house only to find it had disappeared in the howling wind and blowing snow.

They hesitated, not sure what to do. Beulah yelled in Sarah's ear, "put your free hand on my shoulder. Stay right behind me. We don't want to miss the house."

They shuffled along one hand holding their bundle of fuel, Sarah's free hand on Beulah who was groping for the house...any part of the house lost in the endless whiteness. The fifty feet felt like a thousand. Beulah began to despair that they had been blown off course by the brutal wind, their heads turned away, eyes narrowed to tiny slits.

***

"Shall we wait it out here or try to make the house? Tough to say how long it'll last," Silas drawled in his calm baritone, "the ladies will be wondering, won't they?"

"We can probably make it if we go now," Sam said, "the animals are set for a couple of days. Sarah and John are at their house. Mom and Pop Lyon are at their house, I hope. Problem is...it could last a week."

"Well, let's go before that path we dug is filled in, if it isn't already. Here, Sam grab this length of rope, I'll follow behind you."

They walked single file tethered by the rope. Vision was impossible as the wind whipped the snow viciously against their faces. They soon found the path was disappearing; plowing through the drifts was an agony of lifting one leg out to make a foot or two of progress. Exhaustion quickly overtook the older man. No evidence of the house existed before them or the barn behind. Connected only by the rope Sam slogged through the snow, dragging Silas the best he could, trusting instinct to lead them home.

***

In Bloomington, Harold and Autumn were just sitting down to a cup of late afternoon coffee and a look at their account books when the storm crashed into their well-constructed home, banging the unsecured shutters, and shocking the inhabitants with the freight train sound of gale force wind and blowing snow. Harold ran out the door to secure the shutters, shouting for Chief to help. The two girls came from their room frightened by the suddenness of the onslaught.

"What about Bull and Cricket?" Carol asked her eyes glazed with fear. "They'll freeze to death, mother. What can we do?" She began crying, "go try to find them."

"They'll be fine! Get towels and put them on the windowsills to keep the wind out. And get two heavy blankets, we'll cover the outside doors. I'll stoke the fire," she put her hands together in silent prayer for her missing sons.

The large New England style fireplace was almost big enough to fit the entire family and constructed in a way that once heated, the stones retained adequate warmth to keep the main room comfortable. They would be snug and safe with nothing to worry about except the two absent boys. Those thoughts weighed heavy on their minds as the wind battered the house and threatened the livestock still in the pastures. Nothing could be done about it now. They had miscalculated the end of the winter, and everyone was about to pay dearly.

***

"If we're going, we've got to leave right now," Hal said to the group gathered in Doctor Starr's office. The wind was whistling outside, windowpanes rattling, the cold already seeping under the doors, the wood stove not able to keep the room warm.

"My advice is to stay here," Doc admonished while putting away his medical kit, "better be safe than sorry and Ralph really shouldn't be traveling. You men can stay here in the office, there's firewood enough to last for a couple of days. The ladies can come stay with Ruth and I."

"I don't think we have any choice," Eric pointed out the window as the buildings on the other side of the street became nothing but shadows in the blizzard, "Hal, let's get the rigs unhitched and the teams to the stables. Ralphie, you stay here with your dad. We'll be back as soon as we can."

"Ladies, it's not far to my house, just down the hill, but we'd best stay close together. We can follow the boardwalk most of the way. Here, hold this length of ribbon and stay right on my heels." It was the longest 100 yards the 18-year-old girl ever experienced. Wind whipped her skirts, snow stung her eyes until she finally closed them, placed her hand on Doctor Starr's shoulder and prayed for deliverance from the blizzard.

***

Troops from Ft. Leavenworth mustered out as soon as the wind stopped blowing and the snow stopped falling. The storm lasted 48 hours and dumped as much as three feet of snow. They cleared a mile of the road by noon when the clouds blew away leaving the sun to brighten their exhausting job. Hal and Eric were on the road right behind them with the Epcot's hard on their heels. Ralph was weak and in need of rest and his wife's chicken soup. They ate nothing but dried beef and drank melted snow during the storm. Ralph, a teetotaler, even had a shot of whiskey after the pain sharpened on the second night. When they reached the lane to the Epcot place Hal convinced the commanding officer to assign a detachment of soldiers to clear the track about a hundred yards to where the wind scoured the prairie, leaving relatively crusted snow with dormant grass poking through. They reached Ralph's place, helped them get a fire started, their team settled and left with promises to check on Ralph when the snow cleared.

From the Shawnee cutoff to Fish's Ferry was slow going stopping to clear a path in the low spots. About two miles from the ferry, they came upon a wagon trapped in the snow, no team in evidence, a tarp draped on the windward side. Eric and Hal looked at each other, fearing the worst, "Hello the wagon," Hal yelled, climbing down. They would have to dig to reach the trapped pioneers.

"Hello, can you hear us," Eric shouted shoveling snow away from the road. The tragedy they uncovered...it could have been their own families... huddled under the wagon a mother, still alive, two young daughters dead in her arms, "Do you see my husband?" she asked lifelessly, "he left sometime last night."

They dug a path around the wagon, wrapped the two children in the tarp and tied it on the load. The mother, wrapped in a blanket, swayed listlessly between them. She rode in silence, glancing back at times on the remains of her children packed like freight between the construction materials. They came upon her husband frozen in the snow, recognizable only by his arm sticking from under a drift not one hundred yards from the ferry. They dug him out and placed the body with his daughters. The wife showed no emotion.

The mules and men were exhausted when they reached the crossing. It was closed, the barge on the opposite bank and no amount of yelling could raise the ferrymen. Finally, Hal fired his pistol in the air. The attendants, Shawnee's who lived close by, waved acknowledgment and began the process of bringing the raft across not realizing the grizzly cargo they would find.

52

Driving into the village they encountered Blue Jacket and Chief Fish leading a search party for the three hunters. Hal couldn't face going back to Lawrence not knowing Cricket's fate. He joined them, leaving Eric and Mrs. Fish to take the wretched consignment into Lawrence.

***

In the span of fifty feet Beulah and Sarah would have missed the house to the right, overcompensating for the wind, walking almost sideways, had not Margaret realized they were gone to long; She forced the back door open and shouted with all her might. They weren't but ten feet away yet heard just a muffled sound as did Sam. They stumbled into the house near frozen, breathing as though they had run a half-mile, too numb to speak. David and Punch were near tears helping them stack the firewood.

"How could this happen, Papa?"

"I don't know son. Nature is not predictable. We have no way of knowing when the weather will turn bad. This was just worse than most because the past few days have been so pleasant."

"We're alive and that's God's will," Silas drawled. "I'm sore afraid some folk won't be so lucky," he comforted Beulah as best he could. She patted his hand and nodded agreement.

***

The weather warmed steadily from the day the storm blew itself out. The Fish and Barnett families were still worried that the hunters might lose some fingers or toes due to frostbite but that would be a small price to pay for their survival.

The mother who lost her family slept for two days. Sarah rarely left her side. She spoke to her in soothing tones, wrapping warm, damp cloths around her fingers and toes. Sarah wept for the children, preserved, along with the body of the husband, in the smoke house near John T's home. They would be buried when the mother was capable of attending.

"We should put them in the ground now," Reverend Lum said as he viewed the bodies and prayed over them. "The mother will be in no shape to make a decision for quite some time."

Sarah shook her head firmly, "No, we will wait until she can tell us. She may want to take them back east. The poor woman has suffered enough. Let her deal with this her own way."

On the morning of the third day, the patient was on her back, eyes closed when Sarah came with a basin of warm water and a towel.

"I heard you talking to me," she rasped.

Sarah gently bathed her face, "What is your name?"

"Lori Robinson...my girls are dead, aren't they?"

"I'm so sorry."

"I thought I was dreaming. I could hear them laughing," she sobbed almost choking. Sarah helped her turn to the side, held her as she cried herself out.

"Where are they? Did you bury them?"

"No, we waited for you so you can tell us what you want to do?"

Lori composed herself, staring at the ceiling while Sarah continued her sponge bath.

"How long have I been here?"

"This is the third day."

"You're a very nice person. I listened to the things you said, you seem to know what I feel. Have you lost a child?"

Sarah pushed a lock of hair away from Lori's forehead, "No, I don't have no children, but I've seen enough death and heartache to know what it feels like. Do you want to take your family back east for burial?"

"Not Richard, I hate him."

"What do you mean?"

Lori began to sit up. Sarah helped her to the edge of the bed, "He was a terrible man. Beat me and the girls. He was taking us to the wharf at Delaware so we could go back east. I was leaving him, taking the girls. He was glad to be rid of us. Then the storm came. I begged him to wait, not to leave until it was over. He screamed at us. I was afraid he would hurt one of the girls;" she began crying again. "He was drinking," she calmed herself to finish the story. "When the wagon got stuck, I thought he would help keep them warm, but he abandoned us, tried to save himself. He was a terrible man."

"He wasn't going for help?"

"No, he was running away. He thought he could survive alone, without us slowing him down...bury him, I don't care where, but don't never tell anyone. Let his family think he was trying to save the girls. It will be better that way. His Ma is a good person."

They sat quietly, Sarah trying to decide what to do. Finally, Mrs. Robinson said, "I'll help prepare the girls. We'll bury them together." She stood with Sarah's help, "heaven help me to be strong and have the strength to stand alone," she sobbed.

They went to find Reverend Lum.

***

"When did he leave?" Jim Lane stood on the front porch as perplexed as he had been since the Siege of Lawrence, obviously distressed to learn that Sam was gone east on a humanitarian errand while important Territorial matters needed to be resolved. "What about the Free State delegate meeting in Big Spring? He's got to be there," said the tall thin man with piercing eyes squinted in anger.

"Jim, don't you want to come inside to discuss this?"

"Margaret, I've got to get back to Hickory Point. I've got troops over there holding off a bunch of Border Ruffians that just won't leave. I need Sam's help. When will he be back?"

"Just as soon as he can get poor Mrs. Robinson to Springfield and visit with Mr. Lincoln for a day or so. He plans on being back for the Delegate Convention. There's nothing he can do to help you in Hickory Point. Isn't Major Abbott helping?"

Lane turned away almost in disgust. Charlie Robinson wasn't home and now Sam Wood was gone. It felt as though he was taking on all the ills of the Territory single handed, "Tell Sam to get ahold of me as soon as he returns." He mounted his horse, jerked its head around and sprinted hard toward Hickory Point.

***

The Big Springs Free State delegate convention was postponed twice due to the weather. Finally, word spread that the meeting was to be held Monday, February 23. Sam was due home Tuesday the 24th, drop off the boys and Sarah, then leave for the meeting.

'If only things went as planned,' Margaret thought to herself as she stored the shipment of beans and flour received that morning from Brooks Mercantile. Finally, a few supplies were arriving after the storm disruption. "What disaster will be next?" she said out loud.

"What?" Sally asked bringing in more supplies from the gig.

"Just wondering what is going to happen next."

"Something will, no use worrying about it."

Margaret nodded agreement, "I'm worried about Jim Lane. He seemed so distraught when he was here last week looking for Sam. I think the pressure is really affecting him."

"And Charlie being gone doesn't help."

"He's not back yet?"

"No one seems to know when he and Sara will return. Maybe Sam does. I sure hope he gets home on time tomorrow. All those men in Big Springs will be wondering where he is."

They worked quietly setting the house right. When satisfied, Sally said, "Shall we take the gig to my house, unload my things then over to your mom's place. Beulah will be having a fit wondering about us."

"I suppose," Margaret sighed.

"What now?"

"That poor woman, I can't get her out of my mind. Losing her family like that. Frozen to death and she couldn't save the little ones."

"And we almost lost Cricket, Billy and Eudora," Sally added.

"Billy was lucky that he only lost a couple of toes. I hear that Eudora helped save his life."

"Truth is they were all pretty lucky. Hal and Eric too. And Mr. Epcot getting shot by that awful man. This is no way for civilized folk to live, Margaret," Sally looked hard at her best friend, "I'll tell you one thing, I'm thankful Hal and Eric were able to save that woman...But I wonder if I wouldn't rather die with my children and husband," Sally took the reins as they settled in the buggy, clucked the horse on for the short drive to her house.

Margaret hesitated before responding, "Sometimes I question God's plan for us. Freezing children to death..."

"Why Margaret Wood, I've never heard you question God."

"I'm not..." she couldn't finish the thought.

***

By noon on Monday about 20 of the expected 50 delegates had gathered at Constitution Hall in Big Springs. Tap Tappan and Judge Wakefield surveyed the sparse assembly.

Tap pulled his lanky frame to its full six feet four inches and said, "I think we should begin gentlemen. I'm sure Governor Robinson and Lt. Governor Roberts will be here soon."

Clarke Pomeroy, after the Siege of Lawrence moved to Atchison but maintained a room at the Free State Hotel. Brushing his sparce hair over a balding pate, he stood and began gathering his papers, "Tap, what do you suggest we begin doing? We don't have a quorum present...the presiding officers are all absent. Where is Sam, Charlie Robinson and Lt. Governor Roberts? Where is Jim Lane?"

Wakefield stood next to Tappan pleading with the members, all of them preparing to leave, "Sam will be here tomorrow. I don't have a clue where Charlie and Roberts are; but I guaran-damn-t you they have not abandoned us. I won't stand for that kind of talk. On the other hand, Clarke is correct, we don't have a quorum so I suggest we adjourn, go back to our hotel rooms or home whichever the case might be and convene tomorrow at 10 AM."

Chuck Branscomb was livid, "We need to post sentries. I don't want to be surprised like we were last July by Col. Sumner's troops. President Pierce still has a standing order to arrest us if we meet to enact Free State laws..."

Pomeroy interrupted him, "...I spoke to Governor Geary and assured him we would not do anything outside of his authority or against the Organic Law of the Territory. We won't be bothered."

"I rode over here from Council Grove. I'm not going back until we settle this thing. There is no telling where Charlie Robinson is. As far as I know he might have left the Territory, maybe went back to California. And Sam Wood and General Lane...you and Judge Wakefield know those men better than us, Tap. What the hell is going on here?" Tom Ewing pounded his fist on the table before rising to join the other men leaving to find their mounts.

"All I can say is that Charlie and Sam would never abandon us. They are more committed to our cause than anyone and I'll fight the man who calls me a liar. That being said, I don't know where they are, but I promise you I will find out. Just be back here tomorrow," Tap looked to Wake for support.

With nothing further to do the small group of Free State Legislators left for their homes or rooms in Topeka. Quite a few, shall we call them rumors, circulated that Free State Territorial Governor, Charlie Robinson had turned tail, abandoned the Abolitionist cause, and left for California. No one knew enough about the matter to counter that argument successfully. The rank and file of the Kansas Free State Delegation felt abandoned and, even worse, hopeless in the face of Federal intervention and the Border Ruffians.

***

Sam stepped off the train in St. Louis on the Illinois side of the Mississippi; it was Saturday, a day later than scheduled, no way to get to Lawrence on time. Nothing he could do about it now.

"Daddy, what about your valise," David yelled.

60

"Bring it, son."

David, Caleb and Sarah followed him off the car onto the platform.

"We need to get to the dock, see what boat is going upriver and when. I need to get back to Lawrence."

"I'm sorry this trip caused you such problems, Sam, but I feel like Lori would not have survived without our help."

"Don't worry about it Pumpkin, Lori is a strong woman and will be fine, thanks to you. Anyway, I needed to visit with Abe and Salmon about the Republican Caucus we're having in Chicago next fall."

On the Polar Star steaming up the Missouri, they sat on the boiler deck watching the countryside slide by; hills of Osage orange, burr oak and cottonwood trees with occasional fields of wheat, corn or rice when near a settlement.

"I just can't get used to seeing the slaves working in the fields," Sarah said, her white bonnet framing a narrow face with large eyebrows and a gentle gaze that disarmed even the foulest of souls, "it's just so unfair...so wrong."

Sam turned to her as David and Caleb charged down the aft stairs looking for a set of twins they met that morning, "We're doing everything we can, Pumpkin." Looking over the ten or twelve raggedy men and women he wondered if the statement was true. "What's going on with you and Bull? You guys getting married soon?"

She continued staring at the slaves, their heads swiveling to follow the progress of the Steamboat churning up the river, perhaps a faint glimmer of hope in their eyes that they too might be riding the Missouri north to freedom. Sarah turned away wiping a tear from her cheek, "I don't really know, Sam. I haven't even seen him in a month. He's been working on something and then we went east with Lori Robinson. Not a letter, nothing."

Sam placed his arm around his sister, pulled her close, "Well, those Barnett's are an independent minded bunch. I have a feeling...whatever it is that Hal's working on, you figure in his plans somehow."

"Don't you think he should let me in on them?"

***

Tuesday morning arrived cool but sunny. Constitution hall was warmed from the coal stove tended by William's son, Clarence, the custodian of the building. Early risers began arriving by seven. A positive feeling of anticipation permeated the wood paneled walls as the men drank coffee and speculated on what happened to Charlie Robinson.

Esekiel Colman from Kanwaka, Col. J.C. Steele from Bloomington, Reuben Smith from Potawatamie, Isaac Goodnow from Manhattan. Cyrus Haliday from Topeka, Preston Plumb from Emporia, all staunch Abolitionists.

"Even if Robinson and Roberts aren't here, we can organize the two houses; we have the president of the Senate and presiding officer of the House. Sam is supposed to be here today. He can preside until Charlie shows up," Haliday explained.

Clarke Pomeroy arrived at nine, "Charlie's house is still empty and locked. I thought Sara might be home, but she's gone too. I looked into the window and all their furniture is still there.

"Did you stop at Sam's house?"

Tap was going to do that. Isn't he here yet?

The ferry at Big Springs was almost full as Tap and Wake rode up.

"Any news?" Wake spoke first.

"Sam's supposed to be here. Margaret hasn't heard anything different from him. What about Charlie?"

"No sign of him or Sara. Major Abbott is supposed to be checking on Roberts."

"Wake, we've got problems. The rumor is that Charlie has bailed out on us. Headed back to California. What are we gonna do?"

"You and I know that's nonsense. Something bad has happened or he would have been here by now."

They led their horses onto the ferry accompanied by several other legislators all wondering the same thing, 'what is happening to our Free State Government?' They rode up the hill arriving at the meeting hall about 9:30. The street was full of horses, buggies and wagons. The sound of hammers and sawing filled the air, contractors shouting orders and construction workers scurrying about on adjacent buildings under construction.

"I hope we can hear ourselves above all that noise," Wake complained, "Henry Adams will have to run the meeting, he's next in line after Charlie and

Roberts. We have no choice if there's a quorum...nothing else we can do."

***

"Caleb, run over to Charlie Robinson's house and see if he's home. Quick like a rabbit, I'm leaving as soon as I can get Border Ruffian ready. David, go saddle Ruff for me, please... and bring him back here."

David and Caleb dashed out of the house. Sam looked at Margaret, "What a mess. How did things get so bollixed in such a short time?"

"You should have told us about Charlie going to Washington, Sam. We aren't clairvoyant."

"I'm sorry, Meg, it didn't seem important at the time; now I can see where I made a huge mistake. Lt. Governor Roberts has the letter Charlie wrote explaining everything."

Margaret pushed Sam down in a kitchen chair with a cup of coffee. It was five in the morning, "The Roberts' daughter and son-in-law were in a carriage accident in Atchison. He had to go take charge of his grandchildren."

"No... were they badly hurt?"

"I haven't heard. This all just happened in the last few days. I wouldn't have known about it except Mrs. Roberts happened to run into Elvira Brooks on the way out of town. I'm sure they had enough on their minds not to think about Charlie Robinson being in Washington."

Sam blew on his coffee, "I'll get this all straightened out...it's just a misunderstanding.

What's this about Jim Lane fighting Border Ruffians at Hickory Point?"

"I'm not sure, but the rumor is he and Major Abbott had about 20 men fighting a band of Ruffians. Jim didn't say why. I guess they were harassing the settlers...anyway, Harold came by yesterday and said that most of Lane's men were arrested by soldiers from Ft. Leavenworth. He said you need to go to Lecompton and talk to Judge LeCompte to find out why they were arrested and not the Ruffians."

"That doesn't make any sense. Governor Geary must have had them arrested. I just can't believe that Geary would turn on us now. There's got to be more to this story than what you're telling me."

Margaret put her hands on her hips, her mouth pursed in anger, "I'm repeating exactly what happened. You've caused most of these problems by being gone."

"I had no choice..."

"Yes, you did, Sam. It's not like you to shirk your responsibilities."

"I'm not shirking anything, Meg. It doesn't do any good to scold me now..."

"Daddy, Ruff is saddled and ready," David charged in.

Caleb followed hard on his heels, "And Mr. Robinson isn't back yet. His house is locked, and no one is around. I looked in all the windows." Caleb leaned over, hands on knees, trying to catch his breath.

"Did he not say when he would be back, Sam? This is a bad situation and it's your fault."

"Meg, I thought that Charlie had dealt with it. I'll get it all straightened out, but I better leave right now. Have you packed my things?"

Margaret's look warned that the foolish question just added to her frustration. He picked up his bags and left.

***

The California Road was dry, most of the snow melted except for drifts in the sheltered ravines and northern slopes of the hills. The air was cool but bearable dressed as he was in the warm clothes provided by Margaret; clothes he would probably wear the entire trip. Sartorial matters were of no importance when dealing with the critical issue of freeing the slaves, "That's what this is about, Ruff. Freeing the slaves. These other issues are bothersome, not the real problem. I wish everyone felt the way I do about it. They think this is about Kansas, but you and I know it is about freedom, about right and wrong."

They continued another ten minutes in a weighty silence. Suddenly he pulled the reins at the crest of a hill, "Whoa up a minute, Ruff...I've been a fool." He turned in the saddle looking back along the trail just traveled. "I haven't seen Margaret in two weeks then charge out the door with her mad at me." He removed his hat, scratched his head, "Darn it all, without Meg I'm nothing. I'd best ride back and apologize. It might be a week before I see her again. What is wrong with me, Ruff?" Ruff shook his head sensing something amiss. All was silent save the sounds of nature.

The Kansas River valley lay fallow awaiting spring. A line of leafless oak and cottonwood trees rested dark against the green cedar and fir scattered along the river; Lecompton lay nestled in the trees on the opposite side of the narrow basin just above Oakley Creek. Sam felt a tiredness that was more than the sum of his travels the past two weeks. The burdens of the Territory seemed to rest squarely on his shoulders, leaving little time for his family. He looked around at the beautiful Kansas Landscape, the prairie to the south and west, treed hills along the river, fertile bottom lands on the north side. It seemed an unlikely place to be battling over slavery. Before he could decide about turning back, a movement at the base of the hill caught his eye. Someone was crossing the creek headed his way. Sam recognized a familiar black face wearing a broad brimmed hat, riding an old mule. A smile crossed his lips at the sight of his old friend, "William, good to see you."

"Mr. Sam, I was just riding to your house to warn you. We've got big troubles."

Sam laughed, shook his head in frustration then said to William when he recognized the shocked look at Sam's cavalier attituded, "Don't fret, William, I'm not laughing cause it's funny. It seems like everything is going to the devil. Let's sit a spell and talk about it. I was just on my way to Lecompton to find out what in the world is happening. How are you and Jezebel?"

They sat on a rock outcropping to visit.

"We doin' real good, but those Slavery mens is sure stirring up trouble. I can fill you in on most of it. Reason I left is there ain't nobody in Lecompton. Both Judges, LeCompte and Cato gone off... cause more mischef mos likely. The Gobner over in Atchison trying to get them slavery mens under control. Old Sherriff Jones got hisself a Deputy US Marshal name of Frank Pardee to go to Big Springs and arrested most of the delegation yesterday."

"What?" Sam jumped up, "That's crazy! On what charge and by whose authority?"

"Jones got Judge Cato to swear out a bunch of blank writs so's he could charge whoever he wanted for whatever he wanted. I understand he was most unhappy to find that you, Mr. Robinson, General Lane all missing. He charged the rest with unlawful assembly, treason, disturbing the peace, inciting to riot, all kinds of things."

William sat patiently while Sam vented his anger clubbing trees and rocks, surprising Border Ruffian who looked at him with ears pricked. Sam calmed himself, sat next to the old black man. Several new nicks smudged the surface of his fancy cane, "I just bought this in Chicago; had it custom made, feel the weight in the ferrule and heel. Don't have to turn it around in a tight scuffle."

William hefted the walking stick, "That's a formidable weapon, Mr. Sam. I pity the man that challenge it, but it ain't quite as pretty as it was before."

He placed the cane between his knees, took a deep breath, "I plan on cracking a few heads with it if I have any problem with Bogus Jones. I am sorely tired of pacifying these Boarder Ruffians. Tell me, William, where are you getting your information?"

"Most of it I heard from my boy Clarence. He was there at the Hall when the law come riding in, guns drawn. The delegates just sat there, didn't offer no defiance and that made old Jones madder than a hornet. He was countin' on them resistin' so he could call out the army."

"Where are they being held?

"Tecumseh, with General Lanes troops. They also got arrested, over in Hickory Point."

"I heard that story. Who authorized their arrest?"

"The Gobner, cause Lane didn't disband his men like he said he would."

"What about the Border Ruffians?"

"They disappeared back into Missouri."

"What about this new Sheriff, Sherrard? Has that been resolved?"

"Sam, don't you know who that is?"

"Sherrard, no I never met him."

"It's Big Bill... Jones old deputy."

It took a moment to register before Sam roared with laughter, "You mean to tell me the fellow all this fuss is over... is Big Bill? Why that fat tub of guts hasn't got the brains of a frog."

William shrugged, "He may not be very smart but he sure do cause a heap o' trouble. You heard about him shooting Ralph Epcot and he killed a man in Atchison while you was gone. They finally going to have that public hearing next week to talk about his appointment. He told the Gobner he would kill him if they turned him down for the position."

Sam sat there contemplating all of this, slowly got up and mounted Ruff, "I'm going to Tecumseh...get those men out of jail. I'll see you in Lecompton on the way back."

William continued sitting on the rock, "How you plan on doing that?"

"Don't know. Reckon I'll sweet talk Jones into letting them go."

Sam rode off at a lope. William stood up slowly, stretched his back before climbing on the patiently waiting mule, "Jezebel, I've seen Mr. Sam sweet talk folks and it never do turn out well."

***

Tecumseh, Kansas Territory, founded by pro-slavery southerners in the spring of 1854 at a bend in the Kansas River between Tecumseh Creek and Shunganunga Creek. Jones and his deputies made a wise choice incarcerating the Kansas Militia troops of General Lane and the Free-State delegates in the local schoolhouse. Jones recruited pro-slavery guards just daring the Abolitionist scum give them a chance to open fire. The village lay 5 miles east of Topeka's Constitution Hall where the delegate arrests were made. It would take close to three hours to make the 15-mile ride over the hills from Lecompton; a pleasant ride with a dangerous confrontation waiting at the end. "Ruff, I hope they're all there. Jones, Judge Cato, this new marshal and especially Big Bill. I'm tired of pussyfooting around with these fools."

The marital doldrums of that morning vanished in the call to action. "ll make it up to Margaret later. This might be the most important day since we've been here. I've got to get Jones out of the picture for good. Sure do wish that Harold and his boys were here with me."

Sam stopped in the middle of the narrow trail along the ridge of hills, not a road but a well-worn path between Lawrence and Topeka. "Maybe I should go get the Barnett's...No, there's no time. Tap, Caleb Pratt, a lot of good men are in the jailhouse. I've got to do this on my own. I'll bet anything, Jones left a guard detail of farmers or worse, Border Ruffians." He bounded out of the saddle, opened his saddlebags, extracted a copy of the Topeka Constitution, took the preamble and the signature page and put them in his coat pocket.

"This will have to do, Ruff. Let's go get our friends out of jail."

***

The wind blew cold off the Missouri. Governor Geary pulled his coat collar tight around his neck, stood on the gangplank of the chartered riverboat, glanced at the few lingering threads of ice still floating by, then started for the Atchison community center. His entourage consisted of assistant clerk, Shorty Jones, John Gihon and six dragoons from Ft. Leavenworth.

"I haven't been to Atchison since the fall tour," he mentioned to Gihon. "I wish to hell I never had to come here again."

Gihon merely nodded.

"This way Governor," Shorty waved as they reached the meeting venue. He held the door open. The room was full...probably 30 men. Geary expected only David Atchison, General Stringfellow and ex-sheriff Jones. Quite a few others milled about the room; conversation stopped as the Governor entered. He was not popular in pro-slavery Atchison, Kansas Territory.

The town's namesake, ex-Missouri Senator David Atchison gestured for Geary to join him at the head table, "Governor, welcome to Atchison. We appreciate you coming today. I know you are a busy man.

"I didn't expect this many people. I thought this was just you and Stringfellow."

Atchison bristled at the Governor's tone, "You know these men; they are all members of the Territorial Legislature."

"That is a matter of opinion at this point, not a legal reality," Geary retorted.

"Now, now, Governor," General Stringfellow crowed, "let us work together in harmony to resolve our differences of opinion."

"I have made my position clear. No election is final until we have a free and untainted vote with only residents of Kansas Territory participating. And that hasn't happened yet."

Stringfellow and Atchison looked at each other, tension showed around their eyes. They glanced at the soldiers standing guard at the front door and on both sides of the table. Several men had gathered around including the sheriff-elect, or more accurately, sheriff appointee, Big Bill Sherrard. Shorty moved between the governor and Sherrard. The two men hated each other.

"Get out of my way, you little pissant," Sherrard pushed him.

Shorty was not afraid to defend himself, even against the much larger Ruffian, "Keep your hands off me, you drunken lout."

Sherrard laughed and pushed him again, "I ain't drunk you idiot, if I was, you'd be dead."

"You'll never be sheriff in Kansas, as long as I've got anything to say about it," Governor Geary stepped in, towering over all the men in the room. Sherrard, though a few inches shorter, outweighed him by 70 pounds.

"Gentlemen let's deal with the issue at hand," Stringfellow pleaded.

"What is the issue at hand?" Geary challenged, "Why did you ask me here?"

Atchison sat down, indicated a chair for the governor, but Geary continued to stand. Atchison calmly stated, "To validate the Territorial Legislature. That's why. And if you don't validate the election, we'll see to it that you never cause another problem in this territory."

"Or anywhere," Sherrard echoed.

Shorty stood next to the governor's chair aghast at what he had just heard, "Are you threatening the Governor?"

"You might say that you little shit," Sherrard reached out to grab the smaller man. Geary, restrained Sherrard's arm. The would-be sheriff spit in the Governor's face then dared him to do something about it.

"Oh, Bill, for God's sake," Stringfellow groaned.

The room froze for a beat waiting to see the Governor's reaction. The soldiers took a step forward pulling their pistols. Geary held up his hand, calmly took his handkerchief wiped his face, gestured to Gihon and Shorty, nodded to the soldiers, and strolled to the door without a word. Sherrard stood defiantly, fists doubled at his side, "Don't you walk away from me, ya' big chicken-shit." Sherrard turned to his friends, "What a coward."

The soldiers quickly moved to follow Geary. Big Bill swaggered proudly in front of his pro-slavery comrades, grinning like a tenant in a madhouse as the illegally elected Kansas Territorial Legislators pounded him on the back with congratulations.

"Geary's days are numbered in this Territory," Atchison snorted, standing at the open door, watching them walk back to the dock, "one way or the other."

Bogus Jones joined him, "We've run off Reeder and Shannon; Geary is next. I really thought he'd work with us. President Pierce thought so too."

"Run him off, hell," Big Bill laughed, "I'm going to kill him. He's a worthless son-of-a-bitch."

Geary, Gihon and Jones sat in the captain's quarters on board the small paddle-wheeler, Traveler, no one speaking, each with his own thoughts, none of them good.

Shorty tried to gather his wits, obviously shaken by the turn of events at the meeting, "I'm afraid I've got more bad news, Governor."

Geary looked at him.

"Bogus Jones told me they the leadership of the Free-State Legislators in Big Springs two days ago. Being held prisoner in Tecumseh."

"By whose authority...on what charges?"

"Judge Cato evidently issued writs and Deputy Marshall Pardee executed the warrants. Jones orchestrated the entire affair, with Atchison's approval, I would imagine."

Geary buried his face in his hands, "My God, how are we going to stop this madness?"

Shorty waited for Gihon to answer.

"Kansas is going to fall to the pro-slavery people because they are ruthless. This man Sherrard is going to kill one of us, mark my words, unless something is done to stop him."

Gihon sighed deeply, "I think we need to get Sam Wood and John Brown involved. This requires extreme action, and those two men are the only ones capable of fighting Sherrard on his terms."

"We've got to follow the rule of law," Geary pleaded, "I've based my entire term on being fair, ensuring that only Kansas citizens vote. I've been challenged at every turn by the Border Ruffians, the slaveholders, but worst of all, the Territorial judges. I'm not prepared to accuse Judge LeCompte and Judge Cato of being in the pocketbooks of the slaveholders...but,"

"It makes you wonder doesn't it," Gihon finished the thought.

***

Sam sat astride Ruff on a bluff above Tecumseh Creek with a good view of the schoolhouse across the basin, "For being prisoners, they all look pretty friendly, Ruff."

The only way to identify the guards was by the guns. They sat smoking, talking, even laughing at times; all of them, prisoners and guards alike. Sam didn't recognize any of the guards; he identified Henry Adams, President of the Senate, "And there's Tap just coming out the door."

Tappan passed a canteen to one of the guards who took a swig and passed it on to a prisoner. They seemed to be enjoying the sunny morning.

"Looks like a social club down there. No kind of prison I've ever seen. Let's get them and go home," Sam reined Ruff down the gentle slope to the low water crossing. He rode straight to the front door with no challenge, everyone just watching him.

"Hello, Sam, what kept you," Caleb Pratt asked.

"Been busy. You all get your horses and let's go."

"Hold on there, Mister. These men are prisoners."

Sam hooked his left leg across the saddle, "And who might you be?"

"I'm the man guarding these prisoners. Name o' Mordecai Youngblood. Who are you?"

Several of the prisoners laughed. Henry Adams slapped the guard on the knee as they sat together,

"Mordecai that last name of yours went out of style about 60 years ago, didn't it?"

Youngblood laughed along with everyone else. A thin, gnarled old man with broad white whiskers and a stained flop hat, "I may be old Mr. Adams, but I can still put in a full day in the field and take care of mama when I get home."

Sam reached in his coat pocket, "I'm the attorney for all these men. I've got papers releasing them on personal recognizance bail, pending arraignment, nolo contendere process, Nolo prolo, de Jure, habeus corpus, subject to Voir Dire, all signed and approved by the proper authorities. Step over here and I'll show you the papers."

"Now, young fella', I didn't understand a damn thing you just said, and it won't do no good to show me no papers cause' I can't read. Ralston, can you read?"

"Just enough to know if it's my name or not."

Sam eyed them suspiciously, "Well where's the man in charge? Where's Pardee or Jones? I want this all done legal so's there's no confusion about it when the head man gets back."

"They went off to Atchison for a meeting. I reckon I'm in charge and the truth is I'd like to be shed of these prisoners. I ain't got no idea what they done to end up in jail, but they seem like mighty fine gentlemen, and anyway, I got chores to attend at home."

"Me too," Ralston agreed, "what did you all do to get Sheriff Jones so mad at you? He was looking to hang somebody when he rode out of here the other day."

"We didn't do anything, Ralston, just had a meeting."

"Had a meeting? That's all? That don't sound right."

Sam pulled Ralston to a bench, motioned Mordecai over, "It ain't right what they've done to my clients. But it's all straightened out now. To make it legal, Mordecai, I need you to put your X right here attesting that you have released these men on their own recognizance as described in these papers," Sam set the signature pages of his copy of the Topeka Constitution in front of the guard. Mordecai took the pen offered, made an X on the line Sam indicated, "Now, Mr. Ralston, you make an X here as witness to the above."

"I can sign my name."

"Fine, right here next to this X."

Paperwork completed, the guards saddled their horses and departed as quickly as they could, glad to be rid of the responsibility of prisoners, some of whom were neighbors. The prisoners sat silently trying to keep from laughing at the pious antics of their self-appointed legal advisor. Henry Adams, President of the Senate, was a heavy man in his upper body; round with flesh hanging over the waist of his trousers, all supported by thin, chicken like legs. He detested physical labor much like Charlie Robinson, and like him, he had a formidable legal mind, "Sam, what was all that gibberish you just spouted to poor Mordecai? Are we going to get into more trouble over this?"

"I don't know Henry, but I tell you I am fed up to here with molly-coddling these pro-slavery people. The time has come to draw a line in the sand. You tell me, what is this all about?"

They all started talking at once, shouting about Charlie being gone, Bogus Jones arresting them, General Lane leaving in exile. Finally Judge Wakefield stood on the porch and shouted for attention, "Everyone come inside and let's get this sorted out."

The men shuffled into the schoolhouse, sat on the benches in a circle, many grumbling, all of them angry and no one seemed to know what was going on.

George Dietzler spoke first, "Sam, where is Charlie Robinson? I don't believe that he's abandoned us, but I can't think of any reason that would justify him not being here?"

"You mean you don't know?"

Adams responded gruffly, "How could we know, Sam? The only thing readily apparent is that Governor Robinson, Lt. Governor Roberts, General Lane and you were not here three days ago when we convened this convention nor were you here two days ago when US Deputy Marshall Pardee arrested us. Maybe you should fill us in on what you know."

"This is just a misunderstanding. I don't know why you were arrested, but I'll get to the bottom of that. As for Charlie, he's in Washington pleading our case with Stephen Douglas and President Pierce. He felt that he could make them understand the situation here in Kansas by meeting face to face. He left a letter with the Lt. Governor. Didn't Roberts give anyone a copy of the letter?"

"Obviously not," Caleb responded, "we don't know where Roberts is either."

"His daughter and son-in-law were seriously hurt in a carriage accident. He had to go take care of his grandchildren. I guess the letter slipped his mind in the confusion."

The men sat quietly at this news until Reuben Smith began shaking his head, "I don't buy it. Even if that story of going to Washington is true, Charlie should have waited until after this meeting. I still feel that he abandoned us."

Several heads nodded, others grunted agreement, muttering and side conversations threatened to distract the meeting again. Nothing Sam said swayed the men from distrusting the motives of Governor Robinson.

"This is a serious matter gentleman," Sam shook his head in frustration, "we have to trust each other to accomplish our goals."

"It is a serious matter, and right now, I'm not sure what the hell I think. Charlie should be here, Jim Lane should be here, Roberts should be here," George Dietzler lectured with his pompous military bearing on full display.

"I'm just as confused as you folks, but we have to stay focused on what we're trying to do which is make Kansas a Free-State. What have you decided about the delegate convention?" Sam asked.

Adams replied, "After we were arrested, the remaining members voted to postpone the meeting until June. I think that is the best strategy. We'll take the next few months and get this all straightened out then convene in Topeka this summer."

"What about General Lane?" Sam looked around for Lane's men.

Adams responded, "All of them left over the last few days. The guards didn't know how many men were here and didn't seem to care one way or the other. Lane went to Nebraska until this blows over. He'll be back when it's safe."

"We've got to deal with this sheriff," Tap stood and stretched his back, "no way can we let that man be appointed to any kind of office in Kansas."

"There's a meeting next week," Pratt said, "we all need to be there. We can't let the bogus legislature appoint him. Sam, let's you and I go meet with Geary and make certain we're all on the same page."

The men appeared to run out of steam as the various issues were discussed and while not always resolved, at least the concerns were being addressed. Most were tired having slept on the hard plank floor of the schoolhouse or on the benches; all wanted to get home to their families.

Sam prepared to leave, "I'll take care of resolving this illegal incarceration. Don't worry about it. The Governor has to answer some questions about these arrests, but I'm convinced that he'll do the right thing."

The others began moving toward their horses in the corral by the town stables.

"Let us know as soon as Charlie's back. He needs to answer some serious questions about this mess," Preston Plumb picked up his saddle, preparing to ride back to Emporia.

Sam merely nodded. He felt the same way.

***

Harold and Autumn Barnett, along with all five of their offspring rode into Lawrence for church the following Sunday. The first visit since Christmas services, because the storms had wreaked havoc on their farm buildings and livestock. The last month was spent on necessary farm chores, but not attended with the same degree of enthusiasm. Harold, Autumn, Bull and Chief, loved the work. Cricket, Diane and Carol did their part reluctantly because they knew how important it was for survival, yet they wished to be elsewhere. The Sunday break from farm chores was a welcome diversion.

"Bull, are you going to ask Sarah Wood to marry you today," Chief asked his brother.

"I think she just knows we're going to get married. It's common knowledge."

"Bull, you are ignorant when it comes to females," Diane chided her brother.

The Barnett brood sat in the back of the farm wagon rocking with every rut and jolting over every rock on the way to town. Harold and Autumn looked at each other with a silent admonition to avoid the discussion. Autumn listened carefully; she loved Sarah like a daughter but knew that the headstrong girl would not take Bull's nonchalance about marriage with the same degree of tolerance as he did.

Carol Barnett, now ten, still dressing as a boy volunteered, "I don't know why you want to go and get married, Bull. You guys should just be friends and go to the dances and church together."

"You are such a child, Carol," her sister admonished. "Grown men and women have other reasons they want to get married. Like having children."

"Well, they can have children without getting married," Carol announced.

Her brothers and sisters turned on her, "That is a sin. How can you say such a thing?"

"Carol, you watch your mouth young lady," Harold admonished when the chorus of disapproval had halted. "Where are you hearing such filth?"

Carol looked defiantly into the trees bordering the road. She was terribly misunderstood by her family. She only enjoyed life when with her friends in Lawrence, David Wood, Caleb Thompson, Jimmy Pratt and Larry Tappan.

Cricket put his hand on Bull's shoulder, "Brother, I echo the advice of our Shawnee elders. Do not take anything for granted. Especially matters of the heart."

Autumn turned to her youngest son replying in Shawnee, "That was very wise Panther Crouches for Prey."

He basked in the praise from his mother; Her approval was seldom given.

"Eric told me the same thing," Bull ruminated. "I guess maybe I ought to bring the matter up since the new house is over half finished."

"Brother, you had better change your ways or you will lose Sarah Wood to someone else. I heard that there's a new man in town, a dentist who has taken a liking to her," Chief warned.

"Where did you hear that?"

"From Mr. Brooks when I was at the mercantile getting the saws that Pa ordered. He said she's been spending a lot of time with this dentist."

The look on Bull's face warned his brothers and sisters not to mention the matter any further. He jumped down from the wagon to run alongside, glancing up as he breasted his parents. Autumn gave him a look that advised of her own feelings about the matter.

"Ok mother, I'll take care of it today."

"Do you love the girl or not?" she asked.

Bull didn't respond, just kept walking. Harold hurried the team along feeling that the matter was best left alone. Conversation turned to other matters. Bull climbed onto the driver's bench alongside his mother and took the reins to drive the rest of the way into town so that father could join a discussion between Chief and Cricket concerning the advantages of breeding Spanish versus Angora goats, a subject which bored Diane and Carol to exhaustion. Normally Bull would have made his opinion loudly known but he seemed preoccupied and left the arguments to his father and brothers with an occasional comment from Autumn concerning the financial benefits of one idea over another.

***

Two churches were under construction in Lawrence including Reverend Lum's new, much larger Lutheran church. While waiting for the chapel to be completed they shared space with the Baptists in the Community Center, many people attending both services.

"It won't hurt a thing," Rev. Lum told his flock. "A good many of you can use all the salvation you can get. I won't mention any names, but I believe a good old-fashioned dose of Baptist conviction cleanses your soul so that we can join the one and only true Lutheran God in heaven above when the time draws nigh."

This, of course, confused Autumn wondering as she already did if the Lutheran God and Baptist God were one and the same. She intended to discuss a question concerning the Shawnee Great Spirit and the Lutheran God they prayed to on Sunday.

"Mrs. Barnett, there is only one God, and he is most certainly not a heathen God worshiped by savages."

Patient as always, Autumn stood next to the Reverend as he welcomed worshipers to the service, trying his best to maintain a pious good humor in the face of his most challenging parishioner. "Reverend Lum, why can't the Shawnee Great Spirit be the same as the Lutheran God?"

"That is just the way it is, Mrs. Barnett. One God, with one son, born almost two thousand years ago. Your Great Spirit is a figment of some Medicine Man's imagination. Just put your faith in our

Lutheran God. That will suffice, thank you. Let us go inside so that I can begin the service."

"What did he say, mother?" Panther Crouching for Prey asked as she sat between him and Harold.

"He said there is only one God and the Great Spirit is a figment of the imagination of our elders. But I don't believe he knows for sure. He gives the same answer for all of my questions."

"What answer?"

"That's just the way it is."

Cricket nodded, looking for Bull who normally sat with Sarah. Turning completely around he spotted his brother standing in the back of the room, towering above the congregation, an angry look directed toward Sarah, sitting with a tall, bearded gentleman sporting thick brown hair, a dazzling smile and a new wool suit. Cricket nudged his mother nodding toward Sarah and her new beau. She elbowed her husband. Harold sighed deeply wishing only to be left out of the matter. Sam Wood stopped him entering the church and told him to meet after the service to discuss the upcoming indignation meeting about Big Bill Sherrard. Bull's love life was of little concern to Harold Barnett now.

Margaret Wood slumped into the pew, exhausted. She fell asleep in church for the first time in her adult life. Sam smiled fondly then adjusted her bonnet so she rested easily on his shoulder. She worked all day Saturday cooking, cleaning, washing clothes, awaiting Sam who was supposed to be home at noon but didn't arrive until six. Then Meg was up half the night with a sick baby; Flo had the croup, and couldn't sleep without resting in the crook of Margaret's arm. When the baby finally quieted, she and Sam stayed up most of the rest of the night just talking, holding each other, both worn out. They dozed off mid-thought about three in the morning; His comment meant the world to her. "I'll leave all of this behind, Margaret if staying means I would lose you. I love you more than life itself. I'm so sorry for the way I left home. Without you, I'm noth...Margaret?" he snugged the blanket around her shoulders watching her sleep as peacefully as the angel he felt she was. Sam nestled against her arm and fell asleep himself.

Punch looked curiously at his mother having never seen her sleep in church before...a curious sweet smile of contentment graced her lips. He nudged Missy, "Look at Ma."

Any adult, other than Sam, asleep in church was a topic of interest to the children. The last prayer over, Sam woke Margaret for the trip home. They had guests coming but there would be plenty of help from Margaret's mother Elizabeth, Beulah and Sally.

Reverend Lum stopped the Wood family on the way out the door, wouldn't think of letting them leave until he had a chance to discuss a couple of troubling matters, "First of all, Mrs. Wood, are you well?" a sincere expression of concern crinkled the skin around his eyes. He took her hand in his, pressing it gently.

"Just tired Reverend, I'll be fine," she patted his hand trying to reassure him.

"I worry when one of my most devout parishioners falls asleep in church. I hate to think that it might be my sermon," smiling he turned to Sam. "What about this meeting at your house? Are we going to be able to resolve anything or is it just going to be an excuse for everyone to moan and groan about the situation? I've had people through my home all week complaining about one thing or another, one person or another, including you Sam. I'm not going to go if it's just going to be a complaining session."

"I hope you'll come; I have some news that will be of interest."

"Then I'll be there."

The streets on both sides of the Wood home were crowded with wagons, carriages, and saddled horses by the time they trudged up the street from the Community Center. Immediately, Margaret took charge, directing most of the ladies upstairs where Beulah was waiting with Flo, "She hungry, Margaret, we sure glad you here."

"Is she feeling better Beulah? I've been worried about her."

"Oh, she fine. Being hungry a good sign. Here, you take her, I'll go down and help Sarah and Sally gettin' them men organized. I can hear them fussing and fighting from here."

Beulah, a formidable woman under any circumstances, brooked no argument from black or white when her children were challenged in any way. Coming down the stairs, she was appalled to see grown men, maybe 25 or 30 of them, arguing, almost to blows, carrying on like adolescent boys, some of them with the gall to light cigars and pipes. She stopped on the stairs to survey the situation. Sam stood near the back door waving his fist threateningly at George Dietzler; Judge Wakefield tried to mediate. Tap was at the fireplace several men around him screaming with no possible way of understanding what anyone was saying. Reverend Lum tried to restore order with no one paying him any mind. The room was in chaos. Sally and Sarah stood near the cookstove aghast, unable to move let alone try to restore order.

Beulah spotted Sam's club in the corner, retrieved it, moved back up the stairs where she commanded the room and commenced pounding the club on the stair rail getting louder and louder until the men stopped their arguing to see what the commotion could be. When she had their undivided attention she said calmly, "I'm only going to say this one time. You white folks ain't never going to free no slaves when you can't even control yourselves among friends. I've got a sick baby upstairs and children coming in and out of this house hearing you'al carrying on like heathens. I won't allow it. This behavior is embarrassing to us all. John T built a nice flagstone patio in the back of this house. Take your nasty pipes and cigars and your screaming noisy selves out there and you can yell at each other all you want. And I mean right now." She crossed her arms, glowering down at them, daring someone to challenge the order.

No one risked looking up as they filed out, the last being George Dietzler who did not enjoy a good reputation among the black citizens of Lawrence. In this instance, he smiled and nodded his approval then followed the others.

Sam caught the Judges arm, "Wake, take charge, get us organized. Introduce the new dentist then call on me so I can give a report that will help calm things down."

Wakefield hurried to the center of the gathering before they found their voices, "Gentlemen, have you all met our new dentist, Dr. Nathan O'Reilly."

The dentist stood with his hand raised, "Please, gentlemen, just plain Nate. I am so proud to be here in Lawrence and to meet all of you. My practice will be on Massachusetts across from the new bank. I can't wait to get involved in all community affairs, including making Kansas a free state."

Hal Barnett snorted a grunt of derision that caused those around him to question his health. Fortunately, Dr. O'Reilly did not hear.

"Welcome Dr. O'Reilly," Wake continued looking around, "any other new faces? No...then I'll turn it over to Sam. He has some news we all need to hear."

Sam moved to the center of the group, "First, let me also welcome Nate to Lawrence. I've gotten to know him a bit and can tell you he is a fine gentleman, an abolitionist like most of us. I can't attest to his dentistry skills yet, but if I need a tooth pulled, I'd rather trust him than old Doc. Jernigan the veterinarian." Everyone laughed, "oh, yes, and one more thing," Sam added looking straight at Hal, "Nate will be bringing his lovely wife and three children to Lawrence...when is that Nate?"

Hal squealed like a lovestruck teenager and ran toward the house.

Nate watched him, "Must have ate something that disagreed with him. Sam, I'm bringing Maryanne out just as soon as I finish our new home on Indiana Street. John T is going to be putting doors and windows in next week, isn't that right John?"

"I'll put them in just as soon as they get here from Kansas City," John T answered.

Sam continued, "Welcome Nate, I wish things were a bit more settled, but I guarantee you, all of you, that we are going to make Kansas a Free-State. Gentlemen, I want to apologize. A good deal of the confusion that exists today could have been avoided. I'm not even sure where to start, so I'll just dive in and you ask questions as we go. I knew that Charlie Robinson was going back East to try and influence congress and the president to validate the Topeka Constitution. I knew it weeks ago. Charlie gave Lt. Gov. Roberts a letter explaining the entire situation. Then Roberts was sidetracked with a personal tragedy and the letter didn't get delivered. I had to go East for some personal business and to meet with the Republicans planning the 1860 campaign. Here is the letter Charlie wrote. He's supposed to be back any day now. I don't think he's even aware of all the problems we've had here. My point is that Charlie's intentions were good. He was trying to accomplish what we all want and avoid any more bloodshed here in the Territory. It didn't work. The President wouldn't even meet with him and our friends in the House of Representatives are powerless against the Southern Cartel of Senators. I'll let Charlie defend himself when he gets home, but as far as I'm concerned, he's still our Governor."

Henry Adams rose, "I'll reserve judgement on Charlie until I speak with him. But I'm leaning toward a new election. Let the voters decide if he should be governor," murmurs of agreement started amongst the group, "but all that aside, have you spoken to Governor Geary about the arrests?"

"Caleb Pratt and I met with Geary on Friday. He claims he was not aware of this plot that Bogus Jones hatched to arrest all of us. I believe him. Jones did it on his own with the aid of Judge Cato. The Governor and I went yesterday to meet with Cato. He was defiant, claimed that Jones had evidence of crimes, but as usual, he couldn't produce that evidence. Cato agreed to the personal recognizance bail scheme I concocted and Territorial Attorney General McGivers has agreed that no one will be prosecuted as a result of these bogus arrests. Jones is nothing more than a private citizen working with Atchison and Stringfellow to make Kansas a slave state. I really believe they'll change tactics... quit using the Border Ruffians as soldiers and will try and make it happen through the voting booth and the courts. They'll continue sending Missouri citizens into Kansas to vote. We'll organize and see that doesn't happen. My biggest concern right now is this appointment of Big

Bill Sherrard as Douglas County Sheriff. We have to put a stop to that right quick."

"Is the meeting still on for this week?" Tap asked.

"Yes, a public hearing on the matter in Lecompton on Thursday. We all have to be there," Wakefield lit his cigar, glancing toward the house to see if Mrs. Wakefield was near. "This fellow Sherrard is promoted by the Bogus Shawnee Mission legislature; they have the ear of the courts and worse the Territorial Council. We'll have to overwhelm them with numbers. We'll call some witnesses. I know Bull Barnett and Eric McCrea will testify, of course, Ralph Epcot will."

"I sure hope Charlie is back by then," Tap looked tired, "I haven't slept well since the arrests. If we would have resisted, I believe they would have shot us down like dogs."

Sam Walker agreed, "Jones was just waiting for one of you fellas to draw down on them and he would have opened fire. You did the right thing by not resisting arrest," he put his hand on Tap's arm. "Go home, my friend. You seem worn out," he watched Tap walking toward his home on New Hampshire Street. Harold spotted Sam speaking with Caleb Pratt standing next to Caleb's horse, "Where did Bull run off to?"

Caleb and Sam shrugged looking about as if they might spot him where Harold had failed to look. Caleb mounted his horse, "Last time I saw him was when he ran off into the house with a tooth ache or something."

Harold shook his head, "Sometimes I wonder about that boy. Lately he don't seem to have a lick of sense."

***

The morning of the public hearing, low hanging greyish-white clouds hovered over the Territory; a cold drizzle fell matching the mood of the Free-State men.

"There will be trouble," Sam said to Margaret sitting in the warmth of their kitchen, "I'm just not sure what kind of trouble."

"You'll deal with it whatever it turns out to be, Sam," Margaret poured coffee for him and John T. "I just wish that Charlie was back."

John shook his head as he tried to cool the steaming cup, "Charlie won't be any help at this meeting, Margaret. It won't be just angry words. These men will go to blows. That guy Sherrard is a real bad man. I'm going to go, Sam. If there's trouble, I want to help. I know I'll have to wait outside but that might be a good idea to have someone watching your back.

"I'm tempted to have you come inside, John," Sam chuckled, "wouldn't that get Atchison's dander up?"

"What do you think Governor Geary will do?"

"He's on our side. Never will he approve Sherrard's appointment."

A knock at the door, Margaret wiped her hands on her apron to greet the visitors, Eric and Katie McCrea with two-year-old Tammy, "What a pleasant surprise," she exclaimed.

Sam jumped up to grab a chair for Katie, "Come in here, have some coffee."

Sarah hurried down the stairs when she heard the fuss. She squealed with delight and took Tammy in her arms. The little girl laughed to be with her good friend. Katie sat breathlessly hands cupping her stomach, "Whew, that hill gets higher the fatter I get," she smiled at Margaret setting a cup of coffee on the table in front of her, "Eric will have to bring me up in the wagon."

"When are you due?" Sally asked.

"May or June," she took off her bonnet, "I hope before the summer."

Margaret took the bonnet and placed it near the hearth to dry, "You shouldn't be out walking in this wet weather, Katie."

Eric leaned over, elbows on his knees anxious to explain the visit, "Sam, I'm not going to the meeting."

"Why?"

"I told you, Sherrard's friend recognized me. They'll get all stirred up about me shooting Malcolm Clark, even though it was over a year ago..."

"And self-defense," John T offered.

Eric nodded, "If I get up to testify against Big Bill, they'll turn it around to me being a murderer. Anyway, Hal will be a better witness."

"I don't want him to go," Katie said firmly.

"I agree," John added. "I don't want to have to go back to Ft. Leavenworth and get you out again."

"They'll hang me from the nearest tree," Eric emphasized. "No way they take a chance on going to trial."

Sam nodded. A pause in the conversation left only Tammy prattling to Sarah about her new tooth, a soothing sound that Sam focused on, a pleasant interlude compared to the tension he felt about the meeting that afternoon. He said to Eric, "Flo will be good friends with Tammy and your new baby."

Katie smiled at the thought, "Yes, and the Johnsons are expecting. Lawrence will be full of children before you know it."

"I know Tap is talking about building a new school," John added, "I sure wish the colored children could attend. Sally and Mrs. Emery are having classes in the Indian Mission on the Delaware Land until we can build our own school."

"I'm going to insist that all children be able to attend the new school," Margaret announced.

"Good luck with that, Mrs. Wood," Sally scoffed, then added, "I've got to change Flo."

"Here Sally, I'll do it," Katie said standing to take the baby, "Sarah, bring Tammy and come upstairs with me."

As they cared for the two babies Katie asked the question on everyone's mind, "What is going on with you and Hal?"

Tears suddenly appeared in the corners of Sarah's eyes, she placed Tammy on the bed next to Flo so she could watch her change the baby. Sarah sat in the straight-backed rocking chair next to the window, leaned her head back, rocked slowly, "tell me about you and Eric, Katie. You seem to be so much in love. Was your courtship full of romance. How did Eric propose?"

"Sarah, you can't compare Eric and me to you and Hal. You can't compare anyone to you and Hal, you guys are unique. You have to make your own story."

"I know it, Katie, but I'm curious about it. The only other example I have is Sam and Margaret. They fell in love in a day and are so affectionate with each other. I want that for myself. Tell me about you and Eric, was it love at first sight."

She laughed, handed Flo to Sarah and sat on the bed, "Oh my goodness. I hated him the first time I saw him. Daddy had taken him as an apprentice in the shop," she paused to let Tammy crawl into her lap. "That first day, they worked from daybreak until sunset then came to the house for supper. They were both black as the blackest Negro you ever saw; all you could see was teeth. I thought Eric was the foulest creature I'd ever laid eyes on. By the time they finally got cleaned up, he didn't even glance at me, just talked non-stop to Mother and Father, thanking them over and over. He was 14, I was 11. I doubt I said two words to him the next few months. I guess we just kind of grew into each other over the years. He taught me to read. We became each other's best friend. By the time I was 16 we knew that we would be together for the rest of our lives.

The tears flowed down Sarah's cheeks, "What a beautiful story, Katie. Oh, how I envy you."

Katie sat Tammy on the bed and handed Sarah a clean napkin to dry her eyes.

"I'm doomed to be a hopeless romantic in an unromantic world," Sarah applied the cloth to her cheeks.

"What did he say to make you feel so sad, Sarah?"

"He said our new house is almost finished. He said I would have the finest horse and buggy to ride into town whenever I wanted. He described all of his plans, to buy more land with his family, to add on to the house when we had lots of children. He didn't ask me what I thought. Not once. He barely stopped to breath. He didn't say one word about love. It's all business to him."

Katie grimaced, knowing Sarah as she did, a girl with her emotions on display for all to see, so easy to take advantage of, "What did you say to him, Sarah?"

"I couldn't say anything, I was crying too hard. He thought I was crying with happiness," she started tearing up again, "I couldn't get two words out. Then his father came to get him to meet with Sam and talk about the meeting in Lecompton. I haven't spoken to him since. What should I do, Katie?"

"Do you love him?"

"I think so...I don't know. We haven't really seen each other all winter. I just want him to tell me that he cares for me, that he loves me."

Tammy crawled off the bed and lay her head in Sarah's lap patting her leg.

***

A cold February mist coated the prairie grass with icy dew. The horse chestnut and silver maples dripped water from their spidery limbs. The pecan trees on the road to Grasshopper Falls slouched dreary waiting for the sun. Desolate weather for the men riding out of Lawrence to the Lecompton Indignation Meeting; yet the mood brightened as they gathered strength. They were joined by a group from Hickory Point then Bloomington and Palmyra.

Judge Wakefield wrapped a grey scarf carefully about his face leaving only dark eyes peering out from the floppy felt hat dribbling water from the brim, "Doesn't look like the bad weather gonna' keep anybody away," he mumbled. They rode three and four abreast on The California Road, the hills thinning to the river lined with cottonwood and Osage orange. The Kansas River valley bottom on the north side stretched to the hills a few miles away

"I don't think anything will keep our people from this meeting," Sam Walker said. He wore a Bloomington militia uniform coat, an old calvary hat with a hole in the brim cocked back giving little protection from the weather.

"Walker, how many of your militia will be there?"

"Most everyone, except General Lane. I guess he's still in Nebraska."

"He won't be back until Governor Geary rescinds the order for his arrest," George Dietzler said from the row behind, "it's damn unfair to target Lane when he was just trying to protect the neighbors."

Sam reined Border Ruffian around next to Dietzler, Caleb Pratt and Clarke Pomeroy, "I got a letter from Lane yesterday. He's back but staying in Bloomington until things calm down."

Walker nodded, "I heard that too but didn't want to say much."

"Tell me about the skirmish last September when you ran the Border Ruffian Militia out of Lecompton," Sam pulled alongside Walker.

"You mean when you was off hobnobbing with General Fremont and all the bigshots in the east?"

Sam nodded, oblivious to the cynicism.

Walker grinned. He never knew Sam Wood to question his own actions. Sam was the kind of man who acted when action was needed and negotiated when that was appropriate. Wake reminded those who criticized Sam that he didn't hesitate to take blame when his actions were wrong but nine times out of ten he was right where most men did nothing. There had been some animosity toward Sam and a few of the others who were absent during the various Territorial battles after the Siege of Lawrence. There was no use in belaboring the point. Sam was back now. More than could be said for Charlie Robinson.

"Not much to tell," Walker began," there wasn't a shot fired on either side. General Lane divided us up in Lawrence. I was with Colonel Harvey. We rode up the North side of the river, in the bottoms, until we reached Lecompton," he pointed across the river, "the Border Ruffians were under the command of Lincoln Smithers; they could see us over there from quite a way off. Didn't know whether to shit or go blind. We could have wiped em' out. Lane was supposed to signal us when he reached the hill above Lecompton. But he never showed. Finally, we turned back to Lawrence."

"What happened to Lane?"

"He never said."

"You must have scared the Pro-Slavers off."

"That's what I heard. I guess the strategy worked. Evidently Lane showed up about six hours later and the Ruffians had all pie-eyed back to Missouri. But we didn't know it at the time. When we got back to Lawrence, we just went on home."

"Daniel Woodson's to blame for all of the troubles after Shannon left," Wakefield reined around to ride next to Sam, "he called up all the Missouri Militia and ordered Stringfellow to mobilize the Ruffians. They were going to burn Lawrence again, but our boys stopped them at Franklin."

"Old John Brown had a hand in that didn't he," Sam pulled his coat tighter around his ears, "at least that's what he told me."

"He did advise the troops when there weren't any other officers around," Caleb agreed. "He helped the situation considerable until Governor Geary showed up and ordered everyone to back off. That's when Woodson lied about ordering the Missouri Militia to back down. He had never given that order."

The Barnett's joined them coming from Bloomington along with Robert Barber and a large contingent of Palmyra Free State men.

"Hope this little fracas won't amount to much," Wakefield said, welcoming the newcomers.

"What's our strategy, Sam?" Harold asked.

"Strategy? We ask the bogus Territorial Council to withdraw Sherrard's appointment."

"And if they don't?" Walker said.

"Sam can try to sweet talk em'," Tap laughed.

"Not a bad idea," Sam agreed.

They rode on, speaking in low tones as they neared Lecompton. An impressive sight, seventy men on horseback, flowing down the hill. Across the way, visible through the mist, hazy in grey shadows, the Territorial Capital appeared; three-stories high surrounded by wagons, buggies, and horses. Men scattered about in small groups. Governor Geary stood on the landing of the outside stairwell, a cluster of men shouting at him, their voices carried all the way to the riders.

"Wonder what that's about?" Wakefield pointed.

***

Big Bill would always think of ex-sheriff Jones as the boss. 'I owe that man a debt of gratitude I can never repay. He trusts me enough to hand over the job of sheriff of Douglas County, Kansas Territory, the most important job there is right now. I damn sure won't let him down. These rebels won't get away with their illegal ways as long as I'm in charge.'

Yet, when he stopped to think about it riding alone to the meeting, a chill went through his body. He was in way over his head. 'I'll have to bluff them. I've had to bluff my way through everything, all my life. I'll just scare em' into approving me. I'll threaten to kill them. And they know I mean it.' He slapped the reins across the horse's neck, a new look of determination on his unshaven face.

David Atchison and General Stringfellow arrived in a landau accompanied by Bogus Jones on horseback

"Hello fellas," Sherrard shook hands with his friends, "I sure appreciate y'all comin'."

Jones put his hand on Bill's shoulder, "We need to let the rebels know who's in charge around here. This is a formal hearing. It's not going to be just a few farmers getting up to spout off. This is important, Bill. You need to be on your best behavior. I wish you'd have worn a suit or at least a clean shirt."

Big Bill glanced down at his grubby shirt, suspenders barely containing the overhang of a gut he'd developed, "Too much beer lately. I'll work it off when I start sheriffin'." Bill grinned.

Atchison glanced at Jones, "The damned Abolitionists are flooding the territory. It's gonna be harder and harder to rig the elections. This meeting is very important, Bill."

Sam, Harold and Caleb Pratt sat their horses looking at the four men most responsible for the troubles in the Territory. Sam Walker and a few of the others formed a semi-circle around the group. Sam dismounted walked up to Big Bill who towered over him by a good six inches, "There is no way on God's green earth that I'll let you become sheriff of Douglas County."

Bill took a step back, his mouth moved yet no words formed. He gnashed his teeth but couldn't get anything out. To those watching, he seemed afraid of Sam. Walker glanced at Caleb Pratt, "That fat slob's a coward."

Jones sneered at the Free State men surrounding him, "Wood, I've still got warrants for your arrest."

Tap swung his leg over the saddle to stretch his aching back, "You're not even the bogus sheriff anymore. Might as well burn those warrants."

Finally, Bill found his voice, "Well...well, by-God, you ain't really got nothing to say about it, Wood." The big man seemed to move his hand toward his gun.

Sam tapped him on the wrist. "No guns Sherrard. We'll settle this inside. Listen to me, all four of you," he pointed his club, "this man will not be sheriff in Kansas, end of story. It ain't gonna' happen. So, let's settle peaceful, otherwise..." he left the consequences to their imagination.

Stringfellow climbed down from the buggy, "We'll just see about that Mr. Wood," he motioned to his friends to follow him. "Like you say we'll settle it inside."

Four o'clock, the late winter sun settled slowly, floating shadows down the hill darkening the western half of the building. Horses stood motionless, ears back, heads down, water dripping from manes; steam rose from those ridden hard from Franklin and Blue Mound. An icy wind whipped across the hill, swirling up from the river blowing the men, stamping, and shaking water, inside.

Sam and Caleb walked to the south side of the building where Governor Geary and Shorty Jones were coming down the stairs, "What was that all about, Governor?"

He removed his hat, ran his fingers through his hair, "Those men are members of the Territorial Council."

"I know a couple of them," Caleb shook hands with Shorty, "Mr. Stallbaumer isn't a bad sort of fellow."

"None of them are necessarily bad, but they haven't been elected according to the law. That damned Senator Atchison is putting them up to this. I was just trying to talk to sense into them. I'm afraid there's going to be trouble, gentlemen."

Shorty pulled Sam aside as Caleb walked in with the Governor, "Sam, watch Sherrard close, don't let him out of your sight. He's liable to shoot the Governor. He's crazy."

"I heard that, Shorty. I'll stick to him."

By four-thirty the lower level of the Territorial Capital was full of 250 men mostly Free-State. The 60 pro-slavery supporters included all the members of the bogus legislature, the nine associates of the Territorial Council, Judges LeCompte and Cato, and some Border Ruffians summoned by Atchison and Stringfellow. They were heavily armed, crowded around the room backed up against the walls.

Governor Geary called the meeting to order, "Gentlemen, this is a public hearing to discuss the appointment of William T. Sherrard as High Sheriff of Douglas County, Kansas Territory. I have here," he held up a document, "a list of men who wish to speak on this matter."

"Mr. Sherrard, you have the floor to present credentials that qualify you for this position."

Sherrard glanced at Atchison who nodded toward the podium. Bill stood in front of the lectern, a defiant sneer scarred his face, "My credentials are that I've been appointed by the Territorial Legislature and the Territorial Council. Plus, I was deputy sheriff of this county for two years. I don't even know why you all are having this meeting. I'm already the sheriff."

"No, you are not. We don't recognize his appointment. We don't recognize the pro-slavery legislature or Council," Ralph Epcot, pushed through the crowd, arm still in a sling, "You're a low-down drunk. He attacked my children," Ralph turned to the crowd, "he should be run out of the Territory."

Shouts exploded coming from all sides.

Shorty Jones stood on a chair next to the Governor holding both arms above his head, "Quiet gentlemen, quiet please," his thin voice almost a squeak in the excitement of the moment. Sam banged his club on the podium until the chaos subsided. Shorty screeched, "This man is a bully, a murderer, an unconscionable oaf who spit in the Governor's face. He isn't fit to be the town drunk."

"You little pissant. I'll cut your Goddamned tongue out."

"Gentlemen, please let us conduct ourselves with some decorum," Governor Geary stood up, his height normally forceful enough to calm a room.

"I'll show you some decorum," Sherrard bellowed, eyes narrowed in a fierce stare, index finger sweeping the room like a loaded pistol. "Any man speaks out against me, I'll run you out of this Territory if I don't kill you first."

Sam poked his club in Big Bill's chest. Taken by surprise he sat backward into a chair by the podium. Sam glared at the fat bully, club pointed at his nose and shouted, "Where are the members of this so-called Territory Council?" They raised their hands. "You need to vote, right now...withdraw this man's appointment. You can solve this right quick, or we'll go to war over it."

The nervous men of the council looked at each other... so many Free-State men around them; this meeting was advertised as just a formality. Finally, the chairman, John Calhoun from Leavenworth City glanced anxiously at Lecompton, "Judge, you supporting us in this appointment? Was it legal?"

Lecompton nodded yes, looking insolently at the Governor.

"We've made our decision. We stand by the appointment."

"Then I veto it," Geary hammered on the table. Men on both sides began shouting. Sam pounded his cane on the dais. Hal, Caleb Pratt and Sam Walker pushed their way through the crowd. Men were shouting, wildly gesturing, some trying to calm their friends, others urging them to fight. The Boarder

Ruffians pulled guns and knives looking from one side to the other unsure of whose side they were on.

Enter a tall fellow, almost as tall as the governor, still wearing work clothes dirty from his labor, an old slouch hat perched on his head, suspenders holding britches that reached only to his ankles. He raised a calloused hand, shouted for order, "William Sherrard, you godless heathen, do you know who I am?"

The crowd quieted. Those in back stretched to see what was happening.

"No, and I don't give a good Goddamn who you are."

"I'm Elroy Sheppard--you killed my brother, Larry, last week in Atchison. An eye for an eye." He pulled a Harper's Ferry horse pistol from his coat, aimed at Sherrard still sitting in the chair, and fired. The powder charge exploded with a deafening roar of smoke, and sparks. The musket ball missed Sherrard splintering the podium.

Big Bill jumped up, knocking Sam backwards, drew his gun and returned fire. The hall erupted as people dove for cover. Sherrard's meaty arm swatted the club back into Sam's face knocking him senseless. He fell to the floor blood pouring from his nose, reaching out to try and restrain the crazed deputy. Big Bill jerked away firing point blank at Sheppard. The farmer flew backward blood spurting from his chest. Sherrard turned calmly, looked down at Sam, aimed the pistol at his back, then turned and calmly drew a bead on Governor Geary. Shorty pulled his pistol, jumped in front of Geary and began shooting. The room exploded in gunfire from all sides.

Stringfellow and Atchison dove under the table. Bogus Jones bolted out the door. Shots thundered across the room, impossible to see who was shooting or who was hit in the confusion; deafening noise, powder smoke choking the survivors and bodies flying.

Sam lay on the floor a body weighing him down, blood pouring from his nose, eyes blurred, gasping for breath, "Get him off," he gasped.

Caleb yelled, "Sam's wounded."

George Dietzler reached his side, "You hurt bad, Sam?"

"No, I hit myself in the nose with my club."

Caleb helped him to his feet. They stood over the body of Big Bill Sherrard, eyes open staring blankly at the ceiling, a hole in his forehead and blood flowing under his body.

"He's dead," Sam mumbled.

"He appears to be," Caleb helped Sam to a chair. Reverend Lum knelt next to the dead farmer, placed his hand on the man's forehead, closed his lifeless eyes, "Dear Lord, what have you wrought in this God forsaken place."

Men congregated nearby chorused "Amen." They thought he was praying.

It took four strong men to load Sherrard's body into a wagon for the trip back to Leavenworth. Before leaving, General Stringfellow yelled at the Free State men standing nearby, "Someone has to pay for this murder, gentlemen. Those of you who fired shots shall be held accountable."

Sam holding a cloth to his nose mumbled, "Self-defense, Stringfellow. Plenty of witnesses. Big Bill drew down on the Governor. I'll swear out a deposition tomorrow."

Stringfellow glared at him "We'll see about that Mr. Wood. I've got witnesses who saw it different," he spotted Judge LeCompte walking to his home on the hill behind Constitution Hall, "Judge, there'll be an inquest won't there?"

LeCompte hesitated, "I'll look into it tomorrow. I'm a bit shaken right now."

"I shot him," Shorty announced, "and I'll gladly stand trial for it. You saw that he was about to shoot the governor."

Sam took a deep breath, tried to make everyone understand, "Judge, we'll have an inquest about this as soon as you have an inquest about the murder of, Chuck Dow and Thomas Barber and David Buffam. Until then I guarantee you, I'll drag out any legal proceedings until you die of old age."

LeCompte looked at Atchison shook his head and walked away.

Geary came out of the building with a group of Free State men, "You saved my life, Shorty."

"I think he saved my life too, from what I hear," Sam said shaking the little man's hand.

***

That weekend, neighbors gathered at the Wood home drawn like metal filings to a magnet, no formal invitation having been issued. The men and women gravitated for a commonality of purpose, a reassurance that what they witnessed, for those that were there, and what was rumored for those who weren't, was real; but more importantly, 'what did it mean?'

The Free State Citizens experienced a collective sigh of relief over the unexpected death of Big Bill Sherrard. As 'Tap' said riding back to Lawrence in the dark, "Fellas, I hate to say it, but this sure solves a lot of problems." No one disagreed.

Judge Wakefield and Caleb Pratt began to speak at the same time.

"You go ahead, Caleb,"

"No, after you Judge, age before beauty."

"I was just going to say, this does solve one problem, but we have a whole bunch more."

Sam walked off the back porch, paper and pen in hand, "Stringfellow and Atchison aren't going to let the matter drop. They'll make a big deal out of Sherrard being murdered at a Free-State meeting. You know their newspapers are going to spread lies."

He sat on the patio, "Better bring some more benches David, I have a feeling we'll have a crowd today."

David hurried off looking for Caleb to help him with the chores. Sam tried to make some notes, but the wind wouldn't cooperate blowing the notepaper off the stump he was using as a table. He gave up and rested his chin on the palm of his hand, his eyes blackened, and his nose swollen.

"What is Sam so deep in thought about?" Sally asked.

"He's got a lot on his mind. We stayed up half the night just talking. Nobody knows how these troubles affect that man. He puts on a brave front but he's truly worried, Sally."

"He looks like an owl with those two black eyes," she giggled.

David came running back. Margaret opened the door to listen, "Papa, there's a lady out front looking for you."

"A lady? What does she want?"

"I don't know. She just asked if this is where Sam Wood lives. I told her I would get you. She has three kids with her."

"You want me to see who it is Sam?" Margaret asked.

"Come walk around front with me."

"I need to get my bonnet and shawl. Come through the house."

Margaret quickly tied and adjusted her bonnet then draped a dark-grey shawl over her shoulders before they ventured to greet the mystery guest. In the street sat a farm wagon drawn by four mules, a large cask of water on the side, three children in the back, two boys and a girl on their knees peering over the side boards; on the drivers bench a woman dressed much like Margaret. All of them intently watching the Wood's approach.

"Hello, I'm Margaret Wood and this is my husband Sam."

Sam made a slight nod, "I understand you asked for me, do you need some legal advice?" He smiled at the children who turned their gaze on their mother.

Tears formed in her eyes, "I'm Jean Sheppard," she whispered, as though that information was explanation enough.

Sam looked at Margaret as she placed her hand on the woman's arm, "What is it dear? How can we help you and your family?"

"We've been on the road since early yesterday. We don't know where else to turn."

"Sam, go get Sarah," Margaret pushed him toward the Thompson's house where Sarah was helping Beulah with chores. "Mrs. Sheppard get down and come into the house," she could see David and Caleb lingering about trying to eavesdrop, "David, show these children where the outhouse is then bring them into the kitchen. I'm sure they're hungry and thirsty. Sally, will you see to the team." Sam helped Mrs. Sheppard down while the children climbed over the side attended by David and Caleb.

Tap and Pratt, deep in conversation, stopped when they saw the unexpected gathering. Sam motioned them to the back yard, "I'll be right back. Make yourselves comfortable."

Sarah was already walking back when Sam started toward John T's. He explained as best he could the situation, "I don't know what she's upset about, but this is more up your alley than mine. Come tell me what it is when you find out." Sarah broke into a run, always happy to have someone who needed her help.

Wakefield, Dietzler, Harold, Hal and Chief Barnett had joined several others by the time he returned, "Well gentlemen..." Sam left the comment linger not knowing where to start."

"What's the crisis inside," Caleb Pratt nodded toward the house.

"Don't know yet. I'm sure someone will fill us in soon enough. A lady with some kind of problem. Best left for Sarah," Sam explained.

Hal nodded, "She's good at that sort of thing."

Sam opened his mouth to ask something of Hal but, like the early attempt at conversation, he couldn't think of what to say. He still didn't know the status of their marriage plans."

"Most unfortunate business last week," Wakefield lamented. "So many murders and assaults with no consequences. The law is impotent in Kansas."

"There is no law," Tap volunteered, "but I still say we're better off with Bill Sherrard dead."

"True," Harold leaned back in the rocking chair he had commandeered, "I don't care about Sherrard, but that farmer didn't deserve to die that way. I believe the man missed on purpose. How else can you explain it? Him being that close."

"Who was he?" George Dietzler asked, "I don't believe I've heard his name mentioned."

Wakefield pulled a cigar from his coat, stuck it in his mouth but didn't light up, "Name of Sheppard, from over in Doniphan. Squatter, worked the place with his brother before he got killed. Now they're both dead"

Sam stood, "Did you say Sheppard?"

"Yes, Sam. Why?"

"That's the name of the lady in the house," he looked toward the back door as if the answer waited there, "I'd better go see what's up. You fellas go ahead and start without me. I'll be right back."

"Start what?" Chief Barnett asked to blank looks from everyone.

Sally stood at the wood stove waiting for the teapot to boil. She glanced at Sam, put her finger to her mouth shushing him. She motioned, nodding toward the front. They walked down the street a way until Sam said, "What's up, Sally. Why so secretive?"

"Do you know that lady?"

"No, I've never seen her before. I understand she's the wife of the man murdered in Lecompton last week."

"Who told you that?"

"Wake knew the man's name was Sheppard. I just assumed this is his wife."

"This lady is the wife of his brother, the one that Big Bill killed in Atchison a couple of weeks ago. They all lived together somewhere up north of Atchison. When her husband was killed, the brother, the one killed in Lecompton last week, made it his responsibility to take care of Mrs. Sheppard and his niece and nephews. Now both of the men are dead and she has nothing. No way to keep the land. Just an old run-down shack that won't even keep them through next winter. No money, only the wagon and team."

"She doesn't have any other family?"

"A brother back East somewhere. She's written to him. Who knows when or if she'll hear back?"

"Why has she come here?"

Sally shook her head, "That's the sad part," she grasped Sam's hand, "she blames you for her brother-in-law's death. Claims you were supposed to protect him."

"Me? But I didn't even know the man. Never laid eyes on him until the moment he pulled the trigger."

"She's confused, Sam...at her wit's end. We have to help her."

"I'd best go speak with her."

"What are you going to say?"

"I'm going to tell her that her husband is a casualty of war just as if he had been in a battle. He died for a just cause and her brother-in-law tried to do what was right, what he had to do as a brother of a murdered man. They both died in the fight for justice and freedom. She should be proud."

Sally stopped short, "No. You go on about your business. Leave Mrs. Sheppard to the women. That poor lady doesn't need to hear a speech about truth and justice when she hasn't got a clue where her next meal will come from or a roof over her head. Go on now, we'll take care of this. You men make Kansas a free state. Let the women figure out how to live while you're doing it."

Sam watched her walk into the house. He felt worse than he did that morning when he woke. The backyard was teeming with men. 'What in the world can I do to straighten out this mess?'

Bewilderment evidently showed on his face, "Troubled mind, Sam?" John T. asked as he rounded the corner. Sam shrugged his shoulders, "Yes, John. I am concerned, but we've got work to do. Help me get this group organized. We need to set an agenda. No time to get muddled down now." They walked together to the middle of the congregation.

"Let's get started, gentlemen."

***

They seemed relieved, these Kansas pioneers, gathered from Bloomington, Palmyra, Wakarusa, Franklin, and Lawrence. Others in communities further away were waiting to hear the consensus. What do we do now? How do we proceed?

"Has anyone heard from Charlie?" Tap asked.

They looked hopefully at each other.

"Evidently not," Wake stood and stretched his legs, "what do you think, Sam? I'm not questioning his commitment, but this is indefensible."

Dr. O'Reilly removed his suit coat, loosened his string tie, "Fill me in gentlemen, just a quick summary if you please. I've heard so many conflicting rumors, men dead, men wounded...I'm not sure what to believe."

"You can believe that Big Bill Sherrard is deader than a gut-shot Shawnee," George Dietzler said with a serious look.

"Oh, Good God, give me strength," Sam muttered. He turned to censure Dietzler. Hal and Chief Barnett stopped him, "Let it go Sam." Dietzler didn't even realize the slight toward the Barnett Family

"And good riddance I say," Caleb Pratt echoed. "Sherrard is dead. But not before he killed another man name of Sheppard whose wife is in Sam's house right now. Destitute and alone."

"Well then we'll have to help her," O'Reilly ventured.

General agreement sounded through the crowd.

"Agreed, but let's get organized right now," Pratt said with a firmness that belied argument, "Tap, will you act as Secretary."

The tall thin man crawled off the stump he was sitting, stretched his back, "I'd be glad to but don't have paper or a pen. Shall we go in the house."

"No," Sam pointed toward town, "down to the hotel, everyone. Hal and Chief will you go get Ralph Brooks, Riley Tanner and Eric."

"And Mr. Baldwin, he's been mad that we've left him out of the discussions."

The men moved off with a purpose. Sam glanced back at the house. Margaret stood at the back door smiling at him.

"Meg, we're going down to the hotel. Tell us what you need for Mrs. Sheppard. Money, housing, food whatever she needs."

Margaret nodded agreement, "I know that everyone will help. She's just got to decide what she wants to do. But right now is not the time. I've sent David for Reverend Lum. He'll help us counsel her. She's a very religious woman."

"When Lum is done, send him down to the hotel. We'll need a lot of counseling ourselves," Sam drug his feet leaving, glanced at the sky, back at Margaret. She cocked her head, "What?"

"How come she blames me for all of this?"

Margaret stepped off the porch, gathered Sam in her arms, "Once she gets to know you, she'll understand. Yours was the only name she knew in this part of the Territory. I think Mr. Sheppard must have said something like, 'Don't worry, Sam Wood will be there'," with a kiss on his cheek, she sent him on his way, a little lighter of heart.

***

Shalor Eldridge built the new Hotel on the same site as the old Hay Tent. The Free State Hotel, where Sam described the rescue of Jacob Branson; where he met with the Congressional Committee on Territorial Elections; where Governor Shannon negotiated a Peace Treaty between the Abolitionists and the Missouri Militia during the Siege of Lawrence; where Senator Atchison, Bogus Sheriff Jones and their mob of Border Ruffians bombarded the hotel with the Old Sacramento Cannon during the Sack of Lawrence. In the few short years of its existence, it had been burned, torn down, bombarded, and rebuilt three times.

"We've got too many men for an open meeting, Sam. We need to break down into committees," Judge Wakefield observed.

Sam looked over the large crowd gathering in the second-floor ballroom, "Get us organized Wake. I'll chair the State Convention committee."

Wake rapped the flat of his hand on the podium, "Gentlemen, please, quiet'n down."

Sam was about to bang his cane on the table for attention when Caleb Pratt shouted, "HEY, pipe down everyone." Pratt, though younger than most was quickly becoming a well-respected voice for the Abolitionists.

"Thank you, Caleb," Wake nodded to the sturdily built young man. "Let's divide into groups so we can get some work done. This third of the room," he indicated which cluster he meant, "meet over there with Sam Wood to discuss the State Constitution Convention. This middle third meet there," he pointed to tables in the middle of the room, "Caleb Pratt will lead the discussion of Douglas County elections. Needs to be done soon, Caleb; justice of the peace, County Sheriff, Commissioners, the whole gamut. The rest of you men meet over there with Tap. We need Lawrence city elections, again as soon as possible."

Several men began speaking at once, "I'm not from Lawrence; I live in the County; I want to work on the state committee."

Wakefield held up his hands, "Look, you are grown men. You can figure it out. Just try and make the committees have about the same number of people in them. No more than two hours then the Chairmen will read their report to the entire group."

A great deal of grumbling, complaining, and mumbling occurred before they finally settled into the tasks assigned. Sam looked over his committee, sorely worried that Charlie Robinson was not present, "We need to set an agenda for the meeting in June then get the suggested agenda out to all the delegates for their input," he announced to the eager faces staring at him. Most were not delegates to the State Convention, but they were citizens with every right to make their feelings known. 'Forget everything else, Sam. Focus on this matter', he closed his eyes for a moment.

"Sam, maybe you'd best start with what happened at Big Springs and Tecumseh. Some of us may not be privy to the details. That will help us get started," Harold offered.

"Excellent idea, Mr. Barnett," he brightened considerably. Describing the failed state delegate convention and the subsequent arrest of the delegates was right up Sam's alley. By turns they were angry at the temerity of ex-sheriff Jones, then laughing at the bogus legal tactics Sam employed to free the prisoners. When finished the committee was ready to go. The suggestions were clear, concise and constructive. Sam couldn't wait to make his report when they finished at the end of two hours. But he had to wait. Wakefield started with Tap's City of Lawrence report, then Caleb Pratt's Douglas County schedule. When Sam's turn came, he was tired but felt that his words would have to be well chosen or he would throw his friend, Charlie Robinson to the wolves.

'I must be careful. I haven't heard from Charlie, but I know him. Can't let anyone feel that I distrust his motives or actions.'

Sam placed his notes on the podium, "I'll get to the State Agenda in just a moment. It's pretty short. But first, a few words about our Governor. Those of us who know Charlie well, know that his absence in no way defines his commitment to our cause. Something unforeseen is keeping him from being here. That being said, delegates and citizens in other parts of the Territory don't know him as well as we do, and his absence has created doubts in their minds. I can't dissuade their thoughts by mere words. It will take Charlie being here and a valid reason for his absence to sway the doubters. We will discuss it further when Charlie returns.

"Now, to the business at hand, I will prepare a letter to the delegates in all 16 electoral districts in the Territory. The meeting is scheduled for Monday, June 8, 1857, in Topeka at Mr. Halliday's Constitution Hall. The agenda is as follows:

"Discuss the advisability of new elections for all Government officials.

"Re-ratify the Topeka Constitution or re-write?

"Set voter eligibility rules and regulations and form a commission to ratify all votes and the eligibility of the voters. That means only Kansas Citizens are allowed to vote.

"Insist on a new Territorial census and re-assignment of delegates according to the refined numbers. File a protest with Washington over the failure to provide for an accurate census.

"That's pretty much it. Any questions?"

"Sam, what do you think happened to Robinson?"

"I don't know. I sent telegrams to St. Louis and Washington asking for news. All I know is he left Washington two weeks ago. He should have been here by now unless he or Sara took sick. I wish I could tell you more."

***

A fine mist hung in the air, invisible in the gloom of the dark night, felt only as a cold sheen on his face, footfalls the only sound, light from the lantern a soft glow, barely enough to find the lock. He shivered! The cold metal of the key slipped from his hands rattling on the rock steps. "Damnation," he cried, only to take a deep breath then look to the heavens for forgiveness.

"A miserable night to be sneaking around like thieves," Tap observed.

"Not thieves, Brother Tappan, more like messengers of God," Reverend Lum fumbled the lock open.

They made their way to the steeple, took one glance at each other, and began pulling the ropes. It was one o'clock in the morning. The peels of the bell echoed clear in the chill night. Clouds parted at that very moment; a full moon beamed down seeming to Lum a blessing from God. Tap merely glanced outside, satisfied the task would be easier with the bright moon to guide them.

The door banged as more men arrived, "I've been up for an hour," Caleb Pratt complained.

"I never did fall asleep," Sam Walker shook the water from his hat, "Where's Sam?"

"We'll pick him up at his house. Wake, Dietzler, Pomeroy...all the West Lawrence men will be there."

They trudged up the hill, found Eric McCrea with his covered Conestoga wagon. The men who were walking climbed aboard happy to be out of the rain. By the time they reached River Road, they were 40 strong.

"Caleb, Sam Walker...take some men. Find as many of the homesteads as you can. I've drawn maps to those you might not know. Wake, Pomeroy, Bill Speer and I will cross the river to the bottoms and roust those men. Hal and Mr. Barber are in charge of the Bloomington group. Cyrus Haliday and his boys will bring the Big Springs delegation. We'll meet up in Lecompton." Sam waited for questions then reined around to the north when none were asked.

They followed River Road to the Kansas low water crossing thankful the spring thaw had not fully started. Most of Sam's group was on horseback. Those who walked turned toward Lecompton while the others continued their quest. The houses were little more than lean-to's, some dug into the side of a hill. It was dangerous work at night.

A passable muddy road crossed the bottoms then skirted the hills on the north side of the valley near the road to Grasshopper Falls. They turned onto a track that was little more than a footpath, barely wide enough for a farm wagon. The lanterns cast shadows through the trees as though they were swaying in the wind.

"I was only here once. His house is built against a hill, kind of a dugout..."

Close at hand, hidden in the shadows a voice startled them, "Who the hell are you? Quick before we start shooting."

"It's me, Sam Wood. Looking for Tom Mason."

"What in tarnation you doin' Mr. Wood, sneakin' up on a man's home in the middle of the night?"

"We've come to fetch you, Tom, it's election day. We need your vote."

"What?"

"Douglas County elections today," Tap said.

"Who is that?"

"Frank Tappan, Mr. Mason."

"What's the matter with you men? My woman is sick...children all down with ague. We ain't had solid food all winter. I got no dog in that hunt. Go on and leave us be," he stepped into the lantern light accompanied by a young man probably 21.

"Hello, Roscoe," Sam greeted him.

"Hello Mr. Wood, how's Sarah?"

"She's just fine. Sends her regards. Margaret sent this smoked ham and bottle of fresh milk," Sam said extending a bag.

"We don't want no charity. I'm beholdin' to you, but y'all be off. We proud folk in this house."

Sam could see Roscoe's eyes glow in the lantern light. He didn't seem to be of the same opinion as his father.

Tap stepped into the light, "It isn't charity, Mr. Mason. We want your vote. We're trying to keep slavery out of Kansas."

"You mean if I vote the way you want, it'll keep the Niggers out."

"Yes, Sir."

He put his Kentucky Long Rifle down butt first, leaned against it both hands around the barrel, nodded to Roscoe who reached out for the sack, "Take it to Mama. Tell her I've gone to Lecompton with these men. I'll be back shortly."

"Is Roscoe over 21?"

"Yes Sir, I am."

Sam dismounted, rubbed Border Ruffian's nose, reached in his pocket for a dried apple, "We need all the votes we can get. Roscoe comes too."

***

The sunlight peeking over the hills brightened Lecompton into a beehive of activity. 150 Free State men already gathered at Constitution Hall greeted Sam and his group of fifty. The late night canvasing worked better than they expected.

Horses, muddy from the night's outing, stood hitched, scattered along Main Street. Wagons and buggies parked in vacant lots in front of the building. Men were forming a line preparing to prove their eligibility and cast their vote.

"Where are the Pro-Slaver's?" Walker asked.

No one seemed to know.

"Sam," Caleb Pratt shouted, "the judges have all resigned. Said they're afraid of trouble."

"Oh Lord, what next?" Sam unsaddled Border Ruffian. He began rubbing him down with straw from the stable then turned him into the corral.

"I'm going over to Democrat Headquarters and find out what's going on."

"I'll go with you, Sam," Tap trotted to catch him. Others joined as they tramped up the hill. A few trees here and there in the low spots. Mostly ragged buffalo grass in front of the cabins and lean-to's. A good many horses and men lounged about the house the Pro-Slavers called 'Democratic Headquarters'. Broken limbs and rocks defined the walkway of dirt and mud. Conversation ended as the Free State men approached. The Border Ruffians sat on their haunches or astride their mounts watching, no emotion, no sense of what they thought or how they felt about the situation. More curiosity than anything.

"Where's Aaron Walker?" Sam demanded.

"Still asleep."

Sam walked into the house to the bedroom, opened the door, "What are you doing Aaron? Get up out of that bed. I'll not have anyone claim we kept the Pro Slave vote out."

"I'll get up when I've been elected Douglas County Justice of the Peace."

"That'll be the longest sleep you've ever had. You heard of Rip Van Winkle?" Sam laughed so hard he knocked over a chair.

"Is Wood bothering you Mr. Walker?" one of the Border Ruffians rushed into the shabby room.

"No, get the hell out...wait a minute, find my trousers," his dirty nightshirt matched the tangled hair and foul breath from a night of drinking with the Pro-Slavery advocates ready to claim Douglas County for their own.

"We've got to appoint new election judges, right now. The poll opens in 30 minutes," Sam ordered.

"What in the hell happened to Monroe and Ellison?"

"They quit," Tap replied. The small room was filling up. Pro-Slavers and Free State men side by side. The room stank of sweat and smoke.

"Why?"

"Because these Missourians you've got here threatened them."

"These men are all voters."

"No sir, they are not," Caleb countered

"I know every landowner in Douglas County," Sam pointed out the door with his club, "I registered most of the claims. These men are from Missouri."

"Bullshit, they're voters, I vouch for them."

Sam pointed to the burly fellow who asked if he was bothering Walker, "What's your name and where's your claim?"

"Name o' Lyman."

"First or last?"

"First, last name is Leastman."

"Ain't no Lyman Leastman registered in Douglas County is there Sam?"

"No, there is not."

A look of confusion, a glance at Walker," Any man tries to keep me from votin's gonna' pay hell."

"Let's go outside," Sam pushed through the crowd, "I can't breathe in here. We've got to appoint new judges. Tap, Judge Wakefield and Aaron Walker, you are the new judges. Does anybody disagree?"

Thirty or forty Border Ruffians stood around shuffling their feet, chewing tobacco, watching through squinted eyes.

"When do we get to vote?" one of the biggest men asked. He wore rags for clothes, a dirty felt hat, bandoliers crisscrossed his chest with expensive Colt 1855 pistols at his waist. The handle of a large knife stuck above the top of his right boot, a new Sharp's Rifle cradled in his arm.

"Soon as you can prove you are a landowner in Douglas County," Sam Walker explained slowly.

"Bullshit, we was told to come here and vote. Not to let no Abolitionists tell us we can't."

"You believe in the laws of the United States of America?" Sam asked him.

"You better believe I do."

"Well sir, the law says that you have to own land in Kansas Territory to vote in the State election and in Douglas County to vote in the County election," the man started to speak. Sam held his hand up, "not only do you have to own that land, but you have to have homesteaded it for the past three months. Now, do you own land in Douglas County that you have lived on for the past three months?"

The man looked around menacingly, "I ain't saying if I do or don't. I was told to come here and vote."

"What's your name?" Sam asked.

"Jethro."

"Jethro what?"

"Jethro Smith."

"You any kin to the Smiths over in Palmyra?"

A grin spread on his face, more of a sneer, "That's right, my brother."

"What's your brother's name?"

He hesitated, looked at his companions for help. Sam waited a bit then scoffed, "You aren't related to anybody in Kansas, are you?"

"I doubt that's his real name," Tap said.

"I was told to come and vote," he repeated.

"Let me try to explain in a different way," Sam gestured to the other Border Ruffians, "all of you gather around and listen. You have to own a claim in Douglas County to be able to vote; I don't care what someone else told you. And you have to prove that you've lived on that claim for the past three months. I can tell you right now that none of you men qualify to vote. Go on back to Missouri."

"Mr. Atchison told us to come vote," Lyman persisted.

"How much did he pay you?"

They looked at each other getting nervous.

"Where'd you get that new Sharps," Sam asked.

"None of your goddamn business."

"Jethro, if brains were powder, you wouldn't have enough to blow your nose," Sam crowded him trying to provoke a response.

Tap looked at Walker, "This don't look good," to Sam he added, "Maybe we ought to go back and see how the voting is going."

"Don't worry Tap, I'm sure these fellows will see the wisdom of my words. Now, I'm going to try this one more time. Let me make it real clear. None of you men are going to vote in this election."

***

Polls opened at nine. The three judges sat behind a table on the main floor of Constitution Hall in Lecompton, with Douglass County deed records arranged alongside, plus a stack of printed declarations to be signed by each voter attesting to his eligibility. The line stretched from the door at the top of the outside staircase down the street south toward Democratic Headquarters. More than 200 men were in line with others arriving hourly. Voting was by voice. Judge LeCompte kept the tally.

Most men left immediately after declaring their choice. The Lawrence contingent stayed to act as Marshalls. A good many Border Ruffians milled about at Democratic Headquarters watching apprehensively. They were unsure what to do.

"How much they paying you?" Sam asked Lyman.

"Who says they're paying me?" he snapped.

"Why else would you be here?"

"I'm here to guarantee we can bring our Niggers to Kansas just like we do in Alabama."

"You from Alabama?"

"Yeah."

"How many slaves do you own?"

Lyman hesitated, "Don't matter. We gonna make Kansas a Slave State cause it's the right thing to do."

"For who?"

"For everybody."

"Even the slaves?"

Lyman was glaring off in the direction of Constitution Hall. Suddenly, he cast a look of derision on Sam, "You're an Abolitionist ain't you? You think the Nigger's are equal to white people," a gleam of understanding slowly dawned across his face.

"What makes you think they aren't?"

"They dumber than a box of rocks. Can't think for theyselves; got no sense. Wouldn't last a week without a white man tellin' em what to do, when to eat, when to shit. Jesus Christ, you just as dumb as they are," he spit on the ground near Sam's boot.

Sam didn't flinch, "Here's what I think, Mr. Leastman. Senator Atchison paid you to come here and cast your vote for the Pro-Slavery ticket. That's how you bought that Sharp's rifle. Isn't that the truth?"

Lyman looked away but his friends couldn't let that go, "Hell, if Lyman's mouth's movin' he's a lying."

"Yeah, he'll piss on your leg and tell you it's rainin'."

Lyman smiled at his friends, gestured toward the Hall, "We gonna go down there and vote, but not until we're good and ready," he was calm. Didn't make a big fuss about it.

"Why are you doing this?" Sam asked.

Lyman spit a stream of tobacco, squatted on his heels, leaned against his rifle, butt down, both hands on the barrel, "Mr. Wood, you see ole Cooter a standin' there?"

The man indicated didn't flinch, thin pallid face, slack-jawed, droopy eyes, tattered pants that barely reached his ankles.

"Whyn't you ask him if'n he thinks Niggers is equal to white folk."

Sam squatted next to Lyman, "No need. I know what he'd say."

"Do you know why?"

Sam looked at Cooter and Sugg and Bama and all the others and they were the same though some were tall and short, thin and fat; they were still the same, vacant-eyed, raggedy men, down on their luck if they ever had any to begin with; prize possession whatever weapon they carried and possibly a horse. Cooter held the reins to a flop eared old mule that was as shabby as its master.

Sam turned back to Lyman, "Why?"

He looked Sam in the eye, "Cause if Cooter finds out he ain't no better'n a Nigger...well, then he ain't got nothin. He may be poor, ain't got no house, no kin; but all his life he knowed, no matter how bad it gets, he's still a better man than airy a Nigger."

Sam picked up a twig, snapped it then broke it again, "My daddy used to say the same thing. Said that's why the south will fight."

"Your daddy was a smart man."

Sam nodded to Tap and Caleb; they walked back to Constitution Hall.

"What you think's going to happen?" Caleb asked.

"They're going to wait until a little before six o'clock then rush the polls, make the judges hold over until tomorrow. That way they can get word from Atchison about what to do."

Tap nodded, "I think you're right. We'll just have to make sure that doesn't happen."

Come quarter to six the sun was behind the hill, the air turned colder. The last of the voters, a wagonload from Bloomington, drove away leaving the three election judges, Sam and Judge LeCompte preparing to close the polls. Suddenly shouts and gunfire erupted.

"Oh, no, I was afraid of that," LeCompte turned to the commotion, "do something, Sam."

Sam jumped on Border Ruffian, followed by Tap and Sam Walker. They rode hard to the top of the hill. A running battle was waging between the Border Ruffians and the Lawrence men. Harold and Caleb were firing pistols at the bogus voters. Sam rode straight into the Border Ruffians scattering them as he flew by.

He turned and rode back knocking Jethro to the ground.

The firing stopped. Sam leapt down, clubbing men about the shoulders and legs causing them to scream in pain. The Free State men held the Border Ruffians at bay with drawn guns and shouts to back off.

Breathing hard Sam turned to survey the situation, Sam Walker lay on the ground writhing in pain, Tap kneeling beside him.

***

"When General Stephen Watts Kearny inaugurated the American system of justice in the Southwest in 1846, he introduced a judiciary long common to Anglo-American civilization...pioneers did not create new forms

of law and order; rather they continued to use two ancient English institutions: the justice court, headed by the justice of the peace; and a county, or high, sheriff, with powers to collect taxes, deputize citizens, and form a posse." The English roots of this system are reflected in the word "sheriff," where a "shire" is the one-thousand-year-old ancestor of "the modern county in the United States," and "the principal officer of the shire court was the shire reeve."

From the 1789 Judiciary Act, when the office of U.S. Marshal was established, to roughly the 1850s, when the territory of New Mexico was created, the marshal carried out the modern duties of the post office, FBI, and Secret Service. In the antebellum years the marshal enforced the Fugitive Slave Act and postbellum the Civil Rights Act. He was an agent of the courts, a server of subpoenas and warrants of eviction, an overseer of prisoners, supervisor of elections, collector of taxes, and, for some time, most relevant to the historian of family history, the marshal took the census. The inaugural 1790 census was compiled by 650 federal marshals, who spent 18 months trekking the 13 states and enumerated 3.9 million residents."

*--**The New Encyclopedia of the American West.***

***

David, Punch, Caleb and Missy, plus all of their friends, most every child who could walk, waited in Central Park. They ran up and down the sides of the ravine bisecting the city gathering spot, anticipation etched in their faces. A beautiful fall day, sun shining, something was up. Sam looked like the Pied Piper walking from his home to the hotel. A bevy of children followed him, excitement in the air, a festive occasion but the children weren't sure why.

"What is a Justice of the Peace, Papa," Punch asked, grabbing his father's hand.

"Well, it's a mighty important job, Son," Sam had a twinkle in his eye and a wink for his oldest son, David. "I imagine about the most important job in Kansas right now, since Douglas County has the highest population of any place in the state. Except maybe Leavenworth City and maybe Atchison. Well anyway it's an important job. You kids come on and get a seat where you can watch. You'll find out real quick what a Justice of the Peace is and High Sherriff too."

***

"This is the first legally elected court held in Kansas," Sam announced, trying to act judicial but unable to hide his elation, "I didn't ask for the job, but I'm honored, and I promise to execute the responsibility to the best of my ability. Let's get started. Douglas County Court is now in session. What's the first case, Sheriff Walker?"

Sam Walker, newly elected Douglas County Sheriff stood gingerly still hurting from broken ribs suffered at the County elections in Lecompton, "Quite a few cases backlogged, Sam... excuse me, Judge Wood. First off, Lemual Johnson has filed a complaint against Seth Williamson. You fellas step up here, Lem over there and Seth here by me."

The courtroom was packed. It was the first floor of the Eldridge Hotel, but any place would have sufficed for the citizens of Douglas County, Kansas in the Fall of 1857. The elation at having free and honest elections left the citizens feeling giddy. Plenty of troubles between the Free State men and the Pro-Slavery party still existed but the threat of illegal voting was diminished by half.

"Lem, what's the problem?"

"Well Sam...Seth stole my mule."

"Did you steal Lem's mule, Seth?"

"Now Lem, don't go to tellin' tall tales, it was more like I borrowed it."

"What do you mean?"

"I took it back."

"Do you have the mule in your possession, Lem."

"You mean is it back in the corral?"

Sam nodded.

"Yep, but he kept it a week. I didn't know where it was."

Taking a deep breath, Sam puffed his cheeks, blew out the air, "So Seth, If I understand right, you took Lem's mule without his permission then you brought it back. Did, at any time, in the past, let's say six months, did Lem give you permission to use his mule?"

"Nope."

"What possessed you to take it."

"Well...it was like this, me and Uncle Jed and cousin Booger, we needed two mules to pull a stump...all we had was that old mule of Uncle Jed's. My mule got stole two months ago, remember, Sam? So, I went to Lem's house but he weren't around. The mule was. I figured I'd have it back before he got home, but after we pulled that stump, we took a couple of swigs of Uncle Jed's corn likker and I forgot about Lem's mule."

"For a week?"

"Sir?"

"You forgot about the mule for a week?"

"Weeeellll, Uncle Jed had a right smart o' corn likker. But Booger taken care o' Seth's mule right along with Uncle Jed's."

"Lem, was your mule returned to you in the same shape as when it...disappeared?"

"Yep."

"Seth, look me in the eye and tell me you will never again take, Lem's mule without his permission."

"I promise, Sam."

"Promise what?"

"I'll never take Lem's mule without his permission."

"How much money you got on you right now?"

"Bout six bits."

"Seth, you are hereby fined four bits. Two bits goes to Lem for the rent on his mule and the rest to the court for court fees. Pay Caleb Pratt over there. He's the new County Clerk. Next Case."

Part Two

We have got to choose between two results. With these four millions of Negroes, either you must have four millions of disfranchised, disarmed, untaught, landless, thriftless, non-producing, non-consuming, degraded men, or else you must have four millions of land-holding, industrious, arms-bearing, and voting population. Choose between the two! Which will you have?

Richard Henry Dana Jr.

NEW YORK CITY
MAY 1861

The spring sun had not yet crested the buildings along Broadway as Sam strolled along gawking at the throng of early morning commuters. The crowd somehow managed to navigate without injuring anyone jammed as they were on the wooden sidewalks with horses, buggies, and freight wagons buzzing by on the brick street. As was his custom in Kansas, he nodded to the passing gentlemen, tipped his hat to the ladies, but they hurried by, eyes averted, some recoiling in suspicion; a few offered a surprised nod or grunt. The noise, bright colors, the smells of rotting vegetables and animal waste, wagons rattling, shouts of the drivers all created a longing for his quiet home in Lawrence. 'It would take Margaret and the kids a long time to get used to this,' he reflected.

He was run over by a couple of young men hurrying by as though late for an important meeting. Their stove pipe hats made them seem seven feet tall. The well-tailored lads wore black, wide lapeled jackets, long with narrow sleeves; wider trousers than Sam was used to seeing, quite long and tubular with no creases; double-breasted vests in a checked pattern, one red and one yellow, hanging well past the waistline of the trousers. He stared in amazement at the new fashion trend.

The morning sun began to peek between the buildings brightening the ladies as they languished toward the shops in hoop skirts with tatted lace draped over the bodice; parasols twirling stylishly and bonnets of many different colors. Sam stood in front of Mr. Stewart's marble palace on Broadway. Five stories of every conceivable household need or want, every tool, appliance, dish or pot; every fashionable article of attire for men, women and children, ready made in various sizes; or if need be, an army of tailors to make the alterations. He stopped abruptly forcing foot traffic to dodge around as he gazed, open-mouthed at the tall building, like a child seeing the Rocky Mountains for the first time.

His reverie was suddenly interrupted by a man grasping his hand in an aggressive handshake with many slaps on the back jostling him back to reality, "Sam Wood, what a pleasant surprise."

Sam hesitated a moment not sure who was knocking him about in such a manner.

"It's me, Richard Dana. Have I changed that much Sam? What's it been, five years since I last saw you, during the Fremont campaign."

Dana's flowing locks had receded significantly; his face showed the effects of passing years and heavy foods, but the gleam of the famous author and lawyer, was clearly present.

"Richard, please excuse my behavior; this country bumpkin is not used to the big city. I'm making a fool of myself stumbling over everybody."

"We were on our way to your presentation. You know my cousin, don't you? Charles Anderson Dana. Chuck this is the guest of honor, Sam Wood."

Sam grasped the managing editor of the New York Herald Tribune by the hand, "I only know Mr. Dana by reputation. Horace has spoken highly of you. It's a pleasure to finally meet you."

"I can say the same about you, Sam. I'm looking forward to your speech."

"What a difference a few years makes, Sam. Who could have guessed...Kansas, a State and free from slavery. You did it my friend. Accomplished what you said would do," Richard pounded him on the back enthusiastically.

Sam laughed, "I can't take the credit, Richard. It took a lot of people working together to make it happen."

Blocking the sidewalk, causing the commuters to dodge around them proved cumbersome. They began walking toward the Tribune building soon arriving at the corner of Spruce and Nassau. Richard and Charles reached for the door while Sam stood staring at the five story New York Daily Tribune brick office building, "The last time I was in New York the office was a small building with a little printing press not much larger than ours in Lawrence."

He stepped inside. The scene was even more frantic than the bustle on the street. Copy boys dashed from desk to desk, up and down the stairs, answering the calls of reporters, copy editors, proofreaders, and the various news editors. Sam laughed to think of his small newspapers in Kansas with a tiny printing press and one employee.

They approached a desk, "Where is the Sam Wood meeting?" Charles Dana questioned the clerk.

The man didn't look up, just pointed at the stairs, "Third floor."

"I beg your pardon."

The clerk glanced up, shock registering on his face as he recognized his boss. He leapt to his feet, "Oh, I beg YOUR pardon Mr. Dana, please forgive me, I was preoccupied with this story. The meeting is in the large conference room. I believe most everyone has already arrived."

The large conference room took up most of the third floor. It was packed with dignitaries both black and white. Sam nodded to Frederick Douglass and squeezed Sojourner Truth's hand before shaking hands with Horace Greely. Horace was distracted, looking to greet the guests; he handed Sam off to James and Lucretia Mott whom he hadn't seen since the trip to Washington over ten years earlier.

Lucretia shouted into his ear to be heard over the din, "We've kept up with your frontier adventures, Sam. A far cry from the rising young attorney we expected after the Mary Fedder trial in Ohio."

"At times it has been a struggle. I won't deny it."

"We receive regular letters from your mother. She was just in Kansas last month, wasn't she?

"Yes, but with the war beginning, we felt it best she returns to Mt. Gilead. Sarah traveled with her."

They were joined by Susan B. Anthony, "Sam, I don't believe you've met Mrs. Cary. She will also be speaking today."

Mary Ann Shadd Cary gave a slight curtsy. A striking woman with a narrow face, full lips and piercing dark eyes; her dark skin in sharp contrast to the very pale Mrs. Anthony, "I'm pleased to meet you Mr. Wood."

Sam nodded a greeting, "I have not had the pleasure, but I feel I know you through the Provincial Freeman when we were fortunate enough to find a copy. Mail delivery on the frontier is not always reliable. I understand you recently lost your husband. My sincere condolences."

"Thank you."

"I believe you know by brother Stephen."

"Yes, Stephen was present at some of the John Brown planning sessions prior to the raid on Harper's Ferry."

They were interrupted by Horace shouting from the podium, "Ladies and Gentlemen, please take your seats. Those of you scheduled to speak we have chairs on the stage behind me here."

Sam offered Mrs. Cary his arm and escorted her to a seat on the stage.

Horace continued, "Larry, please see that those windows are opened. I've asked our New York's finest to patrol the street down below to keep the noise to a minimum."

"How much did that cost you?" Salmon Chase shouted from the audience. Horace smiled and shrugged his shoulders. Sam took the opportunity to shake the hand of his good friend, "Sal, I'll see you this evening for dinner."

"Quiet please," Horace shouted. "We have so many dignitaries here today that I would have to introduce everyone, and we don't have time for that. But in all fairness, I want to introduce three of President Lincoln's cabinet members. First, our former New York governor and the current Secretary of State, Mr. William Seward."

Seward stood to acknowledge the applause.

"The former governor of Ohio and current Secretary of the Treasury, Mr. Salmon Chase."

Sal waved to the crowd from his front row seat.

"I know I'm missing someone," Horace looked around.

"Ed," Seward pointed to the gentleman next to him in the middle of the crowd.

"Oh, for heaven's sake," Horace slapped his forehead and pointed, "Mr. Edward Bates from Missouri our current Attorney General. My apologies, Ed."

Horace shuffled papers on the podium, "Ladies and Gentlemen, we have statesmen, poets,

Abolitionists, businessmen and women. We have women's rights advocates, Negro rights advocates, States Rights advocates, and every kind of advocate in vogue today. Not everyone agrees on every point, but we can all agree that this war, so long anticipated is now upon us. Today we have invited men and women who have been instrumental in bringing us to this point. Our first speaker needs no introduction other than his name. A gentleman who epitomizes what we fight for. Ladies and gentlemen, Mr. Frederick Douglass."

Douglass, wearing the latest in fashion...dark grey trousers, a black jacket with the tails to his knees, a red and black checked vest with a black tie; his hair combed thick above his forehead, eyes sparkling mischievously, unlike the photographs in which he refuses to smile in fear of being characterized as the happy go lucky, ignorant Negro being stereotyped in the south. His every action, every word was planned to make a certain statement. Douglass was a master at conveying his point of view with an eloquence few men possess.

"Thank you, Horace. It is my great pleasure to be here today. Gatherings like this often make me morose in that I feel I am preaching to the choir. We all differ in our approach to solving the issues inherent in our society, yet we all recognize the universality of the need to eradicate the abomination in its entirety. I see my good friend William Lloyd Garrison sitting in the front row. I wouldn't be here today without his friendship, help and guidance. There in the back I see Mr. Lysander Spoon who so influenced me with his publication of the Unconstitutionality of Slavery which examined the United States Constitution as an anti-slavery document. Mr. Garrison and I disagree on the use of the Constitution as a tool to end slavery, but it is only a disagreement about the means and not the ends.

The same can be said about our departed friend Mr. John Brown. We can disagree with his methods, but never can we doubt his devotion to the cause. I am honored to share the stage today with Mr. Sam Wood who comes weary from the front lines of the battle; a battle that he will attest has raged for six years, not the few months that we claim as the beginning." Douglass walked briskly to Sam and shook his hand vigorously.

Douglass paused to let his words wash over the audience. Applause was heartfelt. He nodded, acknowledging their sincere appreciation, "Ten or eleven years ago I published, in my newspaper, 'The North Star', an editorial asking for suggestions on what could be done to improve life for African Americans. I received a letter from a young lady, only 25 at the time. She said, and I quote, 'We should do more and talk less.' She opined that those speeches were made, and resolutions passed about the evils of slavery and the need for justice for African Americans, yet little tangible in the way of improvements resulted. I published her letter, and she has gone on to become a bright and influential star in the Abolitionist movement. Ladies and Gentlemen, please welcome to the podium Mrs. Mary Ann Shadd Cary."

Douglass stepped to Mary Ann's chair gave her his arm and escorted her to the podium.

"Thank you, Fred, Mr. Greeley, and honored guests. It is with great pleasure and no little satisfaction that I stand before you on this the cusp of a Civil War so long in the making. Some think it unfortunate that it has come to this. I am not of that mindset. Fred, you mention my good friend John Brown, a man who spent his entire life trying to end slavery. A cause that ultimately resulted in his death. So many people, both black and white have given their life to the cause and that number will be increased astronomically with this coming conflict. I had the pleasure of meeting Mr. Sam Wood who will speak of his experiences in Kansas. So many people dedicated to ending slavery and yet there are so many more who cherish that unholy institution.

"I was born free, but I too suffer the whip and the chain, still feel the looks of disgust from my white neighbors, still fear that my brothers and sisters are being worked to death in the south for the pleasure of their white owners. I have traveled extensively in the United States speaking out against slavery, advocating for full racial integration through education and self-reliance. I have advised all blacks to resist unfair treatment and if all else fails to take legal action. I have been spat upon, cursed, attacked, and threatened throughout the states...both north and south. I had to flee to Canada when the fugitive slave act was passed, just as Fred had to flee to Ireland, because the slave catchers were capturing free blacks as well as the enslaved. Now the time has come, and I welcome it. I will volunteer as a nurse, as a soldier, as an ammunition carrier, whatever they will let me do. I beg of you Mr. Chase, Mr. Bates, Mr. Seward please lobby the President to allow the African Americans to fight. It is our war. Don't let the south's battle cry of States rights sway you. The only state right they want is slavery. I beg of you, arm us and let us defend our lives and honor alongside Mr. Wood and the rest of the gallant freedom fighters throughout our great country. Thank you."

The audience stood applauding while she made her way back to the chair on Horace Greeley's arm.

***

Chuck Dana strolled to the podium, "We'll have a fifteen-minute break. The new bathrooms on the second floor are completed...finally. Ladies to the right off the stairs. Men to the left. Refreshments are available in the conference room across the hall."

The noise level rose as chairs were scrapped back, greetings were hailed to old friends, new acquaintances made and the inevitable rush to the refreshments and convenience stations. Fifteen minutes turned into thirty before Horace could get them all re-settled. He walked briskly to the podium. The crowd immediately quieted. He wore his trademark tan overcoat, more suited to the life of a farmer than one of the most influential men in the world, "Ladies and gentlemen, I have known Sam Wood for many years. I knew his mother and father when they were at the front of the Quaker abolitionist movement. Most of you in this room have had a profound influence on the battle for statehood in Kansas, although from afar. Sam, on the other hand, was there, many would say he is the instigator. He has been on the frontier so long he thinks he's Daniel Boone..."

"Or Davey Crockett," shouted Henry Beecher Stowe.

"Let's hope Sam fares better than Colonel Crockett," Horace grimaced, "Sam bear's witness to every event that shaped the new state of Kansas from that fateful day when Stephen Douglas's Kansas-Nebraska Act sprang from the depths of hell, promising to allow the citizens of Kansas to choose her fate. Little did we realize at that time the horrible consequences of popular sovereignty when a lawless element has no intention of following the letter of the law. I know Sam is going to take me to task over comments I made after my tour of the west last year. I won't deprive him of that pleasure by beating him to the punch. I probably deserve his annoyance.

"Ladies and gentlemen, I give you the man termed the Lion of the Evening at the 1856 inaugural Republican National Convention, a man who doesn't know the meaning of the word fear. A man who was present at all the events that led to Kansas statehood. Sam was there from the beginning, brandishing his club, rescuing his fellow citizens, demanding justice, and never backing down. A man who is not afraid to make a decision even though the consequences may hinder his own advancement. A fellow abolitionist, Senator in the state legislature, Colonel in the Kansas Militia, good husband, and father, but most of all a dear friend. Ladies and gentlemen, Mr. Sam Wood.

Sam strolled to the podium after shaking Greeley's hand.

"Where's your club?" Clarke Pomeroy shouted.

Sam turned back to retrieve his cane, "I didn't think I'd need it here among friends," he laughed carrying the cane to the podium, "but then you never know what old enemy might pop out of the bushes...right Clarke?" He pointed to Clarke Pomeroy who was with him in Philadelphia when attacked by Border Ruffians.

"Gentlemen...and ladies, a year ago, Horace honored the, at that time, Territory of Kansas with his presence, first in Leavenworth, then in Lawrence. That week he attended the first Kansas convention of the Republican party in Osawatomie. Then he took his own advice and traveled west, stopping in Salt Lake City where he interviewed Brigham Young and my good friend Orson Pratt who, luck would have it, was on the Sam Cloon with my family as we traveled from Ohio to the Kansas frontier back in 1854. Orson was instrumental in stemming a cholera attack on board and we became good friends despite our differences, especially about multiple wives in the Mormon religion. Horace evidently looked upon that group of polygamists with favor while at the same time demeaning the good citizens of Lawrence. What was it you said Horace?" Sam turned to Greeley, "I believe you said, 'I'm not impressed with Lawrence, Kansas.'"

"Now Sam, you're taking it all out of context," Greeley started for the podium, ready for a debate.

"Calm down, Horace, I understand what you meant. Let me continue. But I will say here that I just spent two days touring your city from Brooklyn to the Battery and Queens to Manhattan. I'm not impressed."

Laugher shook the room. Greeley chuckled while his face turned crimson, "Fair enough, Sam."

"I see several news reporters scribbling furiously over there along the wall. Folks, I'm not Davey Crocket or Daniel Boone. I'm a simple country lawyer."

"Now you sound like, Lincoln," William Lloyd Garrison shouted.

Sam laughed freely, "Lloyd, you know better than that. Abe had it easy compared to us. Life in a rustic log cabin, why, that's like living here in New York compared to life on the frontier. Margaret, the boys, and I slept in a tent with a foot of snow on the ground, no firewood, no food that you here in the city would call edible. I can match Abe story for story; but I fear that I would lose my audience. I'm not as eloquent as he is, plus, I never learned how to compromise. I admit it.

"Margaret and I moved to Kansas with one purpose in mind. End Slavery. And not just in Kansas but in all the states. Horace, I know that you and others in this room, have advocated allowing the South to secede and form another country. I say no, not now, not ever. We will end slavery or die trying. You have just listened to the eloquent words of Mr. Douglass and Mrs. Cary. Do you believe that they or all the other Negros's in the United States give one whit about States' Rights? Do you think I do? Lincoln said he would gladly accept slavery if it would keep the Union together. I say free the slaves and to the devil with States Rights."

Some people applauded and whistled; others shuffled uncomfortably. A few shouts of 'shame' were heard. After the noise quieted, he continued. "The same words were voiced by another Kansas man who was hung by the Federal Government because of his actions at Harper's Ferry just a year ago. John Brown was a valued and staunch ally in the battles throughout Kansas. Did I always agree with him? No, I did not, yet we shared the same goals...end slavery and bring equality to those held in bondage. Most of you in this room feel the same, as do many who couldn't be here. One of them, Henry David Thoreau, was as responsible as any man alive in elevating John Brown to the status of a martyr. How is our friend? I am sorely distressed to hear of the severity of Mr. Thoreau's illness."

Ralph Waldo Emerson rose and addressed the crowd. "Henry is not well. He continues to write as best he can while convalescing at home with friends and family. He sends word that he wished to be here."

"Thank you, Ralph. Please give him my regards. I look at this group of friends and supporters, people who have become successful here in the east and throughout the world. I see Jane Swisshelm, Oliver Wendall Holmes, Henry Wadsworth Longfellow, Bayard Taylor. Mrs. Swisshelm was kind enough to drive me through your new Central Park. What a testament to human ingenuity and the desire to get things done. Much like what happened in Kansas. Horace, I understand your feelings about Lawrence. Those of us who settled there may have been gentlemen when we arrived, but those qualities were quickly knocked out of us. We were idealists prepared to do what was necessary to accomplish our goals; and I include the ladies. Don't think for a minute we could have won the war for statehood without our wives and sisters battling alongside.

"It wasn't a figurative battle of words...no, it was war, where over 150 people lost their lives fighting for a cause they believe in. And that cause was defined in twenty different ways. The opposing camps, Pro-Slave versus Free-State. But those factions were divided and divided again. Some people didn't want any blacks allowed in Kansas, free or slave. Many Free State men wanted to ban slavery in Kansas but allow it in the South. Some believed in the equality of all mankind, many felt that the slaves were a lower form of life from the white race. Everyone had an opinion and finding consensus was another battle altogether.

"I won't bore you with the minor skirmishes. Most of you are aware of the death of Chuck Dow and the rescue of Jacob Branson. How Charlie, Jim Lane and I were branded as traitors and indicted in the Territorial Courts for High Treason. The siege of Lawrence and the Sack of Lawrence were well reported by this very newspaper. I won't rehash the murder of Thomas Barber, so eloquently enshrined in verse by Walt Whitman. Walt, where are you?"

Whitman stood in the back of the room. Those in front turned to see the famous poet.

"Thank you, sir. You brought more attention to that murder than anything we could have done or said in the Territory. Today, these several years later, those murderers have yet to be brought to justice and in fact were exonerated by the Pro-Slavery judges; an affront to civilized men everywhere."

Whitman stood again, "Where is the man who murdered Thomas Barber, Sam? I'm afraid I don't recall his name..."

"George Clarke is his name, and Governor Geary did everything in his power to bring the man to justice. Bogus sheriff Jones refused to serve the warrants sworn out against him. And, to answer your question, he has fled west to the California gold fields." Turning to Greeley, he added, "Another young man taking your advice, Horace."

Taking a sip of water, Sam continued, "Three years ago, in 1858, President Buchanan ratified the pro-slavery Lecompton Constitution which we Free State men repudiated in such a fashion that three more governors were run out of the territory. Governors Shannon, Geary, and Walker all failed to enact the pro-slavery agenda prescribed in Washington. Geary is a fine man and did all he could to meet the conditions of the laws set forth in the Kansas-Nebraska Act, but he failed the Washington power cartel and had to flee the Territory by night just as Governor Reeder and Governor Shannon before him and Governor Walker, then Governor Denver and finally Samuel Medary just last year. All of them appointed by President Pierce or President Buchanan and each failed to satisfy the pro-slavery faction. They chose to follow the law and insist on free and fair voting and that angered the guardians of the pro-slavery creed, the Border Ruffians.

"No description can adequately describe those vile men. I realize I am quick to condemn, faster to action and slow to forgive. I do look for the good qualities of every human I meet, but these creatures are possessed of none. They are void of human compassion, void of any capacity to reason, void of any form of intelligence except for attaining the basest desires," Sam stopped and pointed his cane at the audience, "and, most importantly in their eyes, to ensure the Negro race will forever bear the chains of oppression. The Border Ruffians raped, robbed, and murdered without discrimination. Abolitionists were the foils of their hatred, but they were unable to describe what an Abolitionist was beyond being a 'Nigger Lover'.

"Enough said about them. Horace was not impressed with the people of Lawrence. What did you expect, my friend? Did you expect to see the same parade of dandy's you see here on the streets of New York City? It takes a hardened attitude, if you will, a willingness to get down and dirty with those who try to oppress, and you won't find that quality on the streets of New York or Philadelphia or Washington. Forgive my bluntness but I don't see that quality in this room. Men and women of words and words fail to impress the Border Ruffians. Violence is the only method that stirs their souls. I see here before me brilliant men and women of letters who describe the actions they see on the battlefield from afar, third hand. And let me say here that I am not fond of the Military Conscription Law allowing wealthy men to buy their way out of serving. It goes against all that our country stands for. Without men willing to fight for what they believe, Kansas would be a slave state today rather than the free state it is, and I am proud to be the author of that clause in our first session of the Kansas legislature as a senator, elected Chairman of the Judiciary. Proud to write the clause that banned slavery in Kansas forever. Chase County, Kansas is named after our illustrious Secretary of the Treasury and my valued friend Mr. Salmon Chase, based on a resolution that I introduced just last year," Sam shouted over the applause directed toward Secretary Chase.

Sam examined the audience and pointed at some of the authors, "I don't begrudge your talents. Words are sorely needed to convey what happened. Newspapers are the life blood of our communications. But the events in Kansas demanded a different strategy and the men who faced that enemy...me included...were forced to act immediately...no time to try and reason. It would have fallen on deaf ears...prayers were useless, pleading scoffed at, and reason seen as a sign of weakness."

Sam paused to give himself time to change direction, "Though I have damned you with faint praise let me now lay on a different course, come about, tack into the wind as you eastern sailing men say."

"That's not exactly how we say it, Sam," shouted Reginald Vanderbilt, a well-known yachtsman and businessman in New England.

"Forgive me, Reg, we don't have an abundance of sailing opportunities in Kansas unless you count the Prairie Schooner... we are steamboat men."

Waiting for the laughter to subside, Sam carefully weighed his next comment while surveying the illustrious audience; influential people all. People who made a difference in the politics and policies of the entire nation, even the entire world, "Buchanan and his henchmen thought they could control the election through the artifices of human greed. He offered us a bribe. Can you believe it, ladies and gentlemen? The President of the United States told us that if we approved the Lecompton Constitution, the Federal Government would deed multiple Sections of the public lands for schools plus 72 sections for a state University, 10 for public buildings, in all 5,500,000 acres."

Sam stopped to magnify the significance of this statement, "If we failed to ratify the pro-slavery constitution, he would withhold all these lands, reserve them for the Federal Government forever. Never has a more nefarious scheme of bribery been foisted on the public. And, although it was never announced, certain of us who were leaders of the Free State movement were offered six sections of land each if we would sway the vote. These representatives of the people, guardians of our sacred laws and customs, heirs of George Washington and Thomas Jefferson must have been popping the champaign corks and celebrating their ingenuity...little imagining that the poor farmers and shopkeepers on the Kansas prairie would reject such a bounty of riches. But reject it we did. August 2, 1858, a date that will live forever in the annals of the history of slavery in this country. 11,300 against the Lecompton Constitution and only 1,788 in favor. So, let it be known that we will have a government based upon reason. It is to be a strong government because the qualified voters have ratified it in an open election. Reason will take the place of force, intelligence over ignorance."

Again, applause interrupted his train of thought. The audience was on the edge of their seats; enthralled to hear the first-hand account of events they knew only through newspaper articles well after the fact.

"I want to relate one incident that demonstrates the lack of integrity and compassion in the current administration. This shows the depravity of the pro-slavery Buchanan cabinet. They did not take the defeat of the Lecompton Constitution graciously, shall we say," Sam shook his head depreciatingly as the audience laughed.

Edward Bates shouted, "Come on, Sam, you know Buchanan doesn't have a humorous bone in his body."

Sam nodded agreement, "Nor did his cabinet unless the joke is on the Abolitionists. This happened during the terrible Kansas drought 15 months ago, in the last few months of Buchanan's administration. The Public Lands in Kansas were to be put up for sale by the Federal Government. The squatters were ordered to 'prove up' their land and pay off the debt incurred through the preemption laws. But that was impossible. The lands of Kansas produced no corn, no wheat, no grass for the deer and antelope, let alone the cattle and horses. Desolation was everywhere. We only survived through the kind donations of our friends in the East, including a good many of you in this room. For that I thank you. No one had any ready money and to borrow money at 50% would more than ruin us. I was honored to be nominated to travel to Washington to solve this terrible problem. I called on the President and after the initial pleasantries we got down to it. Many of you already know this story but for those that don't, I will demonstrate his posture during the entire interview." Sam took an armchair from behind the podium and sat staring silently at the audience, his lower lip pouted over his upper like an angry bulldog, chin on chest, his hands folded over his belly to mimic Buchanan's portly gut, his legs splayed forward from the chair like a man about to take a nap. The audience howled.

"Hold still Sam," Thomas Nast shouted, sketching rapidly on his palette, "I want this in tomorrow's edition." They howled at his impression of the taciturn President Buchanan.

Sam jumped up laughing, "When I finished my presentation Buchanan said, 'Whose fault do you think this is, Mr. Wood? Had you adopted the

Lecompton Constitution it would have solved the problem. I wouldn't be inclined to call the debt on the government lands. I pleaded with him...so this is punishment for voting our conscience against your wishes. But isn't that what democracy is all about? A fair and honest vote by the qualified citizens? Again, he glared at me his eyes narrowing to tiny slits. A sinking feeling suddenly came over me...I don't think President Buchannan likes me." Sam held his arms up in surrender.

The room shook with laughter.

"I decided to avoid an argument..."

"Well, that's a first, Sam," Horace said grinning at the audience.

"I avoided an argument by humbly admitting it was our fault. But why punish us now, no good can come of it? I tried to mediate...no really, I did...I was judicial, even conciliatory, but all it did was cause him to send me down to see Jacob Thompson the Secretary of the Interior, 'If Thompson agrees to call off the sale I'll concur,' he told me. So, I trudged down to see Thompson, like a cur dog with my tail between my legs. I made the same presentation, the same plea, and he said, 'go see the president about this matter.'

"I said, 'I did see the President. He told me to come see you'...I'll tell you folks, I felt a like a child. It was embarrassing. Then Thompson said, 'well the way the people of Kansas have acted, they don't deserve any favors from the Federal Government'. He showed me the door and slammed it when I stepped into the hall.

"Thompson resigned last January, and Horace wrote an editorial which I quote," Sam took a sheet of paper from his vest. "'Undertaking to overthrow the Government of which you are a sworn minister may be in accordance with the ideas of cotton-growing chivalry, but to common men cannot be made to appear creditable. These are the acts of a traitor.'" He folded the paper back into his pocket. "I don't know how or when, but someday, in this life or the next, Jacob Thompson will receive just compensation for his retaliation against the people of Kansas."

Sam hesitated once more until the applause abated, "So, ladies and gentlemen, it has come to this. It seems that after 85 years we must fight to preserve our glorious Union of States to which Kansas has just been admitted."

Taking a breath and another sip of water, he leaned on the podium for a few seconds to gather his thoughts, "Our elected territorial representative, Marcus Parrott, arrived in Lawrence on February 8 of this year, bearing official notification to Governor-elect Charles Robinson that Kansas had been admitted. On February 9, Caleb Pratt, the County Clerk of Douglas County, administered the oath of office to the state's first governor. Now, some of you will remember that Robinson went missing back at the beginning of '57' when he came east to plead with Buchanan and his administration to ratify the Topeka Constitution. He had about as much luck with them as I did last year trying to argue against the sale of the public lands. Charlie had been delayed through no fault of his own and by the time we got that mess straightened out half of our Free State people were mad at him. Fortunately, we were able to mitigate the damage and get him re-elected. Robinson's first official act was to call the legislature to meet March 26 at Topeka. We, the new, freely elected Kansas Legislature repealed all the laws passed by the bogus pro-slavery legislature. I was proud to be elected to the State Senate alongside many good friends and neighbor. I was honored to be selected to chair the Committees on the Judiciary and Federal Relations.

"While we organized the new state government, Ft Riley Commandant Nathaniel Lyon moved his troops to St. Louis to prevent Missouri Governor Claiborne Jackson from seizing the federal arsenal in that city. As we now know, Jackson is a staunch Southern sympathizer and refused President Lincoln's request to provide Missouri Militia to aid the Federal Army in securing the arsenal.

"President Lincoln was kind enough to appoint me as Collector of Customs, a position I accepted but was glad to resign when he issued the call to arms of patriots throughout the nation. I was honored to do so and glad that the war is finally here. I recruited a regiment of Kansas men...and boys, including my own son, David who said, "Daddy, I've been on the front line of the war since the day I was born, and you are not leaving me home just because the shooting has commenced."

In a whisper Sam added, "His mother agrees, more or less..."

When the laughter subsided, he continued, "David will enter the War Between the States by my side, in full uniform. I was elected Captain of the First Kansas Rangers and we will join General Lyon as part of the Third Brigade, Army of the West."

Again, he hesitated as the applause slowly subsided, "Many of my friends and neighbors have joined...names you all recognize from the news reports about Kansas over the past seven years. George Dietzler, Caleb Pratt, Sam Walker, Harold Barnett, Sam Tappan; my brother Stephen Wood will serve as our Quartermaster. Ladies and Gentlemen, I thank you for the opportunity to share some of what has happened in Kansas the past few years. We tried to be reasonable, tried to mediate, tried to reason; the time for talking is over. Let the shooting begin."

Part Three
CIVIL WAR

A storyteller, who was there, a grizzled old veteran, white beard flowing, grandchildren at his knee, finally, after a generation has passed, tries to explain it true. But he chokes on the words and the memories overcome him, he looks into the eyes of the babes at his feet, and he cries. They try to comfort him. They cannot understand.

Poets wax poetically; they sound the charge with a cacophony of words; words that hide what was true...the stench of blood and pus; piss and shit from guts ripped open, knives that rip and tear, clubs. Screams of agony and worst of all, the smell of fear; and the noise, how can words describe the noise; shrieks of dying horses, the carrion squeals of rage, men crying out in despair and cannons booming incessantly?

The poets can't express the truth about the moment, the exact instant the bullet cracks into your body ripping your chest open, leaving the brain in denial even as you watch your blood spill out on the battlefield and you try desperately to staunch the flow, yet you know beyond a doubt that you are dead even before you hit the ground. Did I die for God? For country? For an ideal? What is the truth?

The truth can only be known by those who saw it, felt it and tasted it. The senses convey what the words cannot. But we continue to try because the war just won't go away, won't die like it should. It was three months from the April cannonade at Ft. Sumter. America's finest were arrayed against each other from Kansas to New York and south to New Orleans. Spring had wrung itself violently into summer with shots fired in anger across the great nation, the nation of dreams, the nation of hopes, where a man could become anything he wanted. Now it was neighbor against neighbor, father against son.

Thirty-six thousand terrified, schoolteachers, farmers and shopkeepers were about to launch themselves against each other in Virginia at the first Battle of Bull Run. A crazy hodge-podge of nationalities on both sides of the battle lines, in mismatched uniforms and worn-down shoes, bereft of rations and clean water, dying more from sickness and disease than gun shot. It was the beginning of America's darkest hour. Armies scrabbled together from the dregs of society in the slums of New York and New Orleans and aristocrats from Charleston and Philadelphia, all with a romantic vision of what the war would be. Except for the military men. They knew what was coming.

Crashing like an iron hammer on an anvil of prejudice and hatred, boys in blue and boys in grey collided ferociously until bodies and ammunition were exhausted, then with clubs and knives they battled on, face to face, detesting the other with an unreasonable passion, until each looked into the other's eyes and realized, too late, that it was themselves they fought.

***

"They took it for more than it was, or anyhow for more than it said; the container was greater than the thing contained, and Lincoln became at once what he would remain for them, 'the man who freed the slaves'. He would go down to posterity, not primarily as the Preserver of the Republic-which he was-but as the Great Emancipator, which he was not."

Shelby Foote, The Civil War, Vol. 1: Fort Sumter to Perryville

Clinton, Missouri
July 13, 1861
Headquarters of Brigadier General Nathaniel
Lyon
Commander, Union Army of the West

General Lyon sat quietly staring at a map in a commandeered farmhouse while his subordinate officers conferred in hushed tones. The Army of the West was comprised of Missouri, Kansas and Iowa farm boys from the prairies, the flint hill, the high plans, and the Ozarks, called from their homes along the Mississippi, Missouri and Kansas Rivers. They were naïve, poor boys, mostly uneducated, who had no idea what they were fighting for or against and were about to choke on the puke of slavery and the chains of oppression; immigrants who had just disembarked from the ships in New York and Baltimore. Men and boys from Ireland and Scotland, from Germany and England...none of them had a clue who was rebel and who was patriot, nor did they care.

General Lyon had just spent three months with his Fort Riley brigade, the Wide Awakes from St. Louis and volunteers from Kansas securing the Federal Arsenal in St. Louis and securing Jefferson City for the Union. He chased former Governor Price to Springfield and ordered Colonel Siegel to move his troops down from Rolla, Missouri to prepare to confront the enemy.

General Lyon knew the officers on the Confederate side; considered them comrades; considered them brave and dedicated men. They would fight to the death, no quarter given, none asked. Both armies, poorly trained and equipped, were ready to battle over a field that carried no significance whatsoever, except it lie between the hatred of the north and the bigotry of the south, rising barely out of the plain like a glimmer of light in the blackness of an evil soul.

Colonel Franz Sigel tried again to get his attention, "General Lyon, Sir…General, I said that Captain Wood is approaching."

Nathaniel Lyon, a slight man with a full head of brown hair that made him look bigger than he was; an officer respected by his men, stained in uniform, but conscientious of his command. His insignias were tarnished with the grime of campaigns and a focus on getting the job done, not-by-the book regulation. His steady rise through the ranks during the Mexican War and the Indian skirmishes had earned him the rank of Brigadier General and command of Lincolns' Army of the West. His shoes were not shined any more than his insignias, but his men carried out his commands. Lyon was a West Point Man as were several other officers on both sides of Wilson Creek in Missouri that hot summer of 1861.

He was deep in thought about the Confederate Army advancing from the South. Men that he knew well; General Sterling Price and his Missouri Guardsmen; General Benjamin McCulloch with his Texas Confederates and General Bart Pearce with his Arkansas regulars. Lyon had served with all of them in the Mexican American war. They were friends at one time, now bitter enemies.

"General, are you alright?'

"I'm sorry, Franz, what were you saying," he finally answered.

Colonel Franz Sigel was an immigrant, veteran of the German revolutionary forces, rising to the rank of colonel before fleeing Germany in 1852 for America. Siegel combed his thick blonde hair straight back from the forehead, a wispy moustache and goatee further complimented his youthful mien. He was possessed with an insistence on discipline and regimentation that was understood by his German soldiers but resented by the Americans under his command in the 1st Brigade, Army of the West.

"I said that Captain Wood is approaching from the South."

"Finally, we can get some reliable information."

"Who is this Captain Wood that everyone speaks of," Sigel asked in his heavy Germanic accent, 'who ist dis Capitan Vood dat everyvon sprek of?'

"You don't know Sam?" asked Colonel George Deitzler. "He's about as well-known an abolitionist as you'll ever find."

"I know the name," Sigel responded. "But we've never met."

"I'll tell you this Franz, when the fighting starts, you'd best have Sam Wood on your side," General Lyon continued. "I've known him since '54'. He made me understand the slavery issue better than anyone. There is no quit in the man. He's like a bulldog."

"The fighting Quaker," Deitzler laughed.

"Quaker?" Sigel placed his hat on a hook along with his sword, "I thought Quaker's were non-violent. Won't even take up arms."

"Not Sam Wood. He carries a club and he's not afraid to use it. Hell, he's as responsible as any man alive for the Republican Party. I guaran-damn-t you that Lincoln would not be President today without Sam Wood."

"I didn't know it was that Sam Wood," Sigel responded. "Why is he just a captain?"

Lyon laughed, a deep resonant laugh that belied the size of the man. "Sam's not a military man, Colonel Sigel. He's a politician, but he thinks he's a General."

"Hell, he thinks he's the President," Deitzler sat his coffee cup on the floor next to his chair, "I've known Sam since the day he came to Kansas, served with him in the Kansas Legislature and a neighbor of his in Lawrence. He helped me and Charlie Robinson establish the University on Hogback Ridge..."

Sigel interrupted, "You mean Robinson, the Governor of Kansas?"

"Yes, Franz, Charlie, Sam and I were the first settlers in Lawrence. You'll never meet a more humble and unpretentious man than Sam Wood," Deitzler shook his fist in the air. "But God forgive you if you cross him, he's pissed off as many people as like him. He was a good friend of John Brown's. He has influence with Lincoln, Fred Douglass and Harriet Tubman. He and I have crossed swords a couple of times. But at the end of the day...you won't find a better man to stand with you in a fight."

General Lyon moved to the door looking out over the tents of his troops. "Don't cross him, Franz, we need as many men like Sam Wood as we can get. He might not fit your ideal of a soldier, but let it go. Him and his kind will win this war for us."

The two remaining Brigade commanders, Major Sam D. Sturgis and Lt. George Andrews arrived for the staff meeting. The Union position was tenuous, and they knew it; troops were poorly trained and equipped; horses were scarce, as was equipment. Some of the men carried nothing more than farm tools as weapons, but the same was true of the Confederate side.

Major Sturgis shook the dust from his uniform and saluted General Lyon. "That Goldarned Sam Wood is encamping his Negroes right in the middle of my Brigade, on his own hook. Who gave him the right? Them Nigger women got all the boys in sight slaverin' at their doors. There'll be half-Nigger babies from here to St. Louis, for he's done."

"We was just talking about him," Deitzler laughed.

"Well, what we gonna' do 'bout it? He's bringing in Niggers faster than I can recruit solders. He'll have them slaves in uniform if we don't watch out. He ain't makin' any bones about it. That's what he wants;' Lincoln will have your hide, General. I know he's got his spies out here watchin' what's happening."

"Everybody's got spies, Major. The slaves got no place to go. For God's sake, Sam gives em' shelter, he gives em' hope," Lyon said still looking out the door. "Let it go for now. If it becomes a problem, we'll deal with it. I understand that General Sherman has over 2,000 Negroes following him."

"How many men did McCulloch bring?" Major Sturgis looked at the map on the table.

"That's what we're about to find out. Sam took a patrol out three days ago to reconnoiter," Deitzler said.

General Lyon turned to his men and despite his size, immediately commanded the room. "Gentlemen, at first light I want you to mobilize all four Brigades and we'll move to Springfield. George, have you established a forward command post?"

Andrews answered for him, "A scout reported in just an hour ago, General. We'll set up your command at the Willard farmhouse north of Springfield. My men are there now preparing your quarters. There's plenty of wood and game in the area and a clear spring for water."

"I expect McCulloch and Price will outnumber us by a significant margin," Lyon added.

Franz Sigel shook his head, "I don't think so, General. They may have 8,000 men but half of them are the Missouri Guard and they can't be relied on in battle. They have no training and are poorer equipped than we are."

"Franz, don't underestimate those country boys. They'll fight you with guns or knives and pick up rocks if that's all they can find. There won't be any quit in them," Deitzler countered.

Horses and men were heard tramping and snorting outside. The door flew open and a whirlwind backed into the room. He was dressed in yellow trousers with a dirty blue canvas shirt, his pants held up by suspenders, a black slouch hat perched back on his head, carrying a club that he brandished toward whomever he was ordering about. "And I mean now, John T, we can't waste any time. We've got to be ready to move by tomorrow."

Sam came into the room followed by John Thompson, Sam's aide-de-camp a black man of imposing size and demeanor.

"All right, Sam, we'll be ready but what you want me to do with all those negroes coming here. Shall I send them back to Springfield?"

"No, put em up with the rest, we gonna need them before we're through, now get the men packed up and ready to go."

Sam turned to face the startled officers. Franz Sigel stammered, "Shouldn't you salute your superior officers, Captain?"

Sam stared at him.

General Lyon broke the tension, "Sam, how do your men accept taking orders from a colored man?"

"He doesn't order, Nathan, he suggests. Anyway, he's known most of them since we got to Kansas. Gentlemen, I didn't expect such a distinguished group. I feel a little like the lowly dinner guest, in the book of Luke, finds himself at the head of the table. I'll gladly take the foot if it means we win this war, Colonel," Sam looked straight at the rattled officer who was clearly shocked at his behavior. "Now then, Nathaniel. Would you like my report, or shall I come back at a more convenient time?"

"Now will be fine, Sam. I think you know everyone."

"I've not had the pleasure, Colonel Sigel," Sam said walking toward the shaken German officer with his hand outstretched. "But I've heard excellent things from your troops and that's enough for me. We need all the good officers we can get." Siegel failed to offer his hand so Sam gave a friendly slap on the shoulder and the stiff German recoiled in shock.

He acknowledged the other officers in turn then went to the map laying on the table in the center of the room. "George's men have chosen a command post here, just north of Springfield. It's about 5 or 6 miles from there to the James River. McCulloch will move his army to a position south of the James during the next couple of weeks. He's still waiting for some of his command coming up from Shreveport. Most of Price's men are already there. They're itching for a fight. We'll be outnumbered two to one. If we were in Springfield right now, I'd advocate attacking them before they can get to full strength. But we have the same mobilization problems they do. We have to travel by land."

"How did you ascertain all of this, Sam?" Major Sturgis asked.

"I sent David, Caleb and John T down into Price's camp. They weren't even challenged, but if they were, they were going to say that they were looking for David's Pa and John was a slave accompanying him." Sam laughed at the memory, "You should have seen David playing the part, Nathan, he lorded it over John like he was a spoiled southern gentleman, ordering John here and there in front of those southern boys. They were so used to the sight; they didn't think twice."

"Who is David," Sigel asked?

"Why...he's my son," Sam answered.

"What rank is he?"

"Rank? He's a private."

Colonel Deitzler explained to Franz, "David Wood is only, what, Sam, 11 or 12 years old."

"11 going on 20 but you won't find a more dedicated servant of the cause. He did just fine. John asked a colored cook how many soldiers they were feeding. He said that General Price told the cooks to expect to feed 12,000 men."

"I was afraid of that," General Lyon answered. "Well, we've got our work cut out for us. We'll reconvene in Springfield. I'll see to the artillery myself. Let's get to it. Sam, if I could have a moment."

The four Brigade commanders filed out shouting for their aides. Mobilizing 6,000 troops to move at first light would take most of the night. Sam made himself comfortable at the table.

Colonel Sigel stopped Andrews outside. In his heavy Germanic accent he said, "Andrews, what do you make of this man Wood? I don't understand the General not insisting on military decorum and sending his son into the enemy camp. What kind of man is this?"

"Colonel Sigel, all I can tell you is that there wouldn't be a Kansas without Sam Wood. He doesn't give a damn if he fights as a General, a Major or a Private. He's just glad this war is finally here. He'll probably get killed in the first battle anyway. He'll lead every charge and he won't retreat, so you probably don't need to worry about it.

Back inside General Lyon contemplated the map before asking, "I know you don't drink, Sam, but I hope you don't mind if I have a whiskey. I feel like I need it. Can I get you a glass of water?"

"That would be good, Nathan, it was a long ride up from Springfield."

"I guess it looks pretty bleak for us down there?"

"We'll have to create a diversion or hit them when they don't expect it, find some kind of advantage, but don't ask me what that is right now.

We'll have to figure it out when we get to Springfield."

"That's not what I wanted to ask you about, Sam. What are we going to do with all these Negros following you into camp?"

Sam moved to the door to watch the troops mustering for the coming march, "It isn't just the slaves Nathan, the free blacks, southern whites who support the Union... they have no place to go so they follow along in our wake. I understand Grant has over 5,000 following him. But don't worry, they won't be a burden to you. John will coordinate them. They're self-sufficient, they're used to fending for themselves. You'll find them to be more of a help than a hindrance. We need to get the men into uniform, Nathaniel. You know that as well as I do."

"Lincoln is against it. You might get away with it, but, if the President finds out about it, there will be the devil to pay?"

"Some of these slaves can pass for white anyway. Abe knows we'll have to start using them sooner or later, he's just trying to placate some of the Northern Senators. I'm going to arm them and use them in my company until someone tells me not to." He looked at his commanding officer waiting for a response, but General Lyon just shook his head.

Finally, he said, "Let's get to Springfield and let the matter resolve itself."

***

Springfield, Missouri
August 9, 1861

General Lyon's first instinct was to retreat to Rolla, his troops being outnumbered almost two to one. The problem was not one of logistics or strategy it was more personalities. Franz Sigel commanded about 2,500 men almost all of them German and Irish boys. Most didn't speak English. Sigel wanted to attack the Confederates in a pincer movement. He was certain it would work and if it didn't, they could still retreat. Lyon gave in for political rather than tactical reasons. The Junior officers felt the plan would work if Sigel was able to pull off his part by surprising the Confederates from the rear.

Union campfires dotted the land, to the north, as far as the boys could see. General Lyon's 6,000 men were scattered in the arroyos and fields around the Willard farmhouse. Sam's company was bivouacked at the base of a hill on the southern edge of the encampment. Dietzler's Brigade was in the middle, Sigel on the left flank and Sturgis on the right. Major Andrews Brigade was in reserve further north. Men were huddled around the light of the cook fires sharing scuttlebutt and spreading rumors. David and Caleb crawled to the top of the hill without permission, more for something to do than out of mischief.

"I hope we don't come on a snake crawlin' around in the dark," Caleb whispered to David.

"I hope we don't either."

The night was clear, the moon waxing crescent in the western sky, visibility was poor until it cleared the trees. The campfires of the Confederate army could be seen in the distance, with a silver reflection from the dim moon marking the James River.

"There's an almighty bunch of em, Davey."

"A right smart of em, fer sure."

They knew that pickets were scattered all along the hill and further south along Wilson's Creek. "We best get back fore they miss us."

"Nobody'll blow on us. Not since we went down there among em like we did."

"I know, Caleb, but I want to talk to that Irish boy again."

"What fer? You know we ain't supposed to talk to the prisoners."

"I know it Caleb, but that boy don't want to be a soljer. He don't even know what he's a fightin fer. What if it was us they captured."

"They won't capture me, they'll think I'm a slave."

"Yeah, but you're colored. What about me? I'll be a prisoner if I get captured."

"Well, just do like you did when we was in their camp. Say I'm your slave. You seemed to enjoy it. You played it up pretty good, callin me boy and all."

"It was part of the act, Caleb. You know I didn't mean it."

"Let's get Pa and Sam to talk to that Johnny Reb."

"We will, after we figure it out fer ourselves."

The boys reached the cook-fire outside of Sam's field office just as the rain started falling. A group of soldiers were eating and talking low as if the enemy was listening. No one knew what the morning would bring. They had been waiting for five days and nights in Springfield before moving to a forward position. Food was running low. Thankfully water and wood was plentiful. There were no sounds at night except the sentry's patrolling, the horses, restless in their remuda and the occasional bark of a camp dog.

Sergeant Daniel Mullhattur sat on a stump and watched the men smoking and conversing quietly. Occasionally one would address the Sergeant with a variation of the same question, "Sarge, you think we'll be movin out in the morning?"

"Don't know," was the inevitable answer.

The boys charged into the ring of men causing a change in the atmosphere.

"Well, looky here, the porch baby's is back."

"You boys best be hittin the sack, you fixin to see the elephant tomorrow."

"Yessir, them hornets be buzzin round your head come sunup. Johnny Reb'd love to pop a pup like you."

Caleb spoke up, "Them Corncrackers don't scare us none. Just give us a gun and let er rip."

The men laughed and slapped their hats on thighs.

"Them boys got grit, that's for damn sure," Private John Peavler said. He was particularly fond of them since he wasn't much older. In fact, he was glad to have the youngsters take up the slack from his compatriots teasing. Peavler was a Missouri boy from Springfield. He was only 16.

"David, why ain't you selling lemonade? I could use a glass right about now."

"General Lyon reclaimed the ambulance he let me borrow. I left my inventory in Springfield. I'll get it back after we set these Johnny Rebs to running."

Sergeant Mullhattur said, "Boys, there's a bait o hardtack and some embalmed beef yonder, you'd best grab a root whilst ya got a chance." The men took to Mullhattur in a special way. He was tough but fair, honest and didn't play favorites. He mustered into the Regiment in May and rapidly rose through the ranks. The officers, from the commander down, felt that he was A number one. But Sergeant Mullhattur had a secret. One that had been confided to just a single other person in the entire war. Company Commander, Captain Sam Wood knew what it was and he didn't care. But it could never be revealed, not until after this infernal war because the men, regardless of the Sergeant's ability to command, would never accept a woman officer. Sergeant Daniel Mullhattur was a woman disguised as a man.

"Sarge, can we talk to that Irish boy again," David asked?

"What fer ye want tu bother that Reb," Peavler asked?

"It ain't your never-mind, Private," the sergeant warned him. "Davey, Caleb, don't get close to em but you go ahead. That boy's about to piss his pants he's so scared and I don't blame him. Don't know what were gonna do with em when the advance is called. May have to do fer em."

"You don't mean it, Sarge," Caleb said wide-eyed.

"What you want us to do with em? Let em go so's they kin stab ya in the back when we attack?"

"Can't you put em on parole, Sarge?"

"Do you believe they'd just wander off north and not skeedadle back to their lines and pick up a gun agin us? We can't take that chance."

"Come on Caleb, Let's go talk to him again."

Peavler watched them run off, "Why does he get to sell things to the troops. He's a soldier, just like me. He gets his pay, just like me."

"Cause it was his idea. You ain't smart enough to figure out where to get the lemon extract and he got the General to lend him an ambulance when we was on the march. Pretty damned smart, I'd say."

"He got my uniform mended. Some colored woman he hired."

"And he's got a laundry service a goin'. That boy's making more money than the General."

The five confederate soldiers were held in a position behind the command tent. The prisoners called it the bull pit; the Yankee's called it the stockade. It little resembled a true stockade being only a thick chain anchored to two trees and run through the leg shackles of the captives. The men were lying on the ground closely watched by two armed guards, one on each side, but well back from the radius of their range of movement.

It was still early in the war and prisoners were normally held and traded for an equal number of their counterparts, but in this case, there was no time or inclination for a confab, both armies were primed and ready. The prisoners were condemned to the decision of individual commanders or even their guards if the battles overtook them. As they approached the stockade the guard challenged them, "Halt, Davey and Caleb. State your purpose."

"Come on, Milo, you know we're here to talk to Declan."

'Yeah, but Sarge says I gotta say that to whoever comes round here."

"Ok, can we go sit on the stump and parlay with him again?"

"Did you ask Sarge?"

"We did, didn't we Caleb?"

"Sure enough."

"Then I recon ye can."

The boys sat on a log near the captives, close enough that the Irish boy could hear but not close enough to risk being grabbed. Three of the other prisoners were grizzled veterans who eyed everything with suspicion. The man next to Declan, was a fellow Irishman named William who had taken the boy under his wing. They sat quietly watching the sliver of a moon dance in and out among the clouds that were blowing in.

"I wonder how long it's going to rain tonight," William said.

"Yean, might muddy up this little scuffle fixin to start tomorrow," one of the older prisoners laughed.

"How you know it's fixin to start manana, Rob," another asked?

"Experience, from the Mexican War," he said. He couldn't be more than 35 but looked a good deal older. His hair was long and stringy, and a beard which he continually scratched as though it were full of lice. "I kin jus tell. They lookin at us different, tryin to figure out what to do with us." He stopped and scratched at his beard then pointed toward the command tent, "Watch when they come out, they'll look over at us and then look away quick like."

"What will they do with us?" William asked.

"What you think they'll do? They ain't a gonna hand us our rifles and send us on back, I kin tell you that much."

The boys searched for Caleb's father and found him in the camp of the escaped and abandoned slaves, preparing food for the troops and themselves.

"Daddy, we have a problem," Caleb announced.

John T's eyes were bloodshot from the smoke and too little sleep. "Boys, I'm plumb tuckered out so make it quick. I'd like to get an hours sleep before the attack. You boys stay close to me. I don't want you anywhere near the battle when it starts.

"Papa John, There's a boy that we've got to rescue. He ain't a soljer."

"What you talking about, Dave?" John looked toward the prisoners.

"He's a Irish boy, Pa. He don't even know what he's fightin for. He's only 12."

"Who is?" John asked a bit perturbed, "I've got to get these people fed and then ready to move."

"Where we going, Pa?"

"Well, if we win we'll go south, if we lose we'll go north and at a dead run most likely."

"He's a prisoner, Pa. He got off the boat in New Orleans with his family and they put a confederate uniform on him and a gun in his hand. He's a farmer. He never even owned a gun before this."

"Boys, we've got 6,000 soldiers, 400 slaves and about 400 rich white folks complaining that they had to leave their homes because they support the Union. What you want me to do about a Reb prisoner?"

"Let him go and he'll join me and Caleb and help us win the war."

John looked at the two boys, his son, black as the night, and his foster son, white as the driven snow and he loved them both. They were going to see things that young boys ought not to see but John knew it was beyond avoidance. There were youngsters trapped in circumstances on both side of the conflict. The cause was just and the sacrifice inevitable, but it wasn't fair that these two innocents were about to discover the baseness of human existence. The decision had already been made to kill the prisoners if the battle turned against them.

John rubbed his eyes and tried to think, "All right boys, show me quick."

They ran to the stockade and stood near the stump as the guard shouted, "Halt who goes there?"

"Dammit, Milo, quit yelling. You gonna give away our position before the fight starts. By the way, I saw your Pappy in Springfield the other day when I was getting supplies. He said to say 'hey' and your sister had a boy," John answered.

"A boy, damn, don't that beat all. I'm a uncle now. Well, I'll be damned."

"Hello son," John said to the prisoner. "What's your name and where are you from?"

Declan stared at the black man towering over him. They were supposed to be ignorant savages and this one was speaking intelligently and seemed to be friendly. He finally answered, "Declan, sir. I'm from Ireland outside of Wexford. We have a farm there."

"What the hell is this?" the older prisoner screamed. "Now they got Niggers talking to white folk like they equal. What the shit you want here, boy?"

John ignored the man. "How did you get involved in this war, Declan?"

"We had to leave because the potatoes wouldn't grow. When we got to New Orleans, they made my Pa sign a paper and they took me away. Gave me a gun and made me march with the army." He started crying.

"Shut up you sniveling little puissant," the prisoner yelled.

"No, you shut up you asshole. Leave him be, he's just a kid," William leapt to his feet.

"What's all this ruckus here?" Sergeant Mullhattur rushed in glaring angrily at the guards. "The men are trying to get some sleep. We probably gonna need it tomorrow. John T, what's going on? Ya'al go on and leave this be. These prisoners are my responsibility, I'll take care of this."

John turned to Caleb and David, "Boys, you've done all you can. Leave it to Sergeant Mullhattur, he's a good man and will do what's right."

***

The moon had risen in the southwestern sky throwing just enough light for the officers to see where they were going as they exited the smoky command tent. Sam arched his back and stretched his legs as he conversed with Colonel Robert Mitchell, commander of the 2nd Kansas Rangers and Colonel Deitzler, Brigade commander.

They glanced toward the stockade and turned away remorsefully, "Bob, is there any way to save those 5 prisoners?"

Colonel Deitzler answered, "Whatever you do, don't let them go. We've got about 100 of them scattered among the different camps. They can cause us grief if you try to parole them."

Mitchell said, "We'll have to shoot them if it comes down to it, Sam. Let's hope we put the route on these Reb's then we don't have to deal with it."

Other officers joined them as prepared for the dawn attack. Colonel Deitzler said, "Good luck, men. I've got to ride over to General Lyon's camp and brief him on our meeting. We'll have the element of surprise if we time it right. Let's hope Colonel Sigel's Brigade can hold that left flank.

Sam caught site of David and Caleb running toward him as he prepared to order his men to break camp and move to a forward position for the early morning battle. "Dave and Caleb, I'm glad you're here. We're attacking in the morning, and I want you well back when the shooting starts. You can help haul water to the rear guard."

"Pa, we've got to rescue a boy."

"What! Where?"

Caleb spoke up, "Over there, Papa. He's just 12."

Sam walked briskly to the prisoners. His mind was occupied with the coming battle and getting the men into their proper position. Surprise was the key and if the Yankee's could pull it off, they'd have the twelve thousand troops of the South on the run by noon. The five confederate prisoners were a ragged, dirty group. One prisoner was obviously no more than a smooth faced boy with grime on his clothes and fear in his eyes.

"What are you doing here, son?"

"I don't rightly know, sir. I just want to go back and find me Ma."

Sam looked at the other prisoners, met the stare of the hardest looking man he'd seen in some time. The prisoner glared back at him with a sneer, the more menacing with his white teeth gleaming against his dirt covered face. "Hello, Sam Wood," the man said derisively.

"Do I know you?" Sam asked.

"No, but I know you. You killed my brother and I'm gonna' kill you fore this is over."

Caleb and David took a step back, "Pa," David said?

Sam put an arm around each boy and looked down at the Irish boy who was the same age as Caleb, "Who did I kill?"

"Ellis Johnson from Meridian, Mississippi. You killed him in Hagerstown, Maryland and shipped him off to his grieving mother, like a slab a beef."

"So, you're Rob Johnson...an overseer, the sickest kind of human ever made. I imagined you'd be just as I see you here. Captain Johnson was a fine man and he died in the service of the Lord, for a just cause. This boy right here is the son of the fine woman he gave his life for."

Johnson glared at Caleb with hatred in his eyes, "Then, I'll kill him too."

"Who is that man, Papa Sam?"

"He's no one! He has forsaken God and turned his back on everything good. But transgressors and sinners will be crushed together, and those who forsake the Lord will come to an end. That's from Isaiah if you didn't know."

Johnson laughed and spit in the dirt, "I heard you know your verses, but so do I. God is on our side, Wood. "Slaves, obey your earthly masters with deep respect and fear. Serve them sincerely as you would serve Christ."

Sam frowned, "The first time I met your brother, we traded versus. I doubt I have the same effect on you I had on him."

"Ellis was a weak-kneed pussy. He let his own brother steal his girl and he couldn't even see that he was better off without her. She ruin't two good men. I gave him a job and he pissed it off because of you."

"I don't know where you get your information, Johnson, but I don't have time to stand here and

188

argue with you. You kept your slaves in chains and now, sir, how does it feel to be shackled yourself?"

Johnson glared at him with the hatred of a cornered beast. Sam turned to walk away as David asked, "Pa, what about the boy."

Sam came eye to eye with Sergeant Mullhattur, "Captain, these prisoners are my responsibility. I already told the boys that I'll take care of it. Now all of you go on and leave this to me."

The look in her eyes told Sam all he needed to know. "Boys go find John and stay with him until this is over. If something bad happens you go back to Springfield where the reserve force is, you got that?"

"East, Pa, not north?"

"Go to Springfield and wait for me there."

***

"Even as poor a soldier as I am can generally discover mistakes after it is all over. But if I could only induce these wise gentlemen who see them so clearly beforehand to communicate with me in advance, instead of waiting until the evil has come upon us, to let me know that they knew all the time, it would be far better for my reputation, and (what is of more consequence) far better for the cause."

Robert E. Lee

"Who is that guy, Johnson?"

"It's Sam Wood. He's a lawyer. He turned my brother against me. He set a whole family of Niggers free about 8 years ago from a guy I knew, Merle Caldwell from Georgia. Sam Wood is an abolitionist. He's one of the reasons we got this damn war. His kind have ruined this country. Worryin' about the

Niggers stead o' his own kind. I never met a Nigger could last a week without a white man to look out fer em. Not only that, but that son of a bitch is trying to get the vote fer women. I guarantee you; I'll kill him before the sun sets tomorrow."

Sergeant Mullhattur stood nearby listening quietly. As the camp disbanded and the soldiers moved to their positions for the morning attack, the guards were dismissed to join the battle and Mullhattur stayed to guard the prisoners alone.

"Once we whip these Yankees, I'm gonna get me some of them Nigger wenches over there in they camp. There's one or two I'd like to put the wood to," Johnson's friend said.

"That's one thing they good for," Johnson laughed. "Ain't nothing better than a Nigger bitch about 14 or 15, afore they get all blown up like a pig in slop."

Mullhattur sat behind the men and they soon forgot he was there. The battle began at first light. The prisoners grew quiet as they listened to the sounds of war. They could picture the ebb and flow as the Yankees took the Confederates by surprise and drove them back. Then the sound of the Arkansas artillery boomed into a deafening cacophony that brought a cheer from the prisoners. They could sense the shift in momentum. Mullhattur sat quietly puffing on the pipe. Johnson said, "Best let us go and hightail it out of here, Sarge. You fixing to eat lead."

"I believe you're right there, Johnny Reb. It don't sound good for my side."

About 10 AM the Battle of Wilson's Creek had turned bad for the Yankee's. Suddenly the air was full of bugles blowing retreat. Mullhattur leapt up and shouted, "John, come a runnin'."

Thompson and the boys appeared with John carrying a heavy sledge and a chisel. Mullhattur stood with pistols aimed at Johnson and his friends. "Just you boys twitch a muscle. I hope you do cause I don't like you… don't like nothing bout ya. Sit real quiet like. Go ahead John."

He took the mallet and chisel and freed the leg irons from William and Declan. Yankee soldiers were starting to appear from the South, some running, other's helping the wounded, many were moaning in pain.

"Hurry John," Mullhattur urged.

He grabbed the freed rebel soldiers and looked them in the eye, "Boys, we're givin you a chance to live. That's north," he pointed. "You skeedadle as fast as you can. Here's some civilian clothes, they may not fit but they'll save your lives. Now go and don't stop until you get to Canada."

William stuttered and stammered, "Thank you, how can we ever…"

"Just go." And they did, first shedding their Rebel grey and then running as the fleeing soldiers overtook them. Caleb and David followed John to the Negro camp where they jumped on wagons and whipped the mules into a trot, stopping to gather the wounded until they could carry no more.

Mullhattur turned back to the remaining three prisoners with a look of hatred and scorn.

"You son of a bitch," Johnson said.

The Sergeant smiled and dropped her trousers. The men recoiled and looked at each other, "A woman?"

She shot each of them through the heart.

***

Sam left the stockade feeling confident that John would watch his son and Sergeant Mullhattur would manage the prisoners. He turned his full attention to the coming battle. The strategy was simple. Strike before the enemy expected it. The command tent teemed with preparations for battle; lamps lit the table in the smoky, hot tent where colonel Deitzler and his staff discussed plans. Communications were in disarray because the staff had not heard from Segal's people in over an hour. Colonel Deitzler asked, "Sam, do you know if Segal is in position over by Sharp's farm?"

"No, I assume that he is. Did you send a rider to find out?"

"Yes, thirty minutes ago and no word. Damn, I wish we would have strung the telegraph lines."

Lt. Gladstone answered, "There wasn't time, Colonel. Anyway, at first light we can see the troops from the top of the rise. We'll find out right quick if he did."

"We've got to be on the move before then. George, are the drummers in position?"

Deitzler, answered, "Yes and a bugle on a lanyard. We'll begin beating the men forward at 5:45. Major Steele, find General Lyon and see when he'll be back here."

Sam yelled, "Private Logan, get Border Ruffian ready to ride."

"Yessir," the hostler said, "I will sir, but I'm a tryin to find Lt. Pratt's horse for him."

"Where the hell is he, Private?" Caleb shouted.

"I don't know sir."

"Jesus H. Christ, go get Captain Wood's horse."

Sam turned to the Pratt and asked, "What's going on Caleb?"

"I'm not sure, a bunch of the horses are missing. I hope there aren't Reb's behind our lines. I'll jog up to where the men are and commandeer another one."

"When you find a horse, ride over to Colonel Sigel's headquarters and see whats going on. I'll send Munroe over to the right and check on Sturgis position. Since we're smack in the middle, I don't want to start until they're well on the move."

"Alright, Sam. Good luck, my friend. Hell of a thing isn't it? We were sitting in the State House in Topeka a few months ago. I'd just given Charlie the oath of office."

"We knew it was coming, Caleb. I'm glad it's finally here. Let's make the best of it and get back to Kansas as soon as we can." Sam and Pratt shook hands, Caleb jogged up the hill, pausing against the first light of dawn, he turned raised his hat and waved. Sunbeams reflected off his blonde hair, "Good luck, Sam," he shouted.

An involuntary shiver wracked Sam's body as he raised his right hand in a tentative wave, a sense of foreboding like he had never felt before. Yes, he wanted the war, welcomed it, but the realization that shooting would start and men would die triggered a sinister shudder through his body...he glanced back to see if David and Caleb were still in sight. Suddenly the cannons roared, and the shooting began.

***

The Rebels were caught off guard by Sigel's troops in a flanking maneuver from the east. Lyon's and Sturgis troops stretched from Bloody Hill on the west side of Wilson's Creek a mile to the east. Sam's Company I was in the middle with Sigel on the left and Sturgis on the right. Wilson's Creek bisected the battlefield. Trees on both sides of the river offered some cover, but most troops were scattered on the hill dug into redoubts or hunkered down behind a log or their rucksacks.

Bugles blared and drums began beating the men forward at first light. The Federal army advanced boldly with Sigel pinching the left flank and Sturgis following a ridge on the right. Dietzler's troops pushed from the middle. The noise was deafening as the Federal artillery batteries commenced from their positions on the hill and behind Sigel's flanking troops, taking the Confederate Calvary by surprise, setting them on their heels. The strategy appeared sound when Sigel arrived at the rear of the Rebels, but he hesitated and failed to maintain the attack when he mistook the 3rd Louisiana infantry for the 1st Iowa infantry, a mistake that would prove devastating to the Union.

Confederate General McCulloch rallied his troops and began a counterattack that was repulsed by the Union Brigades not once but three times. The turning point came about 10 AM when the Pulaski Arkansas Battery unlimbered and halted any further Union advance.

Sam screamed for his orderly, Corporal Swanson, to ride around the lines and find out why Sigel wasn't firing, "See what's wrong, the Louisiana men are almost on them, why aren't they firing?"

Swanson rode off at a frenzied gallop; Sam turned his attention back to his company dug in on the slope of the hill with Sturgis on his right, holding his own. The position proved ideal for defenses, but the artillery was zeroing in on their location, so Sam shifted his troops further up the hill. He mounted Border Ruffian and rode toward Lyon's position to report on the failure of Sigel to hold the left. As he approached the camp, he saw Lyon dash off toward the front rallying troops as he rode. Sam stopped at the command tent and asked Maj. McElhaney of the Missouri Infantry what he had just witnessed, "Ed, what in the world is General Lyon doing?"

"He just commandeered my horse and rode off to the front. I tried to reason with him, he's badly wounded, Sam, go see if you can get him to come back here."

Sam didn't wait for the rest of the story, he wheeled and pushed Ruff as hard as he could with gunfire coming from all sides; he was just as apt to be killed by friendly fire as the enemy. He reached the summit of Bloody Hill; Lyon was waving his sword and shouting for the Federal troops to advance. He was surrounded by Confederate soldiers. He swung his sword and struck a private in the arm, the man shot the General through the heart with a horse pistol; Lyon pitched back in his saddle, wheeled his horse, recognized Sam on the hill behind him, reached out his hand, tried to speak and fell to the ground dead.

An unnerving silence surrounded the body as the Confederate soldiers gazed down at him, the first time some of them had seen a General. Sam rode up, dismounted, and stood with them looking at the body of his good friend; his voice choked with emotion, "This is General Nathaniel Lyon, Commander of the Army of the West, can I take his body fellas, he was a prince of a man."

"We can't do that Captain," a Sergeant replied, "we need an officer here for that decision. You'd best ride out of here before someone shoots you. He'll be treated with respect."

"I know who you are," a bedraggled private said, "You're Sam Wood, I seen ya in Westport o."

Sam mounted Ruff and took one last look at Nathan's body, saluted the Sergeant, then turned back toward his lines hoping he wouldn't be shot in the back. A patrol sent by McElhaney to find Sam and the General met him at the top of Bloody Hill, "Where's General Lyon?"

"Dead!"

"What shall we do?"

"Ride like the devil, "Sam spurred Ruff toward his men, "and sound retreat."

***

"I am tired of the sickening sight of the battlefield with its mangled corpses & poor suffering wounded. Victory has no charms for men when purchased at such cost."
Union Army Civil War General George McClelland

The First Kansas Infantry was already in retreat when Sam arrived. He made certain that his men were on the move and sent two runners, one each way, to verify all the other companies were falling back. He walked Border Ruffian toward the rear trying to keep his men calm. When he reached the camp headquarters of Dietzler's Brigade, George was already gone. A platoon of infantry commanded by Lt. Henry Clay Wood was dug in along the slope of the hill, overlooking Ray's Cornfield, with a good view of the enemy. Sam knelt down, "Henry, how's Aunt Flo?"

"Hello Sammy, she's fine last I saw her back in April, how's Margaret and the kids? That little gal about five or six now ain't she?"

"She is and I'll bring her around so the family can get to know her better, after we get out of this mess. Say, are you all right? You're wounded," Sam touched his cousin's head.

The Lt. shook him off, "I'm fine, Sam. David was by with that little colored friend of his a couple hours ago, brought us some water. I sent em back and told em to stay there, things was fixin to get messy."

"General Lyon was killed," Sam stood slowly, realizing the impact of the death having said it aloud.

"Nooo, Damn, I hate to hear that, he was a hell of a good man. Who's in charge now? I hope not that asshole, Sigel."

"I imagine...probably, maybe Sturgis...He'll be as bad or worse."

"I heard Sturgis was going to whip some of your Kansas boys for insubordination."

Sam recoiled, "What? Who told you that?"

Before he could answer, gunshots rang out as Wood's platoon opened fire on advancing Arkansas infantry causing them to scurry back to the trees for cover.

"Colonel Dietzler told me to hold em off as long as I can," Lt. Wood stood with Sam's help.

"Well, don't wait too long."

Wood laughed, "These boys all got Sharps and can pick a fly off the ass of a mule at 200 yards. Those Rebs don't stand a chance. Plus, I think they're about out of ammo."

They shook hands, "I'll see you in Springfield, Henry"

"Take care, Sammy."

Sam mounted Border Ruffian and dashed off, looking for George Dietzler to let him know that Nathaniel Lyon was dead.

***

Three lamps failed to brighten the atmosphere or the mood in the smoke-filled room in Springfield where the senior officers gathered in confusion and despair to discuss the repercussions of General Lyon's death. Thirteen hundred of their comrades lay dead along Wilson Creek and Bloody Hill, many unrecognizable from shrapnel, bombs and canon shot. As a detachment of troops and volunteers, including a large contingent of runaway slaves, returned to the battlefield for the bodies; 600 lay wounded in the field hospitals hastily prepared in the dirt streets of Springfield. Yet the officers refused to classify the battle as a defeat.

Captain Wood reported, "We have pretty good intelligence that Price wanted to pursue us, but McCullough was in favor of falling back. That seems to be what they did. Plus, they appear to be short of ammunition."

Sigel nodded, "Then we are all in agreement I will assume command and we'll fall back to Rolla." He hesitated, looking at Sturgis, "If there are no objections, gentlemen, I suggest we proceed with utmost speed in an orderly manner."

Rolla lay 100 miles north and east of Springfield. Its importance magnified by being the western terminus of the Pacific Railroad. Franz Sigel had captured Rolla from the hands of Confederate sympathizers in June prior to joining General Lyon in Springfield.

"I have here a dispatch from President Lincoln," Sigel held a telegram for all to see. "It was addressed to General Lyon, I quote, 'For God's sake, by any means necessary, hold Rolla'."

A knock at the door and Lt. Sam Walker, the former sheriff of Douglas County, Kansas entered, "Sam, we need you urgently."

"Excuse me gentlemen," he saluted and departed the meeting.

***

The early morning air was fresh, but the sunrise orange eastern sky advertised the coming heat of the day. Sam hesitated a moment taking a deep breath. He hadn't slept in over 24 hours. "What is it, Sheriff? Nothing wrong with Davey, I hope. I haven't even had time to talk with him."

"No, David's over in the Negro camp with John T. Someone else is asking for you. Come on, he's near our bivouac."

A tall angular man with a narrow face and days old stubbly grey beard stepped forward when he recognized Sam. They met amidst the smell of cook fires and sounds of men rising from a restless sleep after fleeing the battleground.

"Captain Wood, I'm John S. Phelps," he extended his hand.

Sam stared intently before it dawned on him who he was looking at, "I apologize Representative Phelps, for not recognizing you."

He chuckled, "Well, Sir, none of us are at our best right now, are we?"

"John, this is Sheriff Sam Walker a friend of mine from Lawrence. Sheriff, meet John Phelps. He's been in Washington about 20 years as Chairman of the Committee on Ways and Means. You can thank John Phelps for your cheap postage stamp."

Phelps extended his hand, "Lt. I'm pleased to meet you."

Walker, with a confused look, "Are you a private?"

"When the war started, I left Washington and enlisted with my neighbor, Captain Coleman in the Missouri Infantry...on the Union side," he added with a wry nod of the head. "We were with Colonel Sigel's brigade south of Wilson's Creek. I don't know what Sigel is telling everyone, but he deserted his post as far as I'm concerned. We had McCulloch's troops on the run when Sigel ordered us to fall back to Springfield. But that isn't why I'm here. I'm sure others will tell that story better than me."

"What can I do for you, John?"

"My farm is about two miles south of Springfield, three miles from here. I need you to go over there with me; as soon as possible."

Sam was dead tired, but Representative Phelps's reputation was impeccable with President Lincoln and in Missouri; if he needed something, Sam had no choice. They departed and arrived at the farm about 7:30 that morning. A wagon flanked by three Confederate soldiers stood in front of Phelps pleasant one-story white frame farmhouse. Sam and Lt. Walker hesitated when they saw the rebels.

"Don't worry, they are under a military protection. My company commander is inside."

As they dismounted, a man came out of the farmhouse, a Captain in the Confederate uniform of the Arkansas State Troops commanded by General Bart Pearce. The man extended his hand and greeted Sam cordially, "Hello Colonel Wood."

"I'm Colonel Wood in Kansas, but I'm Captain Wood here. Hello Matt. Sheriff, you remember Matt

Rodgers, Nathanial's second in command at Ft. Riley."

"I'm surprised to see you here Matt, when was the last time we met...It was in January when we were granted statehood."

Rodgers nodded, "Captain Wood, I brought General Lyon's body to Representative Phelps home. He and Mrs. Phelps have agreed to preserve the remains until they can be transported to Rolla and then shipped east to his family. I wanted you to know. I respected the General as much as any man I have ever met... almost like a father to me. He and I spoke often of this coming war. He thought highly of his friendship with you. I never expected it to come to this. It is with a very heavy heart that I fulfill this obligation. Not one I relish, I assure you. General Lyon was my commanding officer and even though we disagreed about the war, he was a good...true friend." Rodgers hesitated and bowed his head, "And now, with your permission, we will return to our lines."

They shook hands. While Rodgers and his men departed, Sam went inside to pay his final respects to General Lyon. Walker and Sam shook hands with Representative Phelps, thanked Mary Phelps profusely for she was the one who prepared the body for transportation to General Lyon's home in Eastford, Connecticut.

"General Lyon was as fine a man I've ever known," Sam felt his eyes clouding with tears. "There is no better man in Heaven."

At nine AM Sam and Sheriff Walker returned to Springfield. They turned their horses over to the hostlers and made their way to camp, both hungry and dead tired. The cook ladled breakfast mush into bowls. They sat eating in silence. Sam finished his coffee, "Did you notice the slaves at Phelps place?"

Walker nodded, "Yeah, I assumed they were slaves. Phelps is a slaveholder?"

"He is. The only reason he's on our side is to protect the Union. Nothing we can do about it now, but it will cause problems later. I think I'll try to catch a couple of hours of sleep. Will you see to getting the men ready to move?"

When Sam reached his tent, George Dietzler was just arriving, a look of despair on his face, "Sam, here is the list of our dead. Would you write the letters to the next of kin? You're better with words than I am...the news isn't good...over a hundred men..." Dietzler put his hand on Sam's shoulder, "Caleb Pratt, Harold Barnett, Harold Barnett, Jr., Eric McRae..." Dietzler turned away. "The list is lengthy, so many of our friends and neighbors...I'm sorry Sam."

Sam stared at the list too shocked at first to reply, "Caleb, Harold...and Hal? Oh, my God!"

Dietzler started to speak, shook his head, turned, and left. David and Caleb waited until the Colonel was gone then entered to find Sam reading the list in detail, his eyes full of tears. "What's the matter, Papa?" He handed the list to David with Caleb reading over his shoulder, "What does it mean, Papa?"

"Men who died at Wilson's Creek. I have to write home and tell their parents, their wives and sweethearts." Sam squeezed his eyes tight, "I'd best write to mother...ask her to do it. She and Sarah they...will know what to say."

Sam sat on the bed, the list dangling from his hand. The boys sat at his side and wept for their friends.

Farewell, my mother!
Bury me in the old churchyard
Beside my eldest brother.
My coffin shall be black,
Six angels at my back,
Two to sing and two to pray
And two to carry my soul away.
James Joyce, 1882-1941

***

Rolla, Missouri

The week following the Battle at Wilson's Creek, the Federal army command in Missouri was transferred back to Sturgis by the new Commander of the Army of the West, General John Fremont, the 1856 Republican candidate for President. Sturgis turned out to be a worse tyrant than Sigel. A Confederate at heart he only fought for the Union as a mercenary. His men despised him.

On the morning of August 15, the men began clearing a hill beside the Springfield-Rolla Road about a mile from the Rolla courthouse. This earthen rectangular fort was fortified by four '32 pounders' shipped by rail from St. Louis. Sam's company was assigned to capture rebel sympathizers in southern Missouri and use them as conscript laborers on the fort. Upon returning from this assignment, he found his men being assembled in the center of the courtyard with ten Kansas volunteers stripped to the waist and tied over the canons as Federal troops prepared to whip them upon orders from Sturgis.

Lt. Walker flagged him down immediately, "Sam what can we do?"

"What are the men accused of?"

"Stealing rations, but it wasn't them. I guarantee it was some of the colored cooks. Sturgis just wants to exert his control over the volunteers...he hates us"

Sam spotted Brigade Commander George Dietzler and rode Border Ruffian to his side, much to the dismay of General Sturgis who was growing angrier by the minute. Dietzler cried out, "He purposefully waited until you were gone to perform this outrage. There is no reasoning with the man. I don't know that we can restrain our boys."

The 2,500 Kansas Rangers, all volunteers, were standing, rifles loaded, prepared to fire on Sturgis and his Federal troops if so ordered by their elected officers. Sam rode Border Ruffian into the middle of the square halting the proceedings. As he dismounted, Regimental Physician Dr. Marvin Patee came running from the field hospital still wearing a blood covered smock.   He demanded that the punishment be halted, "My God, General Sturgis, I'm fighting to save the lives of these brave soldiers and you are demeaning them in public. What is the meaning of this, Sir?"

Sturgis, a youthful looking man of 40, attempted to control his temper. His thick wavy hair, dark handlebar moustache and chin patch gave him the appearance of a thespian. He barked out an order, "Escort Captain Wood and Dr. Patee into my tent...and I mean right NOW." They exited into the General's large command tent. He turned on Sam and Dr. Patee, "Gentlemen consider yourselves under arrest. Guards, take Captain Wood's weapons and place both of these men in the stockade. I will convene a court martial at the proper time and you will be charged with Treason and, if I have my way, you will be shot."

Sturgis' adjutant, Major Frank Bebee interrupted, "General Sturgis, Captain Wood has been promoted to Major Wood. I just received his commission in the dispatch from General Freemont."

"What? Let me see the dispatch. Do you know Freemont?" he asked Sam in a calmer voice.

"Yes, I know him. I didn't know about this promotion, but it is irrelevant to the matter at hand. With all due respect General, I've been accused of Treason before. That threat holds no water with me. I owe my allegiance to my Kansas volunteers...all recruited by me and serving under my command. Let me make this absolutely clear, you will not lay a whip on any of them and if you try to do so they will open fire with my blessing. They have been so ordered."

The guards stepped behind him, one reached for Sam's pistol. He warned them back with one glance, "General Sturgis, I suggest you call this off until we can conduct a proper investigation. Those men are standing out there in 100-degree heat and that in itself is cruel and unjust punishment for volunteers who just fought a bloody battle without complaint, upon your orders."

Patee echoed Sam's sentiments, "General, I agree with Major Wood. If I am to be arrested, so be it, but that will be the death sentence of many of the wounded men. I am already short staffed. I'm using Negroes as orderlies as it is. I cannot stand by while this atrocity is being perpetrated on our own soldiers, men who just lost their friends in a battle that isn't a week old. I don't condone Major Woods threat of force. But I don't want to get mixed up in military affairs. I'm a doctor not a soldier. I beg of you Sir...reconsider while we can still save face."

Sturgis was fuming mad. He stalked to the door, stood staring at the thousands of Kansas volunteers, all of them looking his way. He was between a rock and a hard place, took a deep breath, turned to Sam and Patee, "You Goddamned Kansas fanatics. You caused this war. All over a bunch of Niggers. If I had my way I'd shoot the whole bunch of you." He looked to Major Bebee, who turned away. Finally in a brusque manner, he barked, "You are both dismissed. Major Bebee, dismiss the men and return the prisoners to the guardhouse. Wood, you'll answer for this despite your friendship with General Fremont, I assure you of that, now get out of my sight."

However, two days later, General Fremont reassigned Sturgis to Washington, D.C. where he joined John Pope's army in the Second Battle of Bull Run on Aug. 29, 1861.

***

General Henry W. Halleck was a military genius, not in tactics, but in logistics. On November 9, 1861, he replaced John Fremont as Commanding General, Armies of the West. Halleck's reputation was based on his Military Governorship of California where he helped write the California Constitution prior to it becoming a state in 1851. He was a good friend of current Kansas Governor Charlie Robinson and former Kansas Governor, John Geary. His only combat experience came during the Mexican American War, in 1847, when he helped capture the port of Mazatlán, Sinaloa, Mexico. He was appointed Lt. Governor of the occupied city prior to being transferred to California in 1849.

In December 1861, Halleck appointed General Samuel R. Curtis as Commander of the Army of the Southwest. General Curtis had the appearance of a bank president with a high forehead, bushy eyebrows, and mutton chop sideburns. A man of average height, he commanded with shrewd cunning not by an overpowering presence. Curtis moved his headquarters to Rolla early in 1862. He became a good friend and staunch supporter of the newly promoted Lt. Colonel Sam Wood, commander of Woods Battalion 6th Missouri Calvary.

Missouri remained a bitterly divided state. In October, a rump session of the state legislature passed an ordinance of secession and a few weeks later Missouri became a Confederate state – in name, at least. In reality, the Confederate government of Missouri was a government in exile.

The base in Rolla quickly grew to 25,000 men, sometimes as many as 40,000. Sam and his command of approximately 4,500 Missouri and Kansas volunteers patrolled Southern Missouri and Northern Arkansas. Part of their duty was to ascertain the loyalty of the civilians. In late January 1862 Sam and a detail of about 450 of his Missouri Calvary were returning to Rolla with some 100 prisoners, wagons, mules and livestock confiscated from Confederate sympathizers. On the Lower Rolla-Springfield Road near Corn Creek they encountered a camp with four black women, six black men and four children. One of the men was chained cruelly to a log, his arms bound tightly, a terrible look of pain and anguish etched on his face. Sam ordered the troops to halt. He sat astride Border Ruffian staring at the sight then threw his right leg over the saddle to better ascertain the scene laid out before his troops. The slaves all stopped what they were doing and stared in disbelief at the sudden arrival of the Union Army. Sam shouted, "Lt. Walker."

He rode up at a gallop.

"Sheriff, do these people look happy to you? How about that fellow there," Sam pointed to the enchained man struggling against his bonds.

Walker gazed around, "I can't say they look particularly comfortable, Sam. What you want to do about it?"

A white man came out of the woods hiking his trousers and fastening his suspenders. Shocked at the sudden appearance of so many soldiers, he took a step back looked around carefully, unsure of the situation, "Hello, Colonel, what can I do for you?"

Walker took a step forward, "What is going on here? Don't you know there is a war?"

"I'm taking my slaves back to my plantation over in Fayetteville. We just grabbin' some comestibles then we be on our way. Not that far to go, but the primitives are hungry, and I treat my people good. But I've got to get back to the farm, my wife is ill...with child and I'm a day late as it is."

Sam dismounted, ignored the grubby looking plantation owner, addressing the young man chained to the log, "Hello son, that looks mighty uncomfortable."

"Yessir, it most definitely is."

"What's your name?"

"Roger Beasly, Sir, and he isn't a plantation owner..."

The slave trader took a step forward, "You keep your mouth shut boy..."

Sheriff Walker drew his pistol and pointed it at the man.

Beasly continued, "He bought these people at the slave auction in St. Louis and kidnapped me in Jefferson City. He was avoiding the military base in Rolla. I'm a Canadian Citizen and have the papers to prove it but he stole them. I'm freeborn, Colonel."

Sam nodded, looked about the camp taking in the particulars. The troopers sat their horses, curious to see what was going to happen. He spotted an axe lying next to a pile of firewood by the wagon. With a single blow he broke the chains and helped the young man to his feet.

Sam turned and glared at the slave trader, who held his hands up in protest stammering, "Now...now, hold on there, Colonel. Your orders are to leave the slaves alone. You aren't to interfere. I know my rights. President Lincoln ordered you to stay out of our business. I know the law. I've got a Bill of Sale for these Niggers.

"Lt. Walker, form a detail to escort Mr...?

"Whelan, John Whelan."

"Is that your horse?"

Whelan nodded.

"Lt. Walker, form a detail to saddle Mr. Whelan's horse and escort him five miles south and west until they encounter Telegraph Road. They are to escort him on his way toward his plantation in Fayetteville, say about ten miles...you did say your wife was expecting, didn't you?"

"Well, I..."

"You go on to your plantation, take care of your wife. Your slaves can follow later. They don't ready to travel just yet?"

"Hold on, now, I have rights," he shouted growing red in the face. "This is my property."

Sam took Whelan's saddle bags, rummaged through them, finding the Bill of Sale for the slaves and papers identifying Beasly as a Canadian Citizen traveling to St. Louis on Government business.

"Those are my papers, Sir. You have no right. These are my slaves, ask them, they'll tell you, or, by God, know the reason why."

Sam glared at him trying to control his temper in front of his troops, "If that's the case, Mr. Whelan, I'm sure they will hurry on home as soon as they can." He handed him the Bill of Sale and kept the Canadian papers.

"I'll get you for this, you bastard. I have important friends. You'll live to regret this," Whelan hissed.

Sam picked up the axe, "Go on, I've got no use for the likes of you, never have... if I see you around here again, I will crush your head like a bug and believe me I've had plenty of practice."

The detail rode out at a gallop. Sam addressed the Canadian, "Get the women and children ready and into that wagon. The men will have to walk. Mr. Whelan is correct; I cannot instruct you or help you in any way. Those are my orders. The choice is yours...you are free to follow that man to Fayetteville or follow this rode to Rolla where you will find an encampment of Negros to the tune of about 2,000 people. The camp sits a mile north and east of town. Locate John Thompson, anyone can tell you where to find him. Tell John that Colonel Wood sent you. He'll know what to do."

"I don't know what to say, how to thank you."

"Here are your papers. You need to get on back to Canada as soon as possible. We'll wait here for our men. That will be about four hours. Again, the choice is yours. Good luck and God speed."

The Negroes decamped and started toward Rolla.

***

Union control continued to be shaky in Missouri. After the battle at Wilson's Creek, Confederate Generals Sterling Price and Ben McCulloch fell back into Northern Arkansas claiming victory, refusing to admit that it was at best a stalemate. Price and McColloch were constantly at odds. McCulloch, the former Texas Ranger, was branded a lucky man considering he was part of Colonel Crockets Regiment on the way to the Alamo when he contracted the measles, ended up quarantined in Lockhart and didn't reach the Alamo until Santa Anna left in pursuit of Sam Houston. He was a stout man with thinning blond hair and a full bushy beard who did not like to be challenged when giving orders. As a result, he and Price were constantly at odds. Price, the former Governor of Missouri was just as overbearing only he had the appearance to back it up. Silver hair flowing, a soul patch on his chin, he sat his horse regally looking down on everyone and everything.

Because of the conflict between the two, Confederate President, Jefferson Davis appointed General Earl (Buck) Van Dorn as the supreme commander of the Confederate Army of the West. He established his headquarters in Pocahontas, Arkansas, summoned the two feuding Generals and began consolidating forces for an all-out assault on Union Forces in Missouri. Their goal, sixteen thousand men. The stage was set for the deciding battles that would determine if Missouri would remain tenuously Union or swing back to the Confederacy.

***

Late January 1862. Colonel Wood returned from patrolling Southern Missouri from West Plains to Springfield. A special detachment tasked with obtaining loyalty oaths from private citizens accompanied him. Anyone refusing to sign was transported to Rolla and their property confiscated. If they signed and failed to adhere to the pledge, they were shot. There were no exceptions. The stakes too high. Confederate troops were marauding throughout Kentucky, Mississippi into Arkansas and Missouri.

Rebel troops concentrated their efforts on the Rolla-Springfield Road and the new Telegraph or Wire Road stretching all the way from Rolla to Springfield to Fayetteville. The roads were important to both sides for the transportation of troops, supply lines and lines of communication.

Upon returning to Rolla, Sam was summoned to General Curtis command post in a hastily constructed building on the grounds of the new Fort Wyman.

"Colonel Wood, I commend you; intelligence reports are that southern Missouri is free of Confederate Troops at least to the Arkansas border." Curtis waved him to a chair, "You look tired, Sam. You've been gone what, two weeks?"

"Almost, General. Two hundred and fifty miles plus a stop in West Plains to convince the Rebel sympathizers to sign the loyalty oath. We only took five days rations, so we had to forage along the way. I'm glad to be back."

"That's partly why I wanted to see you. General Halleck forwarded a letter he received from a man down there. I want to read it to you. It's addressed to General Henry Halleck, Supreme Commander Union Army of the West."

With my compliments, General. I am Josephus Walsh, formerly Missouri State Representative from this district in the administration of governor, Sterling Price. My district contained some 1,500 voters 95% being 'Secesh'. In fact, when General McBride and Colonel Coleman of the Rebel army were recruiting in this area over 500 of us gladly joined the southern cause. Then came Lt. Col. Samuel N. Wood of the Federal Army first entering this county at Licking and striking terror into the local citizenry who had been warned the Union army would commit ten thousands of outrages and atrocities. Women would be violated, crops and houses burned.

Col. Coleman, a small man with a brusque but convincing manner assured us that the Federalists would commit these barbarities with impudence and there was no recourse except through their defeat. Coleman regaled us with tails of fighting in the bloody battles in Kansas and, in fact, claimed to have killed John Brown's son Frederick at the battle of Osawatomie.

Colonel Wood ordered everyone into the courthouse to listen to a sermon by a Secesh preacher who had been captured. That poor man was terrified but managed to pull himself together sufficient to offer the text from Matthew, Chapter 5, 17th verse, 'Think not I am come to destroy the law and the prophets. I have not come to destroy, but to fulfill.' Believe me, every man woman and child in that place some 1,500 of them were terrified at what the Federal Army was going to do. Perhaps even burn down the building with us in it.

Colonel Wood took the pulpit and in a clear, calm voice, began by saying that he was no theologian and did not intend to preach a sermon, but if he were, he wanted no better text than that read this morning, for we have not come to destroy the constitution and laws but to enforce them; sustain the constitution and protect the people.

He asked how many owned slaves. Not one hand was raised. One man, my neighbor, Nolan Owens, allowed that he had a colored family living on his place, but they were not slaves and free to leave at any time. They worked the land together and shared the food and profits, if any were ever to be had.

Wood asked the preacher, 'Why are we fighting this war?"

The man, a Southern Methodist, ridiculed the idea of 'secesh' fighting for Southern rights; said he asked two Southern soldiers what they were fighting for. One said, 'for fun'. The other, 'to keep our Niggers from being freed'.

Colonel Wood had a good laugh and told us that his experience was just the same, he supposed they had had fun enough, and to the Niggers—that ragged, barefooted bunch of men and boys composing the rebel army had none to free. That if slaves were fifty cents a dozen, half of them could not buy one at half-price. He spoke for two hours explaining the situation in a way none of those present had ever experienced. In economic terms, how the wealthy landowners who did own slaves were behind this war and *they weren't even fighting. They were using poor, uneducated farmers and shopkeepers to fight their war. They stood to lose $25,000,000 worth of slaves but the resulting increase in value of the land would be four-fold. But regardless of all that, he concluded that if the Union and slavery cannot both exist, which they cannot, then better to stand by the Union and abolish slavery a thousand times.*

He made it very clear that his opinion was that slavery had to be abolished. That he had personal friends of the colored race and, while not everyone agreed with him, there had to be found a middle ground so that we could all coexist within the framework of the Union and the Constitution.

Of the over 1,000 voters there that day, including 90 'secesh' prisoners of war, 964 signed the loyalty oath. I heard many say they had never heard such a powerful speech. The preacher asked Col. Wood what church he belonged to. His reply, 'not any'. The preacher was astounded, 'I thought you are a professor. I've been told you don't drink liquor, you don't smoke, or swear or commit sins of any kind. Are you a saint'?

No, Wood answered, I make no such claims, my actions speak for themselves, but any good qualities I possess are due to my Quaker mother and Margaret, my wife.

Such is the true nature of the notorious marauder and murderer, Colonel Samuel N. Wood, leader of the Kansas Rangers. He was an early settler in Kansas, a Senator, Chairman of the Judiciary in that state. A year ago, he received an important appointment by President Lincoln, a lucrative position, but instead formed a group of soldiers and has fought in Missouri and Arkansas since then. Including the Battle at Wilson's Creek. His current battalion is made up of men from Kansas and Missouri, including many men from our part of the State.

I am not easily swayed from my convictions, General Halleck. It is in that vein I write to tell you that the work done by Colonel Wood in Missouri and Arkansas will be remembered by everyone who has come in contact with him. He was the right man for a difficult job, never flustered, takes time to listen to everyone, yet is a strong but fair disciplinarian. His men reflect the character of their leader.

General Curtis held the letter out to Sam, "And he signs off in the normal manner. This is a copy; General Halleck retained the original. It was also printed in the St. Louis Democrat...I'm certain it would have been picked up by the Kansas newspapers, so your wife is probably aware. You might want to write assuring of your safety."

"Thank you General, I'll send this letter to her. She knows I'll make it through the war. It's our son David that she is concerned about."

Sam left the General intent on getting some much-deserved rest. David drove up in the ambulance he had converted to house his inventory of goods.

"Papa, you're back. We heard about those slaves you rescued. Everybody is calling them Woods Negroes."

Sam smiled, "I didn't really rescue them, son. I just pointed them in the right direction. How's the store business going?"

"Better than ever. I've got three ladies doing laundry and mending uniforms. I even buy fresh lemons when I can get them, for my lemonade and guess what, Pa?"

"What?"

"I change money for the men. I give them change for their five- and ten-dollar bills and charge 25 cents each time. I'm making more money doing that than selling lemonade."

"That makes sense. The large bills don't work so well in poker games."

David laughed and nodded his head, "Well I better get back to work. I'll see you at supper."

Sergeant Mullhattur smiled and waved at David driving off, "That boy is having more fun than a carnival. Colonel Dodge requests your presence in his office as soon as convenient." Colonel Grenville M. Dodge was post commander.

"What is it, Daniel? What does he want? I'm dead tired, as I'm sure you are. We need to get some rest."

"It's that slave trader we ran into some time ago. He's brought a lawyer demanding his property back."

"Is that a fact? Brought a lawyer. Well, this will be fun. Did John T get those people out of here into Kansas?"

"John just got back from St. Louis last night."

At that moment John T rode up, "Sam that slave trader is nosing around looking for his people."

"I just heard. When are you planning on taking them north?"

"It looks like we better get gone right now. I was hoping to re-supply and get a little rest, but we better leave and rest up the trail a way. I'm going to take them to Lawrence. You want me to get a letter to Margaret?"

"How long will you be gone?"

"About two weeks."

"Let me write a quick note. You go on and get organized, I'll go stall Mr. Whelan. Be sure to take that old wagon of his and the mules. I don't want any trace of those people around. Sergeant, go tell Colonel Dodge that I'm still with General Curtis. I'll be there in about an hour. Then see that our men are well fed and have them restock ammunition, wash and repair their clothes. I expect it will get pretty wild. General Curtis told me that Price and McCulloch are itching for a fight, and we are going to give it to them."

"Looks like David is going to have a bunch more business," Mullhattur hurried off to deliver the message.

Sam walked through camp detouring by his cook's fire to see what was in the cook pot. He stopped short as saw her raise a willow branch to one of the children, "Stop this instant, Mrs. Washington."

She turned then threw down the whip seeing Sam approach, the little girl ran crying, "Oh, Colonel

Wood, Colonel Wood, we've missed you so." She threw her arm around his waist.

"Mrs. Washington, this whipping has got to stop. I insist whether I am here or not. No more whipping is that clear? My men are risking their lives to deny the slaveholder the whip and here you are whipping the little ones for some minor offense?"

"You a mighty good man Mr. Wood, but you might near come to spoil ever Nigger child in this camp. I never seen the like."

"Be that as it may, there will be no more of this whipping?"

In the distance the Africans were camped, both freeborn and escaped slaves seeking protection. He strolled that way nodding to those he recognized, listening to their questions, giving hope where he could. While in camp near Rolla they were safe, but eventually they would have to be dispersed as would the white Union sympathizers who had fled their homes for the safety of the army. They were huddled in blankets around campfires. It was cold, spring still just a hint in the air when the sun peeked through.

Sam made certain John T, Caleb and the group of runaway slaves were well on their way before he started for the headquarters of Colonel Dodge, a tall man of average build with a full well-trimmed beard, a volunteer from Iowa trained as a civil engineer. He was itching to get into some real action, planning to join General Curtis and the other battalions in the coming trek into Arkansas. Sam entered the building, spotted Whelan and another man sitting in the hallway, ignored them, and strolled into Dodge's office. His desk was covered with papers and a miniature steam engine from his pre-war duties as chief surveyor for the Union Pacific railroad in Council Bluffs, Iowa.

Sam picked up the engine turning it in his hands, "Mel, how's your leg?"

Dodge laughed, "More embarrassing than anything. How many men do you know that shoot themselves in the leg? I'll have to fib to my grandchildren; tell them it was a war wound... can't let them know it was from my own gun."

Sam nodded with a wry smile, "It happens."

"Sam, that man in there has lodged a complaint against you, even brought a lawyer. Says he's filed an official complaint with General Halleck in St. Louis and sent a copy to Washington. Do you know what he's talking about?"

Sam laughed, "I'm sorry you were bothered with this matter, Mel. Let's get them in here and straighten it out right quick."

Whelan entered, his teeth gritted in anger, waving sheaves of paper as though they were witnesses to the fact, "That's the man. He stole my slaves."

Sam stared at him.

"Have you got anything to say in your defense, Sir," the lawyer said.

"Who are you?" Sam asked sitting down.

"I'm Judge Harrison Reinhold, from Jefferson City, Missouri. I represent Mr. Whelan in this matter."

"You any relation to Maurice Reinhold over in Leavenworth City?"

"Why yes, he's my brother."

"I thought I saw a strong resemblance," Sam sat back crossed his legs putting his hands behind his head. "When was the last time you saw Maurice?"

"It was well before the war. Why?"

"Because he put on about 100 pounds after he got married. He can barely wobble around last I saw him a year ago... let me think, it was when we were celebrating Kansas statehood."

"He always was kind of a runty kid. I guess married life has been good to him."

Whelan looked back and forth between his attorney and Sam disbelieving his eyes and ears, "Are you two old women finished having a gossip session? I want to get my Niggers and get out of here."

"Remind me who you are," Sam leaned forward glaring at Whelan. "I don't remember the circumstances of meeting you. I've run into so many Rebs in the last few months. You all starting to look the same to me."

"Bullshit, you know exactly who I am. You broke the chain of one of my unruly slaves and sent me back to Fayetteville with a group of your soldiers."

"Why sure, I remember you, the plantation owner."

Mr. Reinhold turned to Whelan, "Plantation owner?"

Sam nodded vigorously, "Yes, Mr. Whelan said it was urgent that he get back to his plantation. I had a detachment escort him along so he wouldn't be delayed. Something about his wife being in the family way. His slaves were to follow later. Except for the chained fellow who was a Canadian citizen. I gave that man his papers back sent him by train to the Canadian embassy in St. Louis. Are you saying those loyal slaves of yours didn't make it to Fayetteville? You don't suppose some slave trader captured them and took them to New Orleans? You'll never see them again if they did."

"This is an outrage, Colonel Dodge. I demand satisfaction. This man has taken my slaves illegally."

"I'll tell you something Mr. Whelan, the last man who accused me of something like that didn't fare well. I've got a whole company of men who witnessed me telling those slaves to get on the road as soon as they could. If they didn't go to Fayetteville, it had nothing to do with me."

"Reinhold, say something. What the hell am I paying you for?"

"Well, Mr. Whelan, if what Colonel Wood says is true, I'm afraid you don't have much recourse sir."

"He threatened me with an axe. Said he would bash my head in. I want him arrested."

Dodge tried unsuccessfully to stifle a chuckle, turned to Sam, took a deep breath, "Did you threaten Mr. Whelan with an axe, Sam?"

"Yes, I did."

"There you see," Whelan pointed at his attorney. "Now do something."

Reinhold looked at the ceiling a moment, "What were the circumstances behind this threat, Colonel Wood?"

"The circumstances were that a Canadian Citizen was accusing this man of illegally detaining him. Now, Harrison, as I'm sure you are aware, as Senior Military Officer in the field I have full authority under President Lincoln's declaration of martial law, to conduct investigations, create courts of law and impose restrictions. I am the ultimate legal authority. There was no time, nor was that the place to convene a court of law. I conducted the investigation myself. Upon examining this man's papers, he became irate. I warned him back. When I discovered that the young colored man's Canadian papers were in order, I confiscated them. I returned the Bill of Sale for the slaves to Mr. Whelan."

Sam stood, stretched his legs, "You're welcome to go over to the Negro camp...see if you can find your property, but I'll warn you those people don't take kindly to anyone who smells like a slave trader...and you stink to high heaven. I don't believe you have a plantation in Fayetteville. I believe you misled me. Will there be anything else, Colonel Dodge?"

"Thank you, Colonel Wood, that will be all. And as for you," he pointed at Whelan, "I suggest you go to Washington and pursue your complaint. But, a word of caution, I doubt they give you the same cordial welcome you received here. These specious claims you portray will not be received cordially, we are fighting a war and your personal problems don't become the situation. You are dismissed sir."

February 15, 1862
Springfield, Missouri

General Curtis with 10,000 of his troops advanced to Springfield prepared to engage Confederate General Sterling Price's 8,000 Arkansas and Missouri militia only to have Price beat a rapid retreat to Fayetteville. He combined forces with General McCulloch and General Van Dorn. Their Confederate Army of the Southwest totaled over 16,000 men.

A brilliant orange sunset found the troops of Wood's Brigade huddled around campfires in the new bivouac near Wilson's Creek. They were well rested, well fed, and ready to fight, disappointed in the Confederate retreat. Sam brought two thousand of his troops, leaving the remainder in Rolla as reinforcements.

Private Peavler carried a plate of boiled beans and salted pork to sit near Sargent-Major Daniel Mullhattur, "Sarge, you reckon we going back to Rolla or down to Fayetteville?"

"Don't know, don't care."

"Me, I'd rather go fight. I'm tired of sittin' around."

"Well, you sittin' around on the blood of some boys wish they wouldn't have had to fight last August."

Peavler glanced around, looked down at his boots, placed his fork on the plate, "I've done lost my appetite."

"Sargent-Major, congratulations on your promotion," Sheriff Walker approached from the direction of the latrine. "Have you seen Sam?"

Mullhattur pointed, "Same to you Captain Walker."

Walker acknowledged the compliment as he continued toward the command tent.

"Captain, look at that moon. Ain't it a sight?" Corporal Dawson pointed at the brilliant globe, bright enough to cast shadows.

Walker paused; the vivid moon causing each man a tremor of homesickness.

"A full moon," Peavler marveled.

Mullhattur gazed up for a few seconds, "No boys, it's a waxing moon."

"What does that mean, Sarge?"

"Not quite full see the shadow on the left side?"

They stared in wonder midst the sounds of the crackling fire, of men moving about, the familiar activities of a camp full of men killing time waiting for their next orders.

David sat down by Mullhattur, "You sure are smart, Sarge."

"I paid attention in school. Where's Caleb?"

"He had to go with Papa John to take some slaves to Canada. Their owner filed a complaint to get them back. They left before we came down here to Springfield."

"I bet you miss him."

"Yeah, but I've got a lot of duties to keep me busy."

Mullhattur eyed the young boy with a chuckle, "I guess you do. You must be pretty smart yourself. How did you get into the lemonade business?"

"Everybody was hot and thirsty, so I just got some barrels, filled them with water, bought some lemon extract from my Uncle Stephan. Pa got General Lyon to lend me an ambulance, and things just kind of took off from there. Plus, I can read and write and cipher. Most of the soldiers can't...But I never cheat them," he cautioned.

Mullhattur nodded, agreeing with the assessment, "Well, you are a good soldier. A bit young, but your daddy knows what he's doing, and it don't hurt that your Uncle is the Quartermaster. How's your momma?"

"She's fine. My sister and brother sure are getting big. Punch wanted to come back with us, but momma wouldn't let him. She moved into a new house in Cottonwood Station."

"Where's that?"

"South of Lawrence. Daddy started a newspaper there and in Council Grove."

"I been to Council Grove one time. I was hauling freight for Russel, Majors and Waddell out of Lexington, Missouri. There was a mercantile there in Council Grove. What was that fellas name? He had a black woman for a wife."

"Seth Hayes, he's a friend of mine," David smiled. "You know I had my picture taken?"

"I seen it in the paper. You look pretty good in that uniform. Youngest soldier in the Union Army. I know your mama is proud of you."

Newly appointed Colonel John S. Phelps walked into the firelight accompanied by a detachment of several of his command. They carried lanterns and seemed in a hurry. Phelps formed a battalion of men after the Battle at Wilson's Creek and was appointed Colonel by Abraham Lincoln.

"Sargent, where is Colonel Wood?"

Mullhattur pointed toward Sam's command tent. The flap to the tent was open with several other officers present. Phelps announced, "Gentlemen, we are to report to General Curtis headquarters at six in the morning."

"What's in the works, John?" Sam asked.

"Van Dorn, Price and McColloch are all congregated south of Fayetteville. General Curtis wants to advance on them before they are aware...take them by surprise."

"We're at a heavy disadvantage in manpower," Major Drake of the 5th Iowa Calvary ruminated after Phelps took leave.

The morning brought a light but cold rain. The men proceeded to their drills and assignments, grumbling that they would rather be marching than waiting. All the officers gathered in Curtis's large command tent.

Curtis stood with his hands behind his back watching as Brigadier General Alexander Absoth briefed the men on the battle plan. Absoth commanded the 2nd Division, Franz Siegel the 1st and

Colonel Jefferson C. Davis the third. Sam's battalion as well as former Fort Wyman commandant Colonel Dodge and Colonel Phelps served under Absoth. Within the week they were to strike camp and move on Fayetteville a march of about 110 miles.

"General, we are still waiting on ammunition and field artillery from St. Louis. Any word on the supplies?" Sam asked.

Absoth turned to General Curtis who reported, "Any day now, Sam. We'll have to make do with what we have. I know Van Dorn is in the same situation and his supply lines are longer than ours. Part of our strategy is to draw him up into Missouri if we can. That will stretch his supply lines even further."

***

The cold wet weather hung with them throughout the end of February. By March 5 the army was south of Mount Vernon bivouacking on Honey Creek with about 12,000 men after Curtis had called up his reserves. That afternoon Curtis summoned Sam and Iowa Major William Drake to his tent. Also present were General Absoth and General Sigel.

Absoth began the discussion without formality, indicating the urgency, "Sam, we have a problem. Reports are that Colonel Coleman and a young officer named Posey Woodside have split off from Van Dorn's main force and are circling east trying to flank us. They are gathering recruits as they go. Intelligence tells us they total about 1,500 to 2,000 men, maybe more by now. I'm issuing orders for you to take 450 of your men plus Major Drake's 3rd Iowa Calvary, march East to the Garrison at Militia Springs then scout that country until you intercept them. You can't let them reach Missouri."

General Curtis added, "Their intent is to circle around behind us and cut our supply lines. Your Missouri and Arkansas troopers know the country as well or better than the enemy. Do what you must. Did you find any additional artillery?"

"I have a couple of field artillery pieces, but we need more mules to carry them. I have one howitzer. Stephan is trying to find another. We'll make do."

Curtis continued, "I'm issuing a directive to all of our forces, countersigned by General Halleck. You are to confiscate the animals of any civilian Rebel sympathizer. Mules, horses, oxen, even if you don't need them... deny the enemy their use. Sam, call up as many of your reserves as you need. When you ascertain the size of the enemy send a dispatch to let us know. I've ordered an additional 4,000 men down from Rolla. Reports are that Van Dorn has 16,000 men. We'll be outnumbered but we have the advantage of surprise. They are in a defensive position, but I predict they will advance north when we reach the Arkansas border. We're all short of supplies; your supply sergeant will need to route some of the wagons to the Garrison at Militia Springs. The same with the field hospitals. We don't have enough surgeons as it is. You may have to send your wounded back to Rolla. I don't need to emphasize how much I'm counting on you Sam. Our success in this campaign depends on those supplies getting through."

***

"Prepare your hearts for Death's cold hand! Prepare
Your souls for flight, your bodies for the earth;
Prepare your arms for glorious victory;
Prepare your eyes to meet a holy God!
Prepare, prepare!"
William Blake

Three hundred Calvary on horses worn and thin, two hundred infantry tramping in shoes scrapped and torn, threadbare uniforms for the lucky ones, civilian rags for the rest, one cannon, supply wagons, ambulances, medical staff, cooks, mules, horses, a few cattle, all labored east halting at Militia Springs on March 7. The small garrison was ordered on high alert with a picket line established at several points five miles from town.

On March 10 after a forced march, camp was established at Spring River Mill on the Arkansas border. A courier brought news that Curtis had engaged Van Dorn's Confederate Army north of Fayetteville. Time was of the essence. The message from General Curtis was clear, "Sam, do not allow Coleman to cut our supply lines."

Sam's command tent was packed with officers and their assistants all speaking at once. Sergeant Billy Reynolds an advanced scout, arrived with news. He was from Salem, Arkansas and knew the area well, "I've got spies all through that country. I know what the Rebs are up to. They are east of Salem along the South Fork of Spring River. There's a bunch of em'. Maybe two thousand, I don't rightly know fer sure. We tryin' to get a better count."

Major Drake leaned his palms against the table studying the map, "It looks pretty swampy west of Salem." He glanced at Reynolds.

"Yessir, it is. But Clyde Vetter been huntin' that area since he was a kid. He knows ways to get around."

"What do you think, Sam?" Captain Walker looked at his commanding officer who stood next to Drake studying the situation.

"Our orders are to keep them from advancing north. I'm afraid if we wait to call up reserves from Rolla, they'll be gone. Get the men ready to move immediately. Lt. Nordhal, establish supply and the hospital on this side of Salem," Sam pointed to a location two miles east of the Courthouse."

Captain Walker asked, "What about ammunition, Sam? A good many of Major Drake's men carry the Navy revolver but we don't have much of the .36 caliber ammunition. We've got quite a few Minie Balls. You'll have to ask Stephan about powder. He's at the Magazine right now."

Major Drake frowned. "We have the darndest assortment of rifles you ever saw. Some have the Gibb's carbines, some Enfield; we've got Austrian rifles and British rifles. Even if we get ammunition, it won't fit half the weapons."

Lt. Crawford volunteered, "We have about 100 Sharps, maybe 50 Spencers. I suggest we get those into the hands of the best shots."

Sam glanced at Crawford, a big man with a heavy beard, a scar disfigured his right cheek. Few would cross him. "Excellent suggestion, Lt. Please take the responsibility of seeing to that."

"With your permission, Colonel, I'll begin immediately."

Sam turned to Walker, "Would you ask Stephan to come see me. If there is nothing else, that will be all. Good luck and God speed, gentlemen."

Drake waited as the others left, "Colonel Wood, most of my men are armed with Colt Navy Pistols and little else. We have very few rifles and those are muzzle loaders."

"We'll make do, Bill. Distribute the ammunition as you see fit. Give the most to your best soldiers, those you know won't shy from trouble. Every company has their shirkers. Make your best guess. I'll have Captain Walker do the same."

Drake was a young man, tall and well-built with thick black hair, his eyes framed by dark brows giving him a perpetual look of gravity. A wife and young daughter waited for him in Iowa. He paused at the door, "We missed the battle at Wilson's Creek, Colonel. I hope my men don't let you down."

"I'm not in the least worried, Bill. They'll follow you wherever you lead them. It's in your hands...they won't let you down and neither will I."

The door opened to Stephan Wood, "Major Drake... Colonel Wood," he greeted them.

"Sergeant Wood," Drake acknowledged then left.

Stephan watched him walk away, "Is Drake feeling well, Sam. He looks a little down."

"Battle nerves. He'll be fine tomorrow. Any news on ammunition and artillery?"

"I've got couriers from here to Rolla. I've sent letters, pleas, orders...everyone is short."

"Tomorrow, you keep David with you at the powder magazine or he can help Dr. Patee at the hospital. I don't want him near the shooting."

Stephan nodded. He was taller than Sam but thinner. They didn't look a lot different than they did twelve years ago in Ohio when Sam met Margaret. Stephan chuckled.

"What?" Sam eyed him suspiciously.

"Nothing, big brother, but you look like a pig in slop. You been wanting this war and here it is."

Sam slapped him on the back, "I'm glad you're here with me, Stephan. Keep your head down."

"You do the same, Sammy."

Sergeant Mullhattur stood outside as Stephan exited. The two exchanged words that Sam couldn't hear. Mullhattur entered the tent followed by Stephan, "Colonel there's a delegation of big brass from General Halleck waiting to see you."

"Waiting to see me, about what? Good Lord in heaven, if it's about that idiot slave trader, I'll blow my top. Of all the foolishness, when we're about to go into battle." Sam stormed around the command tent looking for his club.

"Calm down, Sammy," Stephan cautioned. "I don't think that's what it's about. I think they're just observers. Daniel tells me they accompanied the supply wagons, including some ammunition. I'm going to go see what they brought. I'll send the visitors in to see you."

A Colonel, a Major, both well uniformed, and a civilian neatly dressed, carrying a portfolio entered the tent. Sam eyed them warily.

"Colonel Wood, I'm Colonel Blackmon, Major Treadwell and Mr. Jed Lively. We are here strictly as observers. Brigadier General Henry Halleck is interested in recording the realities of war. We will be traveling with you as observers, and Mr. Lively is an artist who will document the action. There will also be some reporters from various newspapers. We will stay out of your way entirely. Pretend that we aren't even here." Blackmon chuckled as did his companions.

Sam stared at them for an uncomfortably long period of time, "Is this a joke of some kind? Do you have written orders from General Halleck?"

Blackmon turned red, "I assure you sir, this is no joke. We, that is General Halleck and I, consider it imperative to provide the citizens with information about the horrors of war; the reality of what is happening."

"Why aren't you observing General Curtis? He's fighting about 15,000 Rebs over in Fayetteville as we speak."

"I believe others from our department are chronicling that engagement," Major Treadwell handed Sam the written orders.

He glanced at the document, handed it back, "Stay well back from the shooting. I'd hate to have to notify Henry of your death. Now, if you'll excuse me, I've got a battle to prepare for."

Taking a deep breath to calm himself, Sam began studying the map again. A knock at the door.

"Come," Sam roared.

"I saw the lamp, Colonel, is there anything else before I see to the rest of my duties?" Sergeant Mullhattur stuck his head in the door.

"Daniel, come in, come in. I didn't mean to shout at you. Those men got my dander up a bit. Where are they?"

"Over by Major Drake's company. They brought four enlisted men to set up their tent and cook their meals."

Sam shook his head, chuckled at the irony, "In the middle of a war. Makes you wonder doesn't it."

"Yes, Sir, it does."

"How are you, Daniel? I often wonder how you're managing."

"I'm getting along fine Sir. Sometimes it's discouraging some of the things I hear said about women, in general, but I let it go in one ear and out the other. I didn't tell you, I found two others like me."

"Where?"

"In Rolla."

"I'll be. Who would have guessed? Maybe someday women will serve in the open alongside the men."

"Not in my lifetime, Sir. Not when we can't even vote or hold office."

"That may be true, but I wouldn't trade you for ten men," Sam said as another knock at the door brought Captain Walker.

"Good, I was about to send for you. See if you can round up Major Drake and Sergeant Reynolds. I want to go over the map again."

***

At dawn the small army advanced into Arkansas, generally following Spring River south. Moving picket lines, a mile each side of the main body and a mile in front, gave advanced notice of engagement with the enemy. They marched approximately five miles when shots were heard from the forward scouts.

"Sergeant Major, bring your squad. Captain Walker..." Sam indicated for Walker to join him. "Major Drake, maintain the advance while we investigate."

Sam rode at a gallop along with the 20-man detachment. They arrived at a point on Janes Creek where a Confederates camp had been hastily abandoned.

"We killed two of them, Colonel," Reynolds pointed to the bodies. "Looks like there were about 40 of them from Coleman's company. They broke camp fast."

"I'm glad you didn't pursue them. It could be a decoy," Sam examined the bodies. We'll wait here for the rest of the men. Sergeant Reynolds, how much further to the enemy position?"

"Probably 10 miles, Sir."

"We'll camp here for the night. Sergeant Mullhattur, have those men identified and buried. Mark their graves well and note the location in your log."

"Yes Sir!"

"We move out at first light."

***

The new day brought a heavy fog darkening the mood of the men as if the fear engraved on their faces was etched by the conditions of the day. Two hundred infantry marched along in silence, eyes scanning for any movement, visibility at times only a few yards. The cavalrymen gave the horses their head trusting them to follow the road. The eerie scene was marked only by the tramping of the soldiers, and clopping of horse's hooves. No one spoke, fearing an ambush at every bend in the rough dirt road. They trekked south and west through forests interrupted at times by fields and meadows. The fog lifted about 10 AM brightening the prospects in all manner. Spirits rose, banter among the men, although subdued, resumed. Scouts were dispatched and returned at fifteen-minute intervals. They passed two hastily abandoned Secesh camps.

"Colonel Wood, we're about a mile from the Reb's," Clyde Vetter galloped back with his report. Vetter, a young man no more than 18, whip-thin with a sparse growth of blonde whiskers on his upper lip sat his horse waiting further orders.

"Major Drake, would you establish our base camp there," Sam indicated a parklike meadow on the south side of a small stream. "I'm going with Private Vetter to see what we're up against." They rode off at a gallop.

Major Drake ordered, "Establish a picket line at a quarter mile, Sentry's surrounding the camp, and a vedette at a half-mile." Captain Walker dismounted and began giving orders.

When he returned, Sam sat his horse, occasionally calling a greeting to one of the men. The early morning clouds and fog gave way to bright sunshine highlighting the routine sights and sounds of the camp being established. Hostlers gathered the horses to graze in the meadow and drink from the stream. The mules and wagons were inspected for any damage, stores and supplies secured. The men spoke quietly and worked efficiently.

"David," Sam shouted when the boy finally arrived on one of the ambulances.

He jumped down to greet his father, "Papa, we almost turned over back there about three miles. The wagon hit a rock and ruined a wheel."

"Was anyone hurt?" Sam put his arm around David who was wearing his new uniform, a Kepi jauntily angled on his head with a Crow feather stuck in the band, the buttons and insignia highly polished. During skirmishes David functioned as an orderly carrying dispatches and messages between the men and officers.

"No, Sir, we were just held up while they made repairs."

"I expect we'll be moving out soon. You'll stay here and help your Uncle Stephan with his duties."

"Yes Sir."

***

Sam, Major Drake, Captain Walker, Lt. Crawford plus several other lesser officers gathered under a large hickory tree on the bank of Horton Branch Creek listening to Reynolds describe the enemy's position.

"There's a reserve force, maybe three hundred of Posey Woodside's men two miles west of Salem, but the main force about 1,200 are a mile and half north of town square in that swampy area part of old man Kildare's farm. It'll be hard to flush em' out of there."

"What do you think, Bill?" Sam asked Major Drake.

"Not very good odds on our side."

"Oh, I think we have them right where we want them," Sam smiled lightening the mood. "Lt. Crawford, how many men are well enough armed to go into battle?"

"About 250 of your company and 100 of Major Drake's."

Sam raised his cane, began taping on a tree gazing up at the blue sky through the branches, "Captain Walker, would you get those 350 men ready to move out. Sergeant Reynolds you'll ride point with Major Drake and I. Sergeant Mullhattur, have the canon brought up. You'll accompany the battery. We'll decide on placement when we encounter the Reb's. Lt. Nordhal, you will be in charge of the reserves at this location. They will also shuttle ammunition, food and water as we need it. Any questions?"

The small force of 250 calvary and 100 infantry, plus one canon, marched east a half mile and turned north on Hunter Road through fields and meadows until they reached the woods where the Reb's blocked the approach with an abatis of trees and branches stretching for 50 yards on each side of the road, leaving a small opening in the center barely large enough for two riders. Sam called a halt to survey the area. A ridge where the river had changed course sometime in the past ran east and west a few hundred yards from the Union position. Sam turned toward the ravine as shots were fired from the just budding trees and behind the breastwork. An infantry man fell mortally wounded. The men dashed for cover or flattened on the ground as an explosion of shots rang out, powder smoke filled the air around the trees. The calvary dismounted and herded their horses further back.

"Daniel," Sam shouted, "The canon there behind that slight rise. Fire at will, shell the breastwork and fire canisters into the woods."

The artillerymen unlimbered the one cannon bombarding the abatis with howitzer shells. The metal balls from the canisters crashed through the trees sending the projectiles into the enemy along with splinters from the shattered branches.

Sam called to Reynolds, "Sergeant is it possible to flank them, get behind them somehow?"

"Yes sir. Clyde knows a way," Reynolds dashed away looking for the local man who was key to their new strategy.

"Bill," Sam put his hand on Major Drakes shoulder, "Take your men, cross the river back downstream a way and circle around behind this bunch. We'll provide a diversion here. Come in from behind them and pour it on with all you've got."

Drake saluted just as Vetter and Reynolds arrived. They ran for their horses as the gunfire from the trees began again in earnest.

"We've got men down, Colonel?"

"Keep your best marksmen here. Have them fire at any puff of smoke. I'm going to take some men around the ridge and charge them to create a diversion, to give Drake's men time to flank them."

"Sam, let me lead the charge. The troops can survive without me but not without you."

"And let you have all the fun. Not hardly, Sheriff. You keep these men firing'

"Colonel Wood," Mullhattur, breathing heavily, grabbed his arm, "we've got to move the cannon out of range of their rifles."

"We're going to create a diversion. Wait until you hear the bugle then move it. You won't have much time."

Sam mounted Border Ruffian with a detachment of 50 of his calvary and advanced on the right side of the breastwork. With the bugler blowing charge, the men stormed out of the ravine screaming and firing at will, while the infantry laid down a barrage of covering fire. Several horses went down, mortally wounded including Border Ruffian who took a musket ball through the eye. Sam leapt to the ground as Ruff stumbled and lay motionless. He and two other men forted up behind the dead horse and fired until they were out of ammunition. Abruptly the canon roared to life sending the Rebs scurrying back to the cover of the forest.

"Blow retreat," he calmly ordered. The men retreated carrying their wounded and dead. Grape shot rattled through the trees. Federal troops could hear the cries and moans of the wounded Rebels. Yet guns from the forest never stopped firing. The noise was deafening and the smoke choking with little wind to disperse it.

Sam ordered the ambulances up and they began loading their dead and wounded. Suddenly David appeared galloping frantically on horseback, "Papa, the Rebs are sending their reserves from Salem. They are almost here."

"Son, ride back and tell Lt. Rankin to intercept those men with half our reserves. Fight them hand to hand if they have to."

David saluted and spurred his horse back to the Union Camp.

"Here they come," Walker screamed as the rebs poured out of the protection of the woods and began rushing the Union position.

"Every man with a gun, follow me," Walker ordered.

They charged over the ridge firing as fast as they could load. The odds were crushing, Sam's forces were about to be overrun. He reloaded his Spencer, sprang to his feet and began running.

Suddenly the Rebs stopped in confusion and began running west back toward the swamp. Major Drake's men charged out of the woods screaming like banshee's, firing their pistols non-stop. A cheer rose from the Union side as the Iowa boys forced the enemy to retreat. Sam and his Missourian's charged ahead joining Drake's men to drive the superior force back into their own advancing reserves who turned tail and ran at the confusing sight of their comrades fleeing.

Sam called a halt at the edge of the swamp to take inventory of the situation.

"We're out of ammunition, Sam," Walker informed him. "I doubt we have 50 rounds left between all of us."

"Gather our wounded and dead. We'll return to camp. I'm not going to risk men wading into that swamp without ammunition."

Sam walked back to Border Ruffian. Several other horses lay dead or wounded, their riders removing personal effects, preparing to dispatch the mortally wounded. He knelt by Ruff's head remembering the many conversations they had riding through the lonely hills and prairies of Kansas; the 4th of July races won, the pride David and Punch took in caring for their prized possession.

"You want me to form a detail to bury them?" Lt. Crawford indicated the dead horses.

Sam nodded, "And get a count on the enemy casualties. Any wounded Rebels, bring them to camp."

Sam cut a large shock of Ruff's mane, put it in his pocket. There was a commotion at the tree line. Several men were milling about arguing over something. He found them standing around a fallen southern soldier, one of Sam's men cradling his head.

"Shoot the son-of a bitch," one infantryman shouted pulling his pistol.

"What's going on here," Sam stepped into the middle of the group.

"Reb soldier, Colonel. I know he's the one shot Butch. I seen him do it."

The rebel soldier, not much more than 16 or 17 was crying. His protector looked up with fear in his eyes, "Colonel, this is my brother, Harry. I've been shooting at him. Please!" He wrapped his arms around the wounded man, blood stained on the front of his tunic.

"You men go on about your business. Go help Lt. Crawford." Sam leaned down to check the wounds. "It doesn't look fatal. Get him into one of the wagons. We'll take him to Dr. Patee."

"You're not going to kill me?" Harry gasped.

"No. But the war is over for you, son."

Walking back to the wagons where soldiers were loading the wounded and dead he spotted something on the ridge behind the battlefield, "Captain Walker," he pointed at the spectacle, "what in the name of everything holy is that?"

Sheriff turned, shielded his eyes trying to make out a silhouette in the sun, "I believe it's that artist fellow. I guess I've seen everything now, Sam. He's painting a picture. You reckon he's been there all through the battle?"

Walking up the ridge Sam encountered Colonel Blackman, "Colonel Wood, my compliments, Sir, on a glorious victory, against overwhelming odds," he shook Sam's hand vigorously. "Rest assured Brigadier General Halleck will receive a most splendid report."

"Thank you, Colonel. Have you been up here this whole time?" Sam walked to the artist sitting in a chair with an easel and drafting paper, putting the final touches on an illustration of the battle.

"Just after we heard the first shots."

Sam watched him make a few lines on the canvas, couldn't think of anything appropriate to say, turned and jogged down to catch a ride on the last ambulance leaving the battlefield. He glanced back up at the artist, "What a strange war."

"Sir?" the driver queried.

"That man up there is drawing a picture of the battle," Sam pointed.

The driver leaned around to see, "That ain't something I ever expected to see."

"Me either."

***

Returning to camp, Sam ordered Walker to arm 25 men with the remaining ammunition and follow the Rebels, "Find out where they are and if they intend to regroup. If they do we'll have to double time out of here."

Walker rode out of camp at a gallop, his command on fresh horses as the remaining officers filed their reports.

"Twenty wounded, five dead, Colonel Wood, including Sergeant Mullhattur."

Sam took a deep breath, "No, not Daniel! Where are the bodies?"

"Makeshift morgue near the field hospital."

"Major Drake, continue the debriefing. I'm going to check on the wounded."

Drake nodded, glanced at Lt. Crawford who shrugged, unsure of Sam's actions so close to the battle and not being confident of where the enemy might be or if a counterattack was coming.

Sam jogged to the makeshift morgue where he found David kneeling by Daniel Mullhattur's body. His eyes brimmed with tears as Sam placed a hand on his shoulder.

"Sergeant Mullhattur is dead," David wiped his eyes on the sleeve of his tunic.

"I'm sorry son. Sergeant Mullhattur was a fine person."

"He is...was my good friend," he cried. Sam took him in his arms.

He sent David back to help Stephan and entered the tent where Dr. Patee was amputating the leg of one of the infantrymen. Sam waited until he was finished then took the young Dr. aside, "When you examine Sergeant Mullhattur's body to prepare for burial, do it privately."

"What do you mean, Colonel?"

"You'll understand when you remove the uniform."

"Female?"

Surprise registered in Sam's eyes, "Yes, how did you know?"

"Just by your tone and I've heard about others from different surgeons here and there. I'll be discreet but I have to notify my superiors."

Sam nodded and walked down the rows of wounded men offering solace where he could before returning to his command tent.

"I've established a picket line around the camp," Drake informed him. "We still haven't received word back from Captain Walker."

"I counted 110 enemy casualties, Sir. We placed the bodies near the road so they could be claimed. Plus 30 wounded under guard at the hospital."

Sam gazed around the area, "We're in a vulnerable position here. No ammunition, food is running short. As soon as the surgeon gets the wounded ready to travel, we'll fall back to Militia Springs."

At that moment Walker returned with 40 prisoners, ten horses and six mules plus two wagons of confiscated weapons, ammunition, and food. "They're skedaddling south, Colonel. Most of these Rebs here are deserters or injured. They claim Coleman is taking his men back to join up with Van Dorn. General Curtis won the battle at Pea Ridge, so the Reb's are all heading to Mississippi."

"That will leave Missouri and Arkansas free from threat, at least for now. We need to prepare to march at first light. We'll return to Militia Springs and await further orders there."

***

Militia Springs Union Garrison
South Central Missouri
March 1862

Fort Wyman, in Rolla, Missouri had grown to a garrison of over 40,000 men. The new commander, Colonel Boyd, a man of considerable political ambition, was responsible for Union forces in Missouri and Arkansas. The Battle of Salem put the spotlight on Colonel Wood due to the illustration published in the New York Tribune and Leslie's Illustrated. Every newspaper in the land picked up the story. Sam was unaware of the publicity, wouldn't have cared about it regardless.

Sam sat alone in the headquarters at Militia Springs reviewing the telegrams and letters received following the battle in Salem. Upon reading the following he had to laugh imagining how it must have irked the author,

March 18, 1862

Ft. Wyman, Rolla, MO.

Headquarters, Col. S. H. Boyd

Col. Wood, I highly congratulate you on such a signal victory in the Battle of Salem. I believe you should not fight against such great odds. Take care of yourself and your gallant command. I will send you reinforcements for

scouting, etc. I send to Halleck telegraph accounts although he had his own observers on-site as you know.
I am, Col., yours most truly, S. H. Boyd.

His contemplation was interrupted by Lt. Crawford, his new aide-de-camp.

"Colonel, another telegram."

It read simply, 'And the legend grows.'

Sam threw his head back and laughed. Crawford smiled, "Good news, Colonel?"

"It's from a friend of mine. John Thompson. He's still in Rolla moving Negroes north. He's financed by a group of free blacks out of St. Louis. It's quite a story. They've saved thousands of lives. He's just ribbing me a little over that article in the newspapers."

Crawford nodded, "Still no word from General Curtis. You think we'll be going south again?"

"You can bet on it."

***

Helena, Arkansas
May 1862

At the conclusion of the victory at Pea Ridge, General Curtis moved his troops across Southern Missouri and Northern Arkansas arriving in Salem on April 1. His 8,000 troops camped in Salem for a week before moving South toward Mississippi. Sam's Battalion was ordered to rendezvous with the main body of the Army of the Southwest on May 15, in Batesville, Arkansas. From there they proceeded south to Helena, with the intent of securing the

Mississippi River for the Union. The combined forces of Curtis' Brigade in Helena totaled 18,000 men.

The victory in the Battle at Pea Ridge or Battle of Elkhorn Tavern as General Curtis preferred to call it, resulted in the Confederate Army retreating south into Mississippi to regroup under General Van Dorn.

The former Texas Ranger, General Ben McColloch's luck ran out in Fayetteville; he was killed in action on the second day of the battle. General Sterling Price, the former Governor of Missouri, survived Pea Ridge and vowed to return and recapture his home state or 'die trying'.

In Helena, Army engineers immediately designed a Fort to function as Union headquarters in Arkansas. The earth and wood redoubt would serve as the Southern Command for the Army of the Southwest. Sam was provided a Steamboat and ordered to cross into Mississippi and secure the area from Memphis to Clarksdale. The new Fort was completed on August 12, 1862. That day found Sam combing the area around Clarksdale, Mississippi where they engaged a band of Bushwalkers or Partisan Rangers, no one could be sure of their affiliation; the truth was it didn't matter, they were wreaking havoc along the river. Renegades who function semi-autonomously outside the command of the Confederate army. They were hated by both sides.

Sam's command steamed down the Mississippi to Friar's Point where the Union had a small garrison. Their bivouac that night was along a ridge near the Matagorda Plantation north of Jonestown,

Mississippi. Sam had a company of 200 men of his 6th Missouri Calvary. They captured 20 Confederate soldiers some horses and mules. In addition, a band of runaway slaves attached themselves to the troops under Wood's promise to transport them across to the Negro camp near Helena.

Sam and David sat back from the campfire enjoying a peaceful meal of hardtack and salt pork in the flickering light. The night was serene yet muggy from the heat and humidity ubiquitous to the Mississippi Delta. The constant buzz of mosquitos kept the men and the horses in misery. The area was a major cotton producing center with more slaves than whites in Coahoma County. In fact, the 1860 census counted only 1,521 whites and 5,085 slaves. Sam took great pride in freeing as many of the slaves as he could, a technical violation of Army regulations but one little enforced.

He watched David closely, "What's the matter, son, you lost your appetite?"

"I guess so Papa, I don't feel like eating."

"That doesn't sound like you. You sick?" He put his hand on David's forehead.

"Maybe."

"We'll have you see Dr. Patee when we get back to the Fort. Why don't you go lay down, get some rest?"

Captain Walker came into the campfire light grinning like he'd won a jackpot. He sat down grabbed David's untouched plate and began eating.

"What is it, Sheriff? You look like you're about to bust a gut to tell me something."

"Walker began shaking with laughter, "You ain't gonna believe this."

"What?"

"Guess who owns the plantation just west of here about 10 miles?"

"No idea, but I suspect you're going to tell me."

"I am, soon as I finish these vittles."

"Come on, Sheriff. I won't be able to eat..."

"Since you won't play my guessing game, I'll tell you...the Honorable Mr. Jacob Thompson former Secretary of the Interior and, as I recall, a man who treated Kansas in a particularly bad way a few years ago."

Sam almost dropped his plate, "Tell me you aren't pulling my leg."

"Swear it on the bible... just heard it from one of the Slaves. Said someone needs to help those people. They've got a terrible owner and an even worse overseer."

Sam jumped up, "That's the best news I've heard in two years. We'll mosey over there tomorrow and have a look for ourselves. Come on Sheriff, I want to speak to the man who told you that."

The group of runaway slaves camped in a sheltered area some 100 yards from the Union troops. Six men, four women and several children. The men, gathered in a group speaking low, stopped when they observed the officers approaching. They lowered their eyes as was the custom among southern slaves when approached by a white person.

Captain Walker indicated a tall, well-formed man of about 40 who took a step back when pointed out. An intelligent gleam in his eyes from the reflected firelight, the pupils dark as the starless night, shirtless, his ebony skin almost invisible in the gloom.

Sam approached cautiously, "I'm Colonel Sam Wood. I'd like a word with you."

"Yessir," he examined Sam carefully.

"What is your name?"

"Tommy."

"Tommy, you mentioned a plantation near here owned by a man named Jacob Thompson. Have you been there?"

His southern slave dialect was prominent causing Sam some difficulty in understanding, "Oh, Yessir! I was born there. That why my last name Thompson."

"Is this the same Jacob Thompson who was Secretary of the Interior?"

"Yes sir. He a General in the Confederate Army now, I believe. Some kind of important man in President Jefferson Davis government in Richmond, Virginia. He don't live on this plantation. He live on the one in Pontotoc but he come here often. His Sister Miz. Sullivan and her children live on this one. The overseer name of Snake Osborne."

"Did you run away from there?"

"No Sir, I was sold to Massah Alcorn, I live on Mound Place Plantation. I going to get my wife; she live on Massah Thompson place. They put us apart and sold our children down the river to New Orleans. Now with this war...I fearful of what gonna happen.

"You've been educated."

He immediately became wary of Sam who said calmly, "You needn't fear me. I'm on your side. That is why I offer passage and protection to any slave desiring to go north."

"I can read and write."

"Will you guide us to the Thompson Plantation?"

He immediately brightened, "Most definitely, Sir especially if you help me rescue my wife."

"We'll leave at first light."

They broke camp at dawn traveling first to Friar's Point where Sam formed a detachment of 25 men to escort the prisoners, slaves, and confiscated mules to Helena. David was extremely lethargic and seemed to be running a fever. Sam debated what to do and finally put a trusted corporal in charge of returning David to Fort Curtis and the immediate care of Dr. Patee. Then to return with the steamboat and report to Sam his condition. Given the nearness of the Thompson plantation he hoped to be back to Friar's Point by the following day, two days at the most.

An older slave woman, thin and gnarled wearing a white wrap around her head and a thin cotton dress to her ankles, approached Sam along with Tommy Thompson who spoke for her, "This is Martha Washington, everyone calls her Auntie, she'd like to go with us and bring her grandchildren back from the Thompson Plantation. She's afraid they won't come if she isn't there."

Sam nodded, "Lt. Crawford, see to a wagon for Mrs. Washington."

A sense of excitement wafted through the ranks. Rumors of a grudge between the Plantation owner, Jacob Thompson, Inspector General of the Confederate Army, and Colonel Wood created additional drama. The men speculated as to the reason more to alleviate the boredom of the march than any concern for the outcome. Thompson's Plantation lay between Jonestown and Clarksdale. The road between the two villages ran unevenly east and west. Tommy Thompson guided them to a rough track leading off the main road into a grove of oak and elm trees ending at a locked iron gate.

"The big house about three miles further up this trail. The trees end in about a mile," Thompson explained.

"Is the gate always locked?" Sam dismounted to inspect.

"This is a new gate. I never seen it before."

"Is there a way to go around?"

"Yes, Sir, but it will take an hour or more."

"Sergeant, have your men open this gate. Even if it means tearing it down."

The chain was removed, the gate opened allowing the procession to continue into fields of corn and cotton as far as they could see.

"Why are there no slaves in the fields?" Captain Walker asked.

Sam turned in the saddle, "I would imagine that gate was to slow us down. A sentry has probably gone ahead to warn them of our arrival."

On a hill in the distance perched a large mansion surrounded by manicured lawns, majestic trees and a circular drive leading to a massive patio large enough for the entire company. They marched onto the grounds; Sam sat his horse surveying several outbuildings including a large stable. A regal lady of about 50 along with two younger women stood on the porch fanning themselves, observing the soldiers in the same manner the soldiers observed them. The two younger ladies about 25, were quite attractive. Their mother nodded agreeably.

Three white men approached from the smaller of the outlying buildings. The older of the three, who Sam took to be the overseer, a coarse man of about six feet, over two hundred pounds, strode ominously to Tommy Thompson, "Thank you gentlemen for returning this runaway. We received word from Mr. Alcorn that this man ran off three days ago."

Osborne reached up and jerked Tommy off the horse and began whipping him with a short-handled leather lash with three metal tipped ends. It took Sam a few seconds to react. He jumped down grabbed the whip and pushed Osborn to the ground.

Osborne jumped up but before he could react, Captain Walker and Lt. Reynolds pulled their pistols and held the three men at gunpoint. Osborne lashed out, "You have no right to interfere with our slaves. I know the law. Lincoln ordered you not restrict our business."

"President Lincoln isn't here right now, I am," Sam brushed off his uniform. "Captain Walker, bind these men and hold them prisoner until I determine what is going on here."

"Lt. Reynolds."

"SIR!"

"Have the men search this plantation until you find the slaves. Confiscate all the animals, any bales of cotton, any harvested corn. Bring it all here."

Several of the domestic slaves joined the white ladies on the porch. Sam climbed the steps removed his hat and nodded to the ladies, "Ma'am, I am Colonel Sam Wood, 6th Missouri Calvary attached to the Army of the Southwest under Brigadier General Samuel Curtis. Perhaps it would be best if you all remained inside the house."

"Please join me, Colonel. I am Maureen Sullivan, and these are my daughters, Abigale and Lisa."

The daughters curtsied then proceeded Sam and their mother into the house.

"I will have Easom bring some lemonade. We can sit on the back patio where the breeze is fresher."

A flower garden with brick walks, trees, statues, all accented by numerous arbors and benches stretched from the house down the hill to the edge of the cotton fields.

"It must take quite an army of gardeners to maintain this," Sam did not mean it as a compliment and Mrs. Sullivan recognized his disgust.

"I know who you are, Sir. We are avid readers of the newspapers. They are delivered weekly at Friar's Point and brought to us as soon as possible. We don't have much in the way of diversion here. Sam Wood is a well-known name in our family. We've followed your adventures in Kansas and, of course, Jacob told us of your chat in Washington."

Easom, a slim, elderly man of mocha colored skin, close cropped curly white hair, wearing a long-tailed beige jacket and trousers, carried a tray with glasses and a pitcher of lemonade, "Will there be anything else, Ma'am?"

"No," Mrs. Sullivan waved him away.

Sam continued to gaze at the incredible garden, "Our chat? Is that what Secretary Thompson called it?"

"No that is how I choose to portray it. We, in the south, are more refined and shall we say cultured, than those who live on the frontier. I can see by your actions with Mr. Osborne that you have a different attitude toward the inferior race. A Southern gentleman would have handled that issue with grace rather than an uncouth physical assault, especially when ladies are present. That is the difference between us. Plus the fact that you fail to understand, Colonel, the Negroes are like these flowers, they must be cultivated, fed and watered. They cannot exist on their own. They would perish. They must be managed with a firm hand, made to understand their...shall we say...place in the order of life."

Sam turned from his observation of the grounds but before he could speak Corporal Dodson came to the door, "Colonel, we need you immediately."

"If you ladies will excuse me," he walked briskly away glad that he did not have to respond to the condescending speech given by Mrs. Sullivan.

The Corporal led the way to the smaller of the buildings below the hill. Made entirely of a dark stained wood, it was a high-ceilinged affair with a stout door and a recently broken lock and chain.

"In here, Colonel."

The interior stank of blood, sweat and offal. With only one small window for light, it took Sam a moment for his eyes to adjust. Moans and low voices in the darkened room created an eerie atmosphere of gloom and foreboding.

"What is this?" Sam covered his nose with his handkerchief.

"Colonel Wood, over here," Bones, the company medical corpsman, called from under the window where he was bent over a form on the floor. Sam peered over his shoulder at a naked woman bleeding from wounds covering her body from neck to foot.

"She's been beaten badly, but she'll survive," Bones held a wet red cloth that he had been using to wipe the worst of the blood away. The woman looked up, her eyes pleading for mercy. Bones pointed to a sheet next to her which he lifted revealing a young slave bruised and bloody, obviously dead. "He died before I could do anything to help. He's all busted up inside; you can see the bruising around his kidneys and spleen," Bones pointed at the worst of the discolorations.

Sam took another look around, "What in God's name is this hell hole?"

"Look here, Colonel," Corporal Dodson pointed at chains and manacles hanging from the ceiling. Five separate pairs, attached to a beam running the length of the room. "They chained the slaves here. These two were hanging, the woman by her wrists and the boy by his ankles. He was still alive when we got him down, but Bones couldn't save him; and look over here, whips and clubs. This one still has blood and hair on it. I've never seen anything like this Sir. It must have been those three men who did it."

Sam nodded, "Go get them, Corporal... Bones, carry this woman to the house. Put her in one of the beds and do what you can for her. I would imagine one of the house slaves will be able to assist you."

Sam knelt by the dead boy and began examining the wounds, "He can't be more than 16 or 17," he turned to find he was alone. Obvious wounds from the whip were crusted with blood or angry red welts. Other wounds from a blunt force object, maybe a club or fists covered his torso. It appeared his jaw had been broken. He must have suffered terribly. The longer Sam looked the angrier he got. Several soldiers arrived, including Lt. Reynolds.

"Chain them to the manacles," Sam ordered.

Reynolds approached the body while his men carried out the orders, "What in heaven's name is this, Colonel."

"Torture chamber of some kind. They beat this man to death," he lifted the sheet.

Reynolds turned his head, "My God, what kind of monster could do that?"

"You're looking at them," Sam turned to the three men hanging in place of the slaves. He turned to Snake Osborne who glared at Sam with an intense hatred, but his face betrayed the fear he felt as he squirmed against the restraints stretching him up on his toes. Sam turned to the younger of the other men, "What is your name?"

"Leonard Dempster," he couldn't look at Sam.

"Did you beat this man to death?"

Dempster looked up with fear in his eyes, "No sir, I never laid a hand on him. It was Snake and Booger done it."

Snake screamed, "Keep your mouth shut. Don't tell them nothing."

Sam turned to Corporal Dodson, "Take Leonard outside, bind him and place a guard on him." Then he took his cane and poked it in the chest of Booger, "What is your real name?"

"Harris English," he was obviously frightened.

"You're the one beat this man to death," Sam lifted the sheet.

"No, I used the whip on him. That's all, I swear."

"That leaves you, Mr. Osborne."

"Nobody in Mississippi gonna do anything about it. Owner of a slave can do anything he want. Even kill em."

The soldiers looked to Sam for confirmation or denial of this statement. Sam glared at the man before ordering, "Leave these men chained in here. Place a guard at the door."

Sam returned to the mansion. The medical corpsman was tending the wounds of the woman aided by one of the house maids, an older woman who seemed accustomed to treating the lashes of a whip.

"Bones, I want you to examine the body again and tell me if he died from that beating or some other cause."

"Colonel, I don't need to look at it again. I can assure you he died from the beating. This woman," he indicated the injured patient, "told me they whipped her because she threatened to run away. They whipped the boy because he said he was too sick to work, then Osborne beat him with the club because he back sassed."

Sam looked at the woman, "What is your name, Missus?"

"Rosetta Thompson."

"Are you wife of Tommy Thompson?"

Her eyes opened to Sam with a brightness that touched him, "Yes Sir. Why do you ask?"

"He is with my troops searching for the other slaves. He came here to take you away from this plantation."

"When I heard he escaped from Mound Place Plantation I tried to run away. But Massah Osborne caught me."

"Did you see Osborne beat the dead man with a club?"

"Yes Sir, it were terrible thing to see. Malcolm begged for him to stop. I couldn't bear it no more. I had to close my eyes."

"Who beat you with the whip?"

"Massah English."

"Did Leonard whip Malcolm or molest you in any way?"

"No sir. He left after they chained us."

"Do what you can in here, Bones. Then join me for a conference in the yard."

Mrs. Sullivan intercepted him in the parlor as he prepared to leave, "Colonel, I must protest putting that Nigger in my daughter's bed. She is bleeding all over the sheets. This is an afront to civilized society and..."

Sam whirled on her with a look of disgust bordering on rage. She clutched the fan to her chest and backed away eyes wide with fear. He took a deep breath and walked to the porch railing looking over garish manicured lawns, bushes and trees, brick walkways and drives all built on the backs of the slaves who received no credit, no pay, no appreciation or blessing for their labors. As if in a trance he looked further to fields of cotton and corn all planted, cultivated, and harvested by the slaves who received not a penny for their efforts, their only reward chains and the lash for not working faster. He closed his eyes and gritted his teeth in anger until he became aware that Captain Walker was speaking to him, "Sam, we've found the slaves."

"Determine who is the head man or woman. Bring them to me... and Tommy," he added as an afterthought.

A look of despair was on Tommy's face as he approached Sam, "My wife not with the others."

"Bones, take Tommy to his wife. Explain her injuries."

Captain Walker and Corporal Dodson approached with a man and woman slave, both in their 40's. Walker explained, "Colonel, this is Carl and his wife Selma, they been identified as the leaders among the slaves."

"I am Sam Wood, Colonel in the Federal Army. Tell me who you are."

In a heavily accented Barbados dalect Carl explained that he and his wife were senior among the slaves. Sam asked, "Why are there no older slaves?"

"Massah Osborne, he don't allow no slaves who can't work."

"What does he do with them?"

"Mostly he trade them away," Carl glanced at his wife who looked away painfully.

"What happens with the ones he doesn't sell or trade?"

Carl looked at his feet refusing to speak. His wife, with a defiant sneer, "He murder them. The graveyard full of dead Niggers by Massah Osborne hand. Including one of Rosetta baby born blind. He were the father. Buried it alive."

"Who was the father?"

"Massah Osborne."

"Can you prove that he murdered the baby?"

"Carl dug the hole."

Sam looked at him questioning the veracity?

"He afraid of Massah Osborne. We all are. But I tired of it. Rather be dead than carry on like this."

"Wait here... Captain Walker, follow me," they returned to Rosetta's side where Tommy was comforting her. "I'm sorry but I need to ask your wife some difficult questions. Was Snake Osborne the father of one of your children?"

She nodded, "He the the father of three of them but one died."

"Was it born dead?"

"No Sir, it were born blind and he took it away. I was told he buried it alive," she began sobbing. Tommy turned to him pleading not to bother her any further.

Sam beckoned to Walker. They walked back to the porch were the husband and wife waited. Activity in the front of the house was frantic as soldiers gathered bales of cotton, wagons of corn, horses, two teams of oxen, mules, pigs and goats. Thirty-five slaves of various ages gathered in a group under a large Elm unsure of what was happening. Sam led Walker to a secluded corner of the wrap-around porch, "Sheriff, this is a bad situation. That man Osborne needs to be dealt with. I can't just let him go."

"I agree with you. We can take him to the Sheriff in Clarksdale, but they won't do anything with him. You're the law here. What do you suggest?"

Sam deliberated for a moment gazing at the fields, then back to the slaves who were watching the two officers closely, "I'm going to convene a court of law and try him for murder. You will be clerk of the court. Handle it just as we did in Lawrence. Lt. Reynolds was a lawyer in New York State, he will act as attorney for the defendants. As I think about it, we'll try all three. Get Sergeant Morris, he will be court reporter. He knows shorthand."

Walker waited for further instructions, "Who should attend the trial?"

"Have Carl and Selma chose five slaves; you choose ten men from the ranks to attend as witnesses plus all the officers. The platoon leaders will continue to guard the premises, prepare the animals and crops for departure. I also want the three white women to attend the trial."

The back patio was shaded by an arbor of large wooden columns and beams. Elm and Oak trees provided additional cover; enough that all the officers of the court and the spectators were out of the sun. A fresh breeze rustled the leaves of the trees. It was not uncomfortable weather, but the seriousness of the situation was evident in the silence of the slaves, the witnesses, and especially the accused who seemed in shock.

Easom, aided by his house staff, provided lemonade or water as requested. A rectangular table served as the podium with a bench from the garden for Sam to sit. The defendants sat to his left facing him with Lt. Reynolds representing all three as counsel for the defense. Captain Walker served as court clerk and bailiff. Sgt. Major Morris, court reporter, sat at a small garden table next to Sam. Mrs. Sullivan and her daughters sat to Sam's right facing him. The witnessing soldiers and slaves gathered in small groups surrounding the main characters.

Walker, Sam and Reynolds conferred inside the house as the others gathered outside in the makeshift court. Armed guards stood behind the bound defendants.

"Sheriff lets proceed as we did in Lawrence," he turned to Lt. Reynolds. "Captain Walker was High

Sheriff in Douglas County and I was Justice of the Peace so we have quite a bit of experience together. But a murder trial… a most unsavory business," Sam sighed. "Lt. Reynolds, we'll have to adlib as we go. I have a copy of George Stroud's book as it pertains to slavery laws. Do you want to review it before we start?"

"I'm familiar enough to begin, I may ask reference to a particular section as we proceed."

Captain Walker walked outside in the eerie daytime silence. He glanced around then ordered, "All rise!"

Sam marched to the bench, nodded to Walker as he sat down.

Walker continued, "This court is convened by the authority of The President of the United States, Abraham Lincoln, providing that martial law is to be enforced in those States, cities, counties, and territories where no Federal Court exists. Lt. Colonel Sam Wood the ranking military authority in this region presiding. You may be seated."

Sam took his pistol, rapped it on the table in place of a gavel, "This court is in session. A few preliminaries before I begin. Spectators and witnesses you will remain silent unless spoken to. No exceptions. As you can see, armed guards are stationed throughout the area. Defendants, you will not utter a single word unless requested to do so by your attorney or by me. Is that understood?" Sam glared at them.

Snake remained silent, Harris grunted, and Leonard said, "Yes Sir."

Captain Walker walked to the defendants, pulled Osborne and Harris to their feet, their hands bound in front, "When you address the court, you say yes sir or no sir." He looked back at Sam.

"One more time. Do you understand the warning I have just given? Defendant Osborne?"

"Yes Sir"

"Defendant English?"

"Yes Sir."

"You may be seated."

Sam began writing as he announced, "The charge is murder of the slave known as Malcolm. Murder in the first degree against all three defendants. I am judge, jury and prosecuting attorney. Lt. Reynolds is the defense attorney. Lt. have you conferred with your clients?"

"Yes Sir."

"How do they plead?"

"Not guilty your honor."

"Call your first witness."

"I call Leonard Dempster...stand and face the court."

Captain Walker stood in front of the accused and because his hands were bound, ordered, "Place both hands on the bible. Do you solemnly swear that you will tell the truth, the whole truth, and nothing but the truth, so help you God, under pains and penalties of perjury?"

In a barely audible voice, "Yes Sir."

"I can't hear him, Colonel," Sergeant Morris interrupted.

"When you address the court, speak in a loud and clear voice. Repeat your answer," Sam looked at all three defendants.

"Yes Sir," Leonard repeated clearly.

Walker held the bible to the defendant's lips. He kissed it.

Reynolds asked, "Mr. Dempster, are you an employee on the Jacob Thompson Plantation?

"Yes Sir."

"How long have you worked here?"

"Three years, Sir."

"Did you murder the slave, Malcolm?"

A shiver of fear shook his body causing him to recoil with surprise. Upon recovering from the shock of the question, he answered in a shaky but firm voice, "No, I had nothing to do with it."

"Then who did murder him?"

"Snake did. He murdered all of them."

Snake started out of his chair; a look of pure hatred directed at the witness caused the ladies, who were on the edge of their seats, to sit back. He began to speak then glanced at Sam. The guard pulled him back into the chair.

"Murdered all of them? Who were the others?"

"Nigger Joe and Granny Alice and old Slow Motion...there might be others. Those are the ones since I been here."

"Why did he murder them?"

"Cause they was old and couldn't work. He said anyone couldn't pull their weight cost him money."

The Lt. looked at Sam, shook his head in disgust, "I have no further questions, Your Honor."

Leonard began to sit down.

"I'll tell you when to sit," Sam stopped him. "Who is your boss?"

"Snake is the Overseer. Mr. Thompson is the big boss."

"Has Mr. Thompson ever told you to murder a slave?"

Leonard shook his head, "No Sir! Mr. Thompson would never do that."

Sam shuffled some papers, made himself a note, "You remain under oath throughout this trial. You may be seated. Counselor, call your next witness."

"Harris English, stand up."

The oath given, Harris, obviously nervous, glanced from Sam to Snake.

Sam pointed at him, "Mr. English, keep your eyes forward. Do not look at Mr. Osborne. Is that clear?"

"Yes Sir."

"How long have you been an employee on this plantation?" Reynolds asked.

"Eight years."

"Did you murder the deceased?"

He bit his lip, shook his head, looked from Sam to Mrs. Sullivan trying to decide what to say; what answer would best benefit him? The spectators could see the turmoil raging in his mind, "No, Sir. I did whip him, but I didn't hit him with the club. That was Snake. I told him he was going to kill that boy. He said any Nigger that back sassed him was a dead Nigger." The words poured out in a torrent.

Snake jumped up and tried to reach the witness, "I told you to keep your mouth shut," he shouted.

The guards pulled him back to the chair.

"Gag him and bind him to the chair," Sam ordered.

English watched them carry out the order trembling with fear, "If he gets lose, he'll kill me, Judge."

Order again restored Lt. Reynolds continued, "Did you see Snake strike the deceased with this weapon?" he showed him the wooden bludgeon found in the shed.

"Yes Sir."

"How many times did he strike him?"

English thought for a moment, "I don't know for sure, but he'd hit him then go do something else then come back and get mad all over. When the boy wouldn't speak, that's when he hit him in the head, I told him he couldn't talk no more, his jaw was busted."

"I have no more questions, Your Honor."

Booger snuck a look at Osborne and scowled with fear. Sam again shuffled papers before asking, "Did you, at any time, during the period that Malcolm was hanging from those manacles, try to stop Mr. Osborne from striking him?"

"Like I said, Judge, I told him he was going to kill the boy. If I would have tried to stop him he would have killed me."

"Have you seen Mr. Osborne murder other slaves?"

"Yes Sir,"

"You remain under oath. Sit down. Lt. call your next witness."

"I call Snake Osborn. Your honor, I suggest the accused remain bound to the chair and testify from there."

"Agreed. Remove the gag. Captain Walker, administer the oath."

After Osborne kissed the bible, Reynolds moved to the front of Sam's table, turned and addressed the accused, "How long have you been in the employee of Jacob Thompson?"

"Some twenty years," his voice betrayed the emotions of his fear and anger.

"Did you murder Malcolm?"

He began breathing hard, looked at his co-defendants with enough rage to murder them if he could get free, "I ain't saying if I did or didn't. But even if I did that ain't murder. The owner of a slave got God control over his property. It ain't against the law to murder a slave...cause he ain't a real person, not a citizen, no rights except what I say. He's a piece of property just like the cattle. I've thought about it, and you've got no right to try me for anything. Owner of a slave can do anything he want to that slave. No court in the south would even try the case."

Reynolds looked at Sam.

Sam asked calmly, "Mr. Osborne, are you an attorney?"

"No... Sir," he added when he saw the look on Sam's face.

"Who told you that an owner can't be tried for murder of a slave?"

"Everyone in the south knows that."

"It might come as a surprise to you, Mr. Osborne," Sam opened the Stroud book, "Just how wrong you are. I quote, 'The State of Mississippi v. Jones, 1840 The question in this case is arising on arrest of judgement transferred on doubts from Adams Superior Court, is, whether, in this state, murder can be committed on a slave. The law determines that said murder is an indictable offense," Sam closed the book, stared long and hard at Osborne, "Do you understand what that means?" Osborne nodded yes.

Sam again opened the book, "John Hoover was executed for killing his slave named Mira in North Carolina in 1839...and there are other precedents." Sam put the book down and continued extemporaneously, "In former times, the murder of a slave in most, if not all the slaveholding regions of this country, was by law, punishable by a pecuniary fine only...You are correct in that an owner's right over the slave is unquestioned, however, the law finds that the willful, malicious, and deliberate murder of a slave, by whomsoever perpetrated, is declared to be punishable with death in every state, including every slaveholding state."

Suddenly Osborne began to see how serious his situation had become. He looked to the ladies, "Mrs. Sullivan do something."

She looked away, took a deep breath, "May I speak?" she looked to Sam.

He nodded, "Once you've sworn to the oath."

"Colonel Wood, I implore you to reconsider your actions. You are in the South Sir; we have our customs and our traditions. I've known Mr. Osborne for twenty years. I must speak to his character. I don't believe for a moment that he is capable of what he is accused."

Sam beckoned to Bones, whispered in his ear, then turned to Mrs. Sullivan, "Who owns the slaves on this plantation?"

She looked a bit confused, "I own the domestic help and Mr. Thompson owns the field hands."

"How much do you think the deceased was worth to Mr. Thompson?"

"Why three or four thousand dollars."

"Three or four thousand dollars? That's more than Mr. Osborne is worth. Would Mr. Thompson give Mr. Osborne carte blanch approval to murder a slave?

"No, I can guarantee that Mr. Thompson has given no such approval."

Four soldiers, carrying a stretcher, walked into the middle of the proceedings accompanied by Bones.

"In front of the ladies," Sam indicated where to stand. "Show them the body."

Bones pulled the sheet back revealing the body.

All three women looked away quickly, "Please Mr. Wood. We are ladies."

"Look at the body," Sam ordered. "Do you still wish to attest to Mr. Osborne's character?"

She sat back, the fan flapping like the wings of a vulture, a look of complete horror on her face. The daughters grew pale and weak; Abigale appeared ready to vomit.

"Bones, take the stand. Captain Walker, administer the oath."

When complete, Sam began, "You are medical officer of this company is that correct."

"Yes Sir."

"What is your opinion of the cause of death of the deceased?"

"A combination of things, including being hung upside down for an extended period. The primary cause was a blow to the side of the head. Contributing causes were fractured ribs...ruptured appendix and spleen, fractured jaw..."

"All caused by the blows from the club?"

"Yes Sir!"

"You spoke with the slave woman, Mrs. Thompson, as part of your examination of her wounds, did you not?"

"Yes Sir!"

"What did she tell you?"

"That Osborne beat the boy to death. That English beat her with the whip and that Leonard was not present."

"Is that all?"

"No Sir! She also told me that Osborne is the father of some of her children and one of the baby's was born blind. Osborne took it and buried it."

"Was the baby dead?"

"No Sir. She claims the baby was buried alive."

The slaves began to cry and moan. The soldiers began talking to each other. Angry voices could be heard on all sides.

Lt. Reynolds stood next to the defendants who were terrified, "Your honor, I object."

"On what grounds?"

"This evidence is hearsay and has no bearing on the case. Secondly, the testimony of a colored person, whether bond or free, is not admissible when that testimony is against a white person. Only white people can testify against whites."

Sam considered for a moment, "Your objection is sustained. Sergeant, strike all of Bones testimony as it pertains to the evidence provided by Mrs. Rosetta Thompson. It will not be considered in the case. Counsel for the defense, do you have anything further?"

"No sir."

"Do any of the defendants have anything you would like to say in your defense?"

They stared at Sam then at Lt. Reynolds. Osborne appealed once more to Mrs. Sullivan, "Please ma'am...do something."

She turned away. But not before giving him a look of pure disgust.

"The defendant Leonard Dempster stand and face the court," Sam ordered. He began writing, "I find you not guilty of the murder of Malcolm. Captain Walker, remove his binds. Mr. Dempster, you are free to go. I suggest you leave this county immediately."

Leonard couldn't believe what he was hearing. He began to speak. Sam shook his head and pointed, "Go."

Leonard disappeared into the trees.

"Harris English, stand and face the court. I find you guilty of accessory to the murder of Malcolm. You will be transferred under guard, to the Federal prison at Helena, Arkansas where you will be confined for a period of no less than three years. Captain assign guards to secure the guilty man."

"Now for Mr. Snake Osborne," Sam hesitated, looked at the people arrayed before the bench, all wondering what he was going to do. Osborne was sweating, his face a mask of dread at the realization of what was happening.

"Mr. Osborne, you claim ignorance of the law that makes murder of a slave illegal. I find that argument self-serving. Perhaps if you were charged with trespassing and claimed unawareness, I would show leniency. You claim that an owner of a slave cannot be held responsible for that slave's death. We have heard testimony here that you are not the owner, solely the owner's representative. I find it improbable that Mr. Thompson authorized you to kill one of his valuable slaves..."

"Malcolm threatened me," Snake interrupted, "said he was going to kill me."

"How in God's name did he threaten you? His jaw was broken. He couldn't speak."

"Well...I know he would have tried if I let him go."

"Mr. Osborne, you placed yourself above these people," Sam pointed at the slaves. "You held yourself out as their God with complete power over them; they had no recourse, no higher authority to appeal your cruel actions. Well, today I sit in judgement of you in the same manner. I, Sam Wood, a mortal man, certainly not God, but a man who has dedicated his life to the law and doing what is right.

"I have examined the evidence, the testimony of the two white employees, what I have seen with my own eyes and the body still warm from the beating you administered. You hung a helpless man...I should say a boy, by the heels and beat him to death with premeditated malice believing that it was justified because he was nothing but chattel, a piece of property no more important than a mule or a cow. Well, you are mistaken sir. I quote again, 'the willful, malicious, and deliberate murder of a slave, by whomsoever perpetrated, is declared to be punishable with death'. I have never witnessed an act of cruelty more malicious than what I have seen today. I find you guilty as charged. You shall be placed before a firing squad and executed. Sentence to be carried out immediately. Captain Walker," Sam shouted further shocking everyone.

"Sir?"

"Can you find seven volunteers among the troops to carry out the sentence?"

"I can find seventy, sir."

"Then draw lots, seven men at 10 paces aim for the heart: three rifles with blanks and four with live ammunition. I and Lt. Reynolds will serve as

280

witnesses as will any slaves who wish to do so. Mrs. Sullivan you will attend the execution. Your daughters are excused."

In stunned silence the onlookers sat as if reality had ceased, and they were witnessing a dream or nightmare. The slaves couldn't believe their ears... could it be true? Was he finally to be punished for his sins. God had heard their prayers.

Osborne dropped to his knees, begging for mercy. Walker ordered the guards to bind his wrists behind his back. Two burly soldiers drug him to the post. The execution took place at the torture shed on the west facing wall to catch the last rays of the evening sun. All the slaves chose to attend.

***

Helena, Arkansas

August 1892

It took a week before they could return to Ft. Curtis. Word of what happened at Jacob Thompson's plantation spread rapidly. Negroes from surrounding farms ran away to join the horde promised free passage to Helena under protection of the Union Army. Sam confiscated Rebel property where it could be identified. The 175 Union soldiers were heavily taxed with responsibility for 60 rebel prisoners, over 200 slaves, mules, oxen, horses, pigs, goats, bales of cotton and wagons of corn.

The only news about David came from a courier three days earlier, "He's in the infirmary, Colonel Wood. Dr. Patee says he is recovering."

"From what?" Sam asked making the messenger quite nervous.

"Sorry, Sir, I didn't think to ask."

It took three trips for the Steamboat to transport all the troops, prisoners, slaves, and confiscated property back to Helena. Sam left Captain Walker in charge at Friar's Point and returned with the first shipment anxious to check on David. He felt a nagging concern that General Curtis would want a full report on the murder trial which had been described in all the newspapers. Before reporting to the General he sought out Dr. Patee at the new hospital near the back edge of the compound.

"He's quite sick, Colonel Wood. I'm afraid that it might be time to contact his mother.

Sam was stunned, "I understood he was recovering."

"He's got malaria...complicated by pneumonia. It would be better if we could find somewhere other than here, in the infirmary," they arrived at David's side. He lay abed in a dormitory style room with nine other cots side by side, all occupied with men ill or wounded, many moaning in pain. Sam was shocked at the change in his son, his face so thin, pale, hair plastered with sweat. They didn't wake the sleeping boy.

A nurse joined them, "Are you David's father?" Sam nodded. "He asks about you every day. I wanted to meet you. My family has a farm north of town. My father, mother and youngest sister still live there. The rest of us are married with homes of our own. Mother has visited me here. She wants to take

David home so he can recover in a... more appropriate setting."

Dr. Patee nodded agreement, "She's a good cook, I can attest to that."

"That would be a great relief to me," Sam whispered.

Arrangements were made and the transfer accomplished that afternoon. The ambulance David used for his business was brought round. He was placed on blankets among the barrels and shelves. Sam was delighted with the Ralston's farm. Mrs. Ralston put her arm around the boy causing him to smile in recognition. David wouldn't let Sam leave until he heard the entire story of the trial, "The southern papers call you the murderer, Papa."

"I expected they would, Son. Some people agree and some disagree. I did what I thought was right."

"You always do the right thing," David whispered as the laudanum took control sending him into a deep sleep. Sam sat watching him, occasionally smoothing his hair while writing a letter to Margaret. Mrs. Ralston entered with a tray of food and water, "I'll set this here for later." She looked at Sam with a motherly understanding. "Is Mrs. Wood aware of the situation?"

"I'm writing a letter now."

"I'm sure he'll be fine, Colonel. I know you're busy with the war and all. You go on about your business. Come back and visit in the morning, he'll be awake then."

***

General Curtis' headquarters occupied a large building at the front portion of the compound facing toward the Mississippi River. Brick buildings were under construction throughout the grounds. Four batteries were strategically placed within a half mile, forming a rectangle around the earthen interior walls. Sam was certain the meeting would be about the Thompson plantation, but Curtis had other things on his mind.

"Sam, we have intelligence that Lieutenant General Theophilus Holmes is gathering troops in anticipation of attacking us."

"Attacking the Fort?"

"Yes."

"I can't imagine that Van Dorn would consider such a tactic."

"Van Dorn has been replaced. He lost the battle at Corinth. I doubt he'll be given another command. This fellow Holmes is gathering forces in an effort to provide some relief for their troops under siege at Vicksburg, Mississippi... and to push us out of Arkansas."

Sam sat listening to Curtis describe the military situation, but his mind was on David. The boy needed to be back in Kansas with his mother. As the general spoke, Sam glanced out the window at the parade grounds where soldiers marched, supply wagons continually traversed the back road while construction crews bricked the powder magazine in the far corner. When he finally looked up Curtis was silent, just staring at him, "Worried about your son, Sam?"

"I am General. I really need to take him back to his mother in Kansas... just as soon as he's capable of traveling."

"When do you think that will be?"

"Dr. Patee says it could be a week. It could just as easily be a month."

"Well, here's some more bad news. Jacob Thompson has petitioned the President to have his slaves returned and have you tried for the murder of his overseer."

Sam chuckled, "I expected something of the sort."

"The whole incident has created problems for Abe. He's preparing a document to free the slaves, calling it an Emancipation Proclamation. The former senators from the South are up in arms about your actions."

"What do you want me to do?"

"Are the newspaper reports accurate?"

"The northern papers are. The south skewed the facts, as usual."

Curtis walked to the window gazing at the frenzied activity as the soldiers strengthened the fortifications, "Was the man guilty?"

"As sin."

Curtis nodded, thought a bit before turning to face him, "Sam, I'm as ardent an abolitionist as you are. The President is not. He would ignore slavery if it meant preserving the Union. So would John Phelps."

"John Phelps? What has he got to do with it?"

"Lincoln appointed Phelps Military Governor of Arkansas. Then passed the buck to him. Your orders are to go to Little Rock and confer with Phelps about the matter. His decision will stand, and Phelps is pro-slavery as you know."

"Somehow, I knew Phelps' position on slavery would come back to haunt me. I don't know where Thompson's slaves are. I would imagine they've gone to Rolla. Regardless, General, I'll deal with this matter. It was my decision and I'll resolve it one way or the other. I'll go to Little Rock while David is recuperating. General, with your permission, I'd like to take him home when I get back."

"Whatever you need Sam, just let me know."

***

The heavy army coach was pulled by eight large draft horses. The road between Helena and Little Rock was recently graded after the spring rains. Sam sat comfortably listening to two officers discussing the latest gossip. Rumors were as common in the army as the truth, probably more so.

"I heard from a friend in Washington that Pinkerton's detectives have uncovered a plot to kill Lincoln."

Sam perked up hearing his good friends name mentioned. He hadn't seen Pinkerton since the 1860 presidential election but was well aware of Allan's rise to be a trusted advisor of the President. Plots against Lincoln were common as they were toward Jefferson Davis. He glanced out the window watching the tree covered hills roll by. The peaceful scenery belied the war raging not many miles away.

His thoughts turned to David. The boy had been a constant companion proving himself time and again. His role as a sutler keeping him busy during the long boring hours in camp waiting for the next skirmish. There was some resentment from other sutler's and even from the soldiers themselves. Such a young boy setting himself up as a merchant and drawing army pay at the same time. Ten dollars a month as a private. That income supplemented by his traveling store. But the soldiers were more than happy to have access to the lemonade, soap, needles and thread, combs, razors, tin plates and cups, books, newspapers, and tobacco that David provided. There were undercurrents of unrest that he was shown favoritism because his father was a Colonel and General Lyon had blessed the arrangement, even providing an ambulance for him to set up his stores.

'No question about it, David is a smart boy,' Sam thought to himself. 'It's true he wouldn't have been able to set up his business without our friendship with General Lyon. How I miss that man. He was a good friend for many years.'

The coach pulled to a stop bringing him back to reality. A private opened the door, "Watering the horses, gentlemen, if you would like to stretch your legs."

"Where are we?" the Major bent his head under the door frame.

"About fifteen miles from Little Rock, Sir. We'll be there in three hours or so."

***

John S. Phelps occupied an office in a brick building, formerly the City Hall, now serving as headquarters for the Military government of Arkansas. He advanced quickly after joining the Missouri Militia in the battle at Wilson's Creek, from a private in that battle to a Colonel leading his own battalion in the Battle of Pea Ridge. Because of his service in the Federal Government as a Representative from Missouri, more importantly because he joined the Federal Army in hopes of keeping the Union together, President Lincoln appointed him Military Governor of the Confederate State of Arkansas. But the fact remained that Phelps was a slaveholder and believed in the institution. His stance on the matter caused serious conflict between the Governor and Brigadier General Curtis who was a staunch abolitionist. That conflict came to a head over the Thompson Plantation incident with Sam Wood, as usual, smack in the middle of the disagreement.

Phelps' office was sparse with a desk, two chairs placed in front and a six-person conference table and chairs off to the side. Phelps, Thompson, and his lawyer were seated at the table when Sam arrived. It was obvious from their demeanor; the men were good friends.

'Stands to reason,' Sam thought to himself as he took measure of the three. Thompson was Secretary of the Interior while Phelps was a Representative in Congress. ''They've been plotting something.'

Thompson, a tight-lipped, puckered up man displayed a no-nonsense bearing. He ignored Sam.

Sam greeted Phelps, "Hello John, good to see you again. You've come up in the world since your days as a private at Wilson's Creek." Sam smiled warmly, not wishing to start the meeting off on a sour note.

"Hello, Colonel Wood. I believe you know Secretary Thompson..." Sam was taken aback by the reference to his former cabinet position given the fact that he was now the Inspector General of the Confederacy. Phelps continued, "And this is former Attorney General, Jeremiah Black, acting as Mr. Thompson's attorney. I assume General Curtis informed you they are under military protection while here."

Black took command without consulting Thompson who sat staring out the window as if he weren't interested in the proceedings at all, "Colonel Wood, this is a most trying time in the history of our great country. But we must continue to observe the rule of law, wouldn't you agree?"

Sam nodded pleasantly, "I couldn't agree more."

Black forged ahead, "We are willing to overlook the unfortunate circumstances leading to you murdering, Secretary Thompson's foreman...if you will agree to return his personal property...immediately."

Sam glanced at each man letting his eyes rest on Phelps the longest, causing the Governor to turn away uncomfortably. Thompson hadn't said a word, in fact, appeared bored with the entire affair. Sam gathered his thoughts, "Mr. Black, murder is a strong term and I take umbrage at the insinuation. I assert that my actions were governed by the law. I have a transcript of the trial if you would like to review it." He turned to Phelps, "John, what do you make of this matter?"

Phelps hesitated a moment, "Jacob is a friend of mine, yet we find ourselves in opposite camps over this question of States Rights. I am of the same mind as Jacob concerning the matter of slavery. However, I fight for the preservation of the Union while Jacob prefers secession," he contemplated his hands for a moment trying to find an inspiration. "I'm not certain of the proper protocol here but President Lincoln has placed the matter in my hands. It seems to me... if Secretary Thompson is willing to drop the murder charge... you should be willing to return his property."

"His property meaning the mules and oxen?" Sam clarified.

"We want all of his property returned," Black snapped unpleasantly, "especially his slaves. They are quite valuable, and President Lincoln has agreed not to interfere with the plantation owner's property."

Sam answered firmly, "My orders were to confiscate all rebel animals and crops. As for the Negroes, I'm not sure if they followed the mules, or the mules followed them. As you point out, they are nothing but property. I don't know where the mules or the Negroes are. They left of their own accord and judging by what I saw they were wise to do so. Here is my response to your demands, tell Mr. Thompson that the way the people of Mississippi have behaved.

They don't deserve any favors from the Federal Government."

Sam stood preparing to leave.

"Governor, what do you plan to do about this?" Black demanded.

"Wait a moment, Sam. What did you mean by that last comment?"

"Ask Mr. Thompson."

Thompson scowled refusing to look at Sam, "He's still angry over a decision I made concerning the public lands in Kansas. He's being very trifling; just the attitude he accused me of. I made a decision in my capacity as Secretary of the Interior. President Buchanan agreed with me. That should have been the end of it."

Sam turned on him, "Sir, I made a decision in my capacity as Military commander of the Federal Army and my superior General Curtis agrees with me," then to Phelps he asked, still standing, "Governor Phelps, do you require anything further of me regarding this matter

Phelps seemed defeated, "I'm not well gentlemen. In fact, I've submitted my letter of resignation to President Lincoln. I hate to leave this problem for my successor." He paused looking at Thompson, "Jacob, I'm sorry but Colonel Wood is correct in this matter. You'll have deal with your property issues after the war."

Sam walked out not bothering to wait for a reply.

***

Council Grove, Kansas

June 1863

After surviving the Sack of Lawrence in May of 1856 and the Siege of Lawrence in September of that year, the Wood family felt it wise to move out of Lawrence. In addition, Sam started newspapers in Falls Township on the Cottonwood River and in Council Grove on the Neosho River. Stephan Wood and his family moved to Elmwood, near Falls Township which some settlers were calling Cottonwood Falls, where the brothers started a cattle operation next to land Seth Hayes owned on Diamond Creek.

Sam and Margaret's new home on Main Street in Council Grove was just south of Hayes trading post and his new restaurant, the Hayes House. The Wood home was a two-story clapboard affair set back from the street on a lot outlined by a picket fence graced with a perpetually off-hinge gate. One fine spring day in early June, Sam and Margaret sat holding hands on the porch watching David, Punch and Flo play in the yard with neighborhood children. Council Grove had grown with over 200 permanent residents, a school and other businesses catering to the growing flood of settlers moving west along the Santa Fe trail.

"Aren't the honeysuckle beautiful," Margaret pointed to the trees lining the Neosho.

Sam glanced and grunted.

"They've bloomed late this year."

"What have, my love?"

"The trees! Aren't they beautiful?"

He glanced at the river, back at the children watching the wagon train rumbling by on its way west, "I hope the kids don't run out in front of one of those wagons."

Margaret smiled. Sam took very little interest in the conditions of the day other than how it might affect politics and his vision of what the world should be.

"Good morning Sam... Margaret... I've got a letter for you...from the Governor," Seth Hayes climbed the steps then squatted by the porch swing with the envelope extended. He waited patiently while Sam read it before handing it to Margaret.

Knowing that Seth wouldn't leave until he knew what the Governor wanted, Sam explained, "Wants me to go see him in Topeka."

Seth nodded, waiting patiently.

"He's worried about Quantrill."

"Ain't we all?" Seth agreed, taking his tobacco pouch from a side pocket.

Margaret glanced up from reading the letter. He knew what was coming.

"The Governor is going to make you Brigadier General of the Kansas Militia?"

"Maybe it's just an honorary thing, Meg."

"Oh, Sam, you know he expects you to organize the militia and get back into the war. Haven't you done enough already?" She handed the letter back.

Seth looked from Margaret to Sam. He lit his pipe, carefully following the conversation. Seth knew everybody and everything that happened in Council Grove and everything that happened to the people passing on their way west. He prided himself on his knowledge of world affairs and Sam Wood was the best source for information he ever met. Just a week ago a letter had come from Abraham Lincoln himself.

Sam glanced back at the children running and screaming alongside the last of the wagons rumbling by, pulled by six hulking oxen, "You've got more competition in town, Seth."

"Yep, opening a mercantile right across from me," he nodded to the buildings being constructed across the street.

Margaret patted Sam on the arm, "I better go do the wash. You'll need to leave first thing in the morning."

Seth sat in Margaret's vacant spot on the swing next to Sam, "I'm mighty worried, Sam. It's bad enough with the war over in Missouri, but if it comes to us... we've got no defenses against it."

Sam nodded, "I'll go see the Governor. If it looks like Quantrill is going to bring his raiders into Kansas, we'll have to apply to Ft. Riley for troops to help us. I'm not sure who the new commander is since we lost Nathanial."

Seth stood, puffed on his pipe staring at the competition awhile, then tapped the tobacco out, blew through the stem and placed it in his coat pocket, "We can get thirty or forty men together, but they won't be much of an army. Mostly shopkeepers and farmers."

"We'll make do with what we have, Seth. If I'm going to oversee the militia, we'll make sure the small towns are protected."

Seth started down the steps shaking his head, "Sometimes I think I ought to pull up and head west with those pilgrims."

Margaret strolled back wiping her hands on a towel, "Seth get all the information he needed?" she laughed.

"He's a good man, especially in times like these. We'll need to organize a militia here just in case some of the bushwhackers head this way."

She sat down watching him reread the letter, "Sam?"

"Hmmmm?"

"Do you ever wish you would have married someone else?"

He looked sideways to see if she was kidding.

"I mean in your travels. Do you ever see girls that are prettier or smarter and wish you would have waited to marry?" She twisted the towel gazing at the children.

"What brought this on, Meg?"

"Nothing special... surely you must see beautiful women in New York City and Philadelphia. All the places you travel and all the people you know."

He looked down the street at the children trooping back from escorting the wagon train out of town, "I could travel the whole world over and I would never find someone I love more than you." He put his arm around her, "You are my sweetheart whether I'm in Topeka or in New York... my entire reason for living and don't you ever forget it."

***

Tom Carney succeeded Charlie Robinson as Governor of Kansas a few months prior to receiving Sam in Constitution Hall, the official State Capital building in Topeka. Carney was a tall man. A bald pate fringed with bushy brown hair and a full beard gave him the appearance of a hard-working farmer, which he was. He also owned a successful mercantile in Leavenworth, not to mention a bank. He enjoyed talking business more than government affairs. After some pleasantries and discussion about mutual acquaintances they got down to the crux of the meeting, "We do live in a difficulty time, Governor," Sam agreed as they discussed the ravages of war.

Carney had heavy eyebrows framing deep set eyes sodden with the turmoil he faced, "Jim Lane is forming a brigade. Are you going to join him?"

"I haven't decided yet what I'm going to do. General Curtis has been reassigned as Director of Indian Affairs in the west. He asked me to join him. I fully expect he'll be assigned as supreme commander in Missouri."

"Well, as I mentioned in the letter, I'm promoting you to Brigadier General of the Kansas Militia. President Lincoln insists that you continue your military service and not resign completely."

Sam looked out the window at the Kansas River. New buildings were being constructed up and down Main Street belying the fact that Kansas was embroiled in the Civil War. General Sterling Price made good his promise to return to Missouri and re-establish the Confederacy in his home state. Rumors were rife that he would bring the war to the 'abolitionist scum' in Lawrence. Jim Lane organized a militia commanding a large army stationed in Kansas City hoping to keep him out of Kansas.

"Governor, I'm not sure I want to serve with Jim Lane. He and Charlie Robinson are at loggerheads. I have no interest in getting in the middle of that dispute. My son David is just now recovering from Malaria. I have a newspaper in Council Grove...another in Falls Township. I'll play my part, but I need to decide where I can best serve and what part the Kansas militia can play."

"We may not have the luxury of time, General. I just received a report that Quantrill has advanced into Westport."

"That's not good news," Sam grimaced.

"Rumor is he is going after General Lane. Wants to destroy Lawrence...blames us for the women who died in that building collapse in Kansas City."

"That was a terrible mistake. Who ordered them arrested? Seems to me that jailing the girlfriends and wives of Quantrill's raiders was going a bit far outside of reason, not to mention the law."

"I agree, Sam. I'm not sure who ordered the arrests. They were imprisoned in George Bingham's house in Kansas City...I was told the women were crammed into two small rooms and Lane's soldiers wanted to create more space. They took out some of the support beams...the whole thing crashed down and seven of the women died in the accident."

Sam shook his head in frustration, "Quantrill is a dangerous man...no scruples whatsoever. That foolish mistake just makes the situation worse;

added fuel to the fire. One of the reasons Margaret and I moved to Council Grove. I still have a house in Lawrence, but we don't want to live there right now. I'm also worried that the bushwhackers will start attacking the smaller towns, like Council Grove. If the situation is that serious, I'll..."

"Hold on Sam... Mrs. Harrison, what is all that ruckus?"

The governor's private secretary appeared at the door wringing her hands, fear etched on her face, "A messenger from Lawrence..."

A short heavy-set man dashed out of breath into the room, "Quantrill is burning Lawrence. They were killing every man and boy they saw. I barely got out alive...we've got to notify Ft. Riley."

Sam jumped up knocking over his chair, "I've got to get to Council Grove."

"That's where they were headed next."

The Governor stood in shock. Sam didn't even shake hands goodbye. He dashed out the door running for the stable, 'Please Lord, don't let me be too late'.

About the Author

Henry E. Peavler

The author has a home in Texas, near his five children. Against all odds, he continues to write.